THE

NOVELS

OF

CHARLES BROCKDEN BROWN,

CONSISTING OF

WIELAND; OR, THE TRANSFORMATION.
ARTHUR MERVYN; OR, MEMOIRS OF THE YEAR 1793.
EDGAR HUNTLY; OR, MEMOIRS OF A SLEEP-WALKER.
JANE TALBOT.
ORMOND; OR, THE SECRET WITNESS.
CLARA HOWARD; OR, THE ENTHUSIASM OF LOVE.

With a Memoir of the Author.

COMPLETE AND REVISED EDITION.

VOL. II.

PHILADELPHIA:
J. B. LIPPINCOTT & CO.
M. POLOCK, 406 COMMERCE ST.
1859.

ARTHUR MERVYN;

OR,

MEMOIRS OF THE YEAR 1793.

BY

CHARLES BROCKDEN BROWN.

IN TWO VOLUMES.

VOL. I.

PHILADELPHIA:
PUBLISHED BY M. POLOCK,
No. 6 COMMERCE STREET.
1857.

PREFACE.

The evils of pestilence by which this city has lately been afflicted will probably form an era in its history. The schemes of reformation and improvement to which they will give birth, or, if no efforts of human wisdom can avail to avert the periodical visitations of this calamity, the change in manners and population which they will produce, will be, in the highest degree, memorable. They have already supplied new and copious materials for reflection to the physician and the political economist. They have not been less fertile of instruction to the moral observer, to whom they have furnished new displays of the influence of human passions and motives.

Amidst the medical and political discussions which are now afloat in the community relative to this topic, the author of these remarks has ventured to methodize his own reflections, and to weave into an humble narrative such incidents as appeared to him most instructive and remarkable among those which came within the sphere of his own observation. It is every one's duty to profit by all opportunities of inculcating on mankind the lessons of justice and humanity. The influences of hope and fear, the trials of fortitude and constancy, which took place in this city in the autumn of 1793, have, perhaps, never been exceeded in any age. It is but just to snatch some of these from oblivion, and to deliver to posterity a brief but faithful sketch of the condition of this metropolis during that calamitous period. Men only require to be made acquainted with distress for their compassion and their charity to be awakened. He that depicts, in lively colours, the evils of disease and poverty, performs an eminent service to the sufferers, by calling forth benevolence in those who are able to afford relief; and he who portrays examples of disinterestedness and intrepidity confers on virtue the notoriety and homage that are due to it, and rouses in the spectators the spirit of salutary emulation.

In the following tale a particular series of adventures is brought to a close; but these are necessarily connected with the events which happened subsequent to the period here described. These events are not less memorable than those which form the subject of the present volume, and may hereafter be published, either separately or in addition to this.

C. B. B.

ARTHUR MERVYN.

CHAPTER I.

I WAS resident in this city during the year 1793. Many motives contributed to detain me, though departure was easy and commodious, and my friends were generally solicitous for me to go. It is not my purpose to enumerate these motives, or to dwell on my present concerns and transactions, but merely to compose a narrative of some incidents with which my situation made me acquainted.

Returning one evening, somewhat later than usual, to my own house, my attention was attracted, just as I entered the porch, by the figure of a man reclining against the wall at a few paces distant. My sight was imperfectly assisted by a far-off lamp; but the posture in which he sat, the hour, and the place, immediately suggested the idea of one disabled by sickness. It was obvious to conclude that his disease was pestilential. This did not deter me from approaching and examining him more closely.

He leaned his head against the wall; his eyes were shut, his hands clasped in each other, and his body seemed to be sustained in an upright position merely by the cellar-door against which he rested his left shoulder. The lethargy into which he was sunk seemed scarcely interrupted by my feeling his hand and his forehead. His throbbing temples and burning skin indicated a fever, and his form, already emaciated, seemed to prove that it had not been of short duration.

There was only one circumstance that hindered me from forming an immediate determination in what manner this person should be treated. My family consisted of my wife and a young child. Our servant-maid had been seized, three days before, by the reigning malady, and, at her own request, had been conveyed to the hospital. We ourselves enjoyed good health, and were hopeful of escaping with our lives. Our measures for this end had been cautiously taken and carefully adhered to. They did not consist in avoiding the receptacles of infection, for my office required me to go daily into the midst of them; nor in filling the house with the exhalations of gunpowder, vinegar, or tar. They consisted in cleanliness, reasonable exercise, and wholesome diet. Custom had likewise blunted the edge of our apprehensions. To take this person into my house, and bestow upon him the requisite attendance, was the scheme that first occurred to me. In this, however, the advice of my wife was to govern me.

I mentioned the incident to her. I pointed out the danger which was to be dreaded from such an inmate. I desired her to decide with caution, and mentioned my resolution to conform myself implicitly to her decision. Should we refuse to harbour him, we must not forget that there was a hospital to which he would, perhaps, consent to be carried, and where he would be accommodated in the best manner the times would admit.

"Nay," said she, "talk not of hospitals. At least, let him have his choice. I have no fear about me, for my part, in a case where the injunctions of duty are so obvious. Let us take the poor, unfortunate wretch into our protection and care, and leave the consequences to Heaven."

I expected and was pleased with this proposal. I returned to the sick man, and, on rousing him from his stupor, found him still in possession of his reason. With a candle near, I had an opportunity of viewing him more accurately.

His garb was plain, careless, and denoted rusticity. His aspect was simple and ingenuous, and his decayed visage still retained traces of uncommon but manlike beauty. He had all the appearances of mere youth, unspoiled by luxury and uninured to misfortune. I scarcely ever beheld an object which laid so powerful and sudden a claim to my affection and succour.

"You are sick," said I, in as cheerful a tone as I could assume. "Cold bricks and night-airs are comfortless attendants for one in your condition. Rise, I pray you, and come into the house. We will try to supply you with accommodations a little more suitable."

At this address he fixed his languid eyes upon me. "What would you have?" said he. "I am very well as I am. While I breathe, which will not be long, I shall breathe with more freedom here than elsewhere. Let me alone—I am very well as I am."

"Nay," said I, "this situation is unsuitable to a sick man. I only ask you to come into my house, and receive all the kindness that it is in our power to bestow. Pluck up courage, and I will answer for your recovery, provided you submit to directions, and do as we would have you. Rise, and come along with me. We will find you a physician and a nurse, and all we ask in return is good spirits and compliance."

"Do you not know," he replied, "what my disease is? Why should you risk your safety for the sake of one whom your kindness cannot benefit, and who has nothing to give in return?"

There was something in the style of this remark, that heightened my prepossession in his favour, and made me pursue my purpose with more zeal. "Let us try what we can do for you," I answered. "If we save your life, we shall have done you some service, and, as for recompense, we will look to that."

It was with considerable difficulty that he was persuaded to accept our invitation. He was conducted to a chamber, and, the criticalness of his case requiring unusual attention, I spent the night at his bedside.

My wife was encumbered with the care both of her infant and her family. The charming babe was in perfect health, but her mother's constitution was frail and delicate. We simplified the household duties as much as possible, but still these duties were considerably burdensome to one not used to the performance, and luxuriously educated. The addition of a sick man was likely to be productive of much fatigue. My engagements would not allow me to be always at home, and the state of my patient, and the remedies necessary to be prescribed, were attended with many noxious and disgustful circumstances. My fortune would not allow me to hire assistance. My wife, with a feeble frame and a mind shrinking, on ordinary occasions, from such offices, with fastidious scrupulousness, was to be his only or principal nurse.

My neighbours were fervent in their well-meant zeal, and loud in their remonstrances on the imprudence and rashness of my conduct. They called me presumptuous and cruel in exposing my wife and child, as well as myself, to such imminent hazard, for the sake of one, too, who most probably was worthless, and whose disease had doubtless been, by negligence or mistreatment, rendered incurable.

I did not turn a deaf ear to these censurers. I was aware of all the inconveniences and perils to which I thus spontaneously exposed myself. No one knew better the value of that woman whom I called mine, or set a higher price upon her life, her health, and her ease. The virulence and activity of this contagion, the dangerous condition of my patient, and the dubiousness of his character, were not forgotten by me; but still my conduct in this affair received my own entire approbation. All objections on the score of my friends were removed by her own willingness and even solicitude to undertake the province. I had more confidence than others in the vincibility of this disease, and in the success of those measures which we had used for our defence against it. But, whatever were the evils to accrue to us, we were sure of one thing: namely, that the consciousness of having neglected this unfortunate person would be a source of more unhappiness than could possibly redound from the attendance and care that he would claim.

The more we saw of him, indeed, the more did we congratulate ourselves on our proceeding. His torments were acute and tedious; but, in the midst even of delirium, his heart seemed to overflow with gratitude, and to be actuated by no wish but to alleviate our toil and our danger. He made prodigious exertions to perform necessary offices for himself. He suppressed his feelings and struggled to maintain a cheerful tone and countenance, that he might prevent that anxiety which the sight of his sufferings produced in us. He was perpetually furnishing reasons why his nurse should leave him alone, and betrayed dissatisfaction whenever she entered his apartment.

In a few days, there were reasons to conclude him out of danger; and, in a fortnight, nothing but exercise and nourishment were wanting to complete his restoration. Meanwhile nothing was obtained from him but general information, that his place of abode was Chester county, and that some momentous engagement induced him to hazard his safety by coming to the city in the height of the epidemic.

He was far from being talkative. His silence seemed to be the joint result of modesty and unpleasing remembrances. His features were characterized by pathetic seriousness, and his deportment by a gravity very unusual at his age. According to his own representation, he was no more than eighteen years old, but the depth of his remarks indicated a much greater advance. His name was Arthur Mervyn. He described himself as having passed his life at the plough-tail and the threshing-floor; as being destitute of all scholastic instruction; and as being long since bereft of the affectionate regards of parents and kinsmen.

When questioned as to the course of life which he meant to pursue upon his recovery, he professed himself without any precise object. He was willing to be guided by the advice of others, and by the lights which experience should furnish. The country was open to him, and he supposed that there was no part of it in which food could not be purchased by his labour. He was unqualified, by his education, for any liberal profession. His poverty was likewise an insuperable impediment. He could afford to spend no time in the acquisition of a trade. He must labour, not for future emolument, but for immediate subsistence. The only pursuit which his present circumstances would allow him to adopt was that which, he was inclined to believe, was likewise the most eligible. Without doubt his experience was slender, and it seemed absurd to pronounce concerning that of which he had no direct knowledge; but so it was, he could not outroot from his mind the persuasion that to plough, to sow, and to reap, were employments most befitting a reasonable creature, and from which the truest pleasure and the least pollution would flow. He contemplated no other scheme than to return, as soon as his health should permit, into the country, seek employment where it was to be had, and acquit himself in his engagements with fidelity and diligence.

I pointed out to him various ways in which the city might furnish employment to one with his qualifications. He had said that he was somewhat accustomed to the pen. There were stations in which the possession of a legible hand was all that was requisite. He might add to this a knowledge of accounts, and thereby procure himself a post in some mercantile or public office.

To this he objected, that experience had shown him unfit for the life of a penman. This had been his chief occupation for a little while, and he found it wholly incompatible with his health. He must not sacrifice the end for the means. Starving was a disease preferable to consumption. Besides, he laboured merely for the sake of living, and he lived merely for the sake of pleasure. If his tasks should enable him to live, but, at the same time, bereave him of all satisfaction, they inflicted injury, and were to be shunned as worse evils than death.

I asked to what species of pleasure he alluded, with which the business of a clerk was inconsistent.

He answered that he scarcely knew how to describe it. He read books when they came in his way. He had lighted upon few, and, perhaps, the pleasure they afforded him was owing to their fewness; yet he confessed that a mode of life which entirely forbade him to read was by no means to his taste. But this was trivial. He knew how to value the thoughts of other people, but he could not part with the privilege of observing and thinking for himself. He wanted business which would suffer at least nine-tenths of his attention to go free. If it afforded agreeable employment to that part of his attention which it applied to its own use, so much the better; but, if it did not, he should not repine. He should be content with a life whose pleasures were to its pains as nine are to one. He had tried the trade of a copyist, and in circumstances more favourable than it was likely he should ever again have an opportunity of trying it, and he had found that it did not fulfil the requisite conditions. Whereas the trade of ploughman was friendly to health, liberty, and pleasure.

The pestilence, if it may so be called, was now declining. The health of my young friend allowed him to breathe the fresh air and to walk. A friend of mine, by name Wortley, who had spent two months from the city, and to whom, in the course of a familiar correspondence, I had mentioned the foregoing particulars, returned from his rural excursion. He was posting, on the evening of the day of his arrival, with a friendly expedition, to my house, when he overtook Mervyn going in the same direction. He was surprised to find him go before him into my dwelling, and to discover, which he speedily did, that this was the youth whom I had so frequently mentioned to him. I was present at their meeting.

There was a strange mixture in the countenance of Wortley when they were presented to each other. His satisfaction was mingled with surprise, and his surprise with anger. Mervyn, in his turn, betrayed considerable embarrassment. Wortley's thoughts were too earnest on some topic to allow him to converse. He shortly made some excuse for taking leave, and, rising, addressed himself to the youth with a request that he would walk home with him. This invitation, delivered in a tone which left it doubtful whether a compliment or menace were meant, augmented Mervyn's confusion. He complied without speaking, and they went out together;—my wife and I were left to comment upon the scene.

It could not fail to excite uneasiness. They were evidently no strangers to each other. The indignation that flashed from the eyes of Wortley, and the trembling consciousness of Mervyn, were unwelcome tokens. The former was my dearest friend, and venerable for his discernment and integrity. The latter appeared to have drawn upon himself the anger and disdain of this man. We already anticipated the shock which the discovery of his unworthiness would produce.

In a half-hour Mervyn returned. His embarrassment had given place to dejection. He was always serious, but his features were now overcast by the deepest gloom. The anxiety which I felt would not allow me to hesitate long.

"Arthur," said I, "something is the matter with you. Will you not disclose it to us? Perhaps you have brought yourself into some dilemma out of which we may help you to escape. Has any thing of an unpleasant nature passed between you and Wortley?"

The youth did not readily answer. He seemed at a loss for a suitable reply. At length he said that something disagreeable had indeed passed between him and Wortley. He had had the misfortune to be connected with a man by whom Wortley conceived himself to be injured. He had borne no part in inflicting this injury, but had nevertheless been threatened with ill treatment if he did not make disclosures which, indeed, it was in his power to make, but which he was bound, by every sanction, to withhold. This disclosure would be of no benefit to Wortley. It would rather operate injuriously than otherwise; yet it was endeavoured to be wrested from him by the heaviest menaces. There he paused.

We were naturally inquisitive as to the scope of these menaces; but Mervyn entreated us to forbear any further discussion of this topic. He foresaw the difficulties to which his silence would subject him. One of its most fearful consequences would be the loss of our good opinion. He knew not what he had to dread from the enmity of Wortley. Mr. Wortley's violence was not without excuse. It was his mishap to be exposed to suspicions which could only be obviated by breaking his faith. But, indeed, he knew not whether any degree of explicitness would confute the charges that were made against him; whether, by trampling on his sacred promise, he should not multiply his perils instead of lessening their number. A difficult part had been assigned to him; by much too difficult for one young, improvident, and inexperienced as he was.

Sincerity, perhaps, was the best course. Perhaps, after having had an opportunity for deliberation, he should conclude to adopt it; meanwhile he entreated permission to retire to his chamber. He was unable to exclude from his mind ideas which yet could, with no propriety, at least at present, be made the theme of conversation.

These words were accompanied with simplicity and pathos, and with tokens of unaffected distress.

"Arthur," said I, "you are master of your actions and time in this house. Retire when you please; but you will naturally suppose us anxious to dispel this mystery. Whatever shall tend to obscure or malign your character will of course excite our solicitude. Wortley is not short-sighted or hasty to condemn. So great is my confidence in his integrity that I will not promise my esteem to one who has irrecoverably lost that of Wortley. I am not acquainted with your motives to concealment, or what it is you conceal; but take the word of one who possesses that experience which you complain of wanting, that sincerity is always safest."

As soon as he had retired, my curiosity prompted me to pay an immediate visit to Wortley. I found him at home. He was no less desirous of an interview, and answered my inquiries with as much eagerness as they were made.

"You know," said he, "my disastrous connection with Thomas Welbeck. You recollect his sudden disappearance last July, by which I was reduced to the brink of ruin. Nay, I am, even now, far from certain that I shall survive that event. I spoke to you about the youth who lived with him, and by what means that youth was discovered to have crossed the river in his company on the night of his departure. This is that very youth.

"This will account for my emotion at meeting him at your house; I brought him out with me. His confusion sufficiently indicated his knowledge of transactions between Welbeck and me. I questioned him as to the fate of that man. To own the truth, I expected some well-digested lie; but he merely said that he had promised secrecy on that subject, and must therefore be excused from giving me any information. I asked him if he knew that his master, or accomplice, or whatever was his relation to him, absconded in my debt? He answered that he knew it well; but still pleaded a promise of inviolable secrecy as to his hiding-place. This conduct justly exasperated me, and I treated him with the severity which he deserved. I am half ashamed to confess the excesses of my passion; I even went so far as to strike him. He bore my insults with the utmost patience. No doubt the young villain is well instructed in his lesson. He knows that he may safely defy my power. From threats I descended to entreaties. I even endeavoured to wind the truth from him by artifice. I promised him a part of the debt if he would enable me to recover the whole. I offered him a considerable reward if he would merely afford me a clue by which I might trace him to his retreat; but all was insufficient. He merely put on an air of perplexity and shook his head in token of non-compliance."

Such was my friend's account of this interview. His suspicions were unquestionably plausible; but I was disposed to put a more favourable construction on Mervyn's behaviour. I recollected the desolate and penniless condition in which I found him, and the uniform complacency and rectitude of his deportment for the period during which we had witnessed it. These ideas had considerable influence on my judgment, and indisposed me to follow the advice of my friend, which was to turn him forth from my doors that very night.

My wife's prepossessions were still more powerful advocates of this youth. She would vouch, she said, before any tribunal, for his innocence; but she willingly concurred with me in allowing him the continuance of our friendship on no other condition than that of a disclosure of the truth. To entitle ourselves to this confidence we were willing to engage, in our turn, for the observance of secrecy, so far that no detriment should accrue from this disclosure to himself or his friend.

Next morning, at breakfast, our guest appeared with

a countenance less expressive of embarrassment than on the last evening. His attention was chiefly engaged by his own thoughts, and little was said till the breakfast was removed. I then reminded him of the incidents of the former day, and mentioned that the uneasiness which thence arose to us had rather been increased than diminished by time.

"It is in your power, my young friend," continued I, "to add still more to this uneasiness, or to take it entirely away. I had no personal acquaintance with Thomas Welbeck. I have been informed by others that his character, for a certain period, was respectable, but that, at length, he contracted large debts, and, instead of paying them, absconded. You, it seems, lived with him. On the night of his departure you are known to have accompanied him across the river, and this, it seems, is the first of your reappearance on the stage. Welbeck's conduct was dishonest. He ought doubtless to be pursued to his asylum and be compelled to refund his winnings. You confess yourself to know his place of refuge, but urge a promise of secrecy. Know you not that to assist or connive at the escape of this man was wrong? To have promised to favour his concealment and impunity by silence was only an aggravation of this wrong. That, however, is past. Your youth, and circumstances, hitherto unexplained, may apologize for that misconduct; but it is certainly your duty to repair it to the utmost of your power. Think whether, by disclosing what you know, you will not repair it."

"I have spent most of last night," said the youth, "in reflecting on this subject. I had come to a resolution, before you spoke, of confiding to you my simple tale. I perceive in what circumstances I am placed, and that I can keep my hold of your good opinion only by a candid deportment. I have indeed given a promise which it was wrong, or rather absurd, in another to exact, and in me to give; yet none but considerations of the highest importance would persuade me to break my promise. No injury will accrue from my disclosure to Welbeck. If there should, dishonest as he was, that would be a sufficient reason for my silence. Wortley will not, in any degree, be benefited by any communication that I can make. Whether I grant or withhold information, my conduct will have influence only on my own happiness, and that influence will justify me in granting it.

"I received your protection when I was friendless and forlorn. You have a right to know whom it is that you protected. My own fate is connected with the fate of Welbeck, and that connection, together with the interest you are pleased to take in my concerns, because they are mine, will render a tale worthy of attention which will not be recommended by variety of facts or skill in the display of them.

"Wortley, though passionate, and, with regard to me, unjust, may yet be a good man; but I have no desire to make him one of my auditors. You, sir, may, if you think proper, relate to him afterwards what particulars concerning Welbeck it may be of importance for him to know; but at present it will be well if your indulgence shall support me to the end of a tedious but humble tale."

The eyes of my Eliza sparkled with delight at this proposal. She regarded this youth with a sisterly affection, and considered his candour, in this respect, as an unerring test of his rectitude. She was prepared to hear and to forgive the errors of inexperience and precipitation. I did not fully participate in her satisfaction, but was nevertheless most zealously disposed to listen to his narrative.

My engagements obliged me to postpone this rehearsal till late in the evening. Collected then round a cheerful hearth, exempt from all likelihood of interruption from without, and our babe's unpractised senses shut up in the sweetest and profoundest sleep, Mervyn, after a pause of recollection, began.

CHAPTER II.

My natal soil is Chester county. My father had a small farm, on which he has been able, by industry, to maintain himself and a numerous family. He has had many children, but some defect in the constitution of our mother has been fatal to all of them but me. They died successively as they attained the age of nineteen or twenty, and, since I have not yet reached that age, I may reasonably look for the same premature fate. In the spring of last year my mother followed her fifth child to the grave, and three months afterwards died herself.

My constitution has always been frail, and, till the death of my mother, I enjoyed unlimited indulgence. I cheerfully sustained my portion of labour, for that necessity prescribed; but the intervals were always at my own disposal, and, in whatever manner I thought proper to employ them, my plans were encouraged and assisted. Fond appellations, tones of mildness, solicitous attendance when I was sick, deference to my opinions, and veneration for my talents, compose the image which I still retain of my mother. I had the thoughtlessness and presumption of youth, and, now that she is gone, my compunction is awakened by a thousand recollections of my treatment of her. I was indeed guilty of no flagrant acts of contempt or rebellion. Perhaps her deportment was inevitably calculated to instil into me a froward and refractory spirit. My faults, however, were speedily followed by repentance, and, in the midst of impatience and passion, a look of tender upbraiding from her was always sufficient to melt me into tears and make me ductile to her will. If sorrow for her loss be an atonement for the offences which I committed during her life, ample atonement has been made.

My father is a man of slender capacity, but of a temper easy and flexible. He was sober and industrious by habit. He was content to be guided by the superior intelligence of his wife. Under this guidance he prospered; but, when that was withdrawn, his affairs soon began to betray marks of unskilfulness and negligence. My understanding, perhaps, qualified me to counsel and assist my father, but I was wholly unaccustomed to the task of superintendence. Besides, gentleness and fortitude did not descend to me from my mother, and these were indispensable attributes in a boy who desires to dictate to his gray-headed parent. Time, perhaps, might have conferred dexterity on me, or prudence on him, had not a most unexpected event given a different direction to my views.

Betty Lawrence was a wild girl from the pine-forests of New Jersey. At the age of ten years she became a bound servant in this city, and, after the expiration of her time, came into my father's neighbourhood in search of employment. She was hired in our family as milk-maid and market-woman. Her features were coarse, her frame robust, her mind totally unlettered, and her morals defective in that point in which female excellence is supposed chiefly to consist. She possessed superabundant health and good-humour, and was quite a supportable companion in the hay-field or the barnyard.

On the death of my mother, she was exalted to a somewhat higher station. The same tasks fell to her lot; but the time and manner of performing them were, in some degree, submitted to her own choice. The cows and the dairy were still her province; but in this no one interfered with her or pretended to prescribe her measures. For this province she seemed not unqualified, and, as long as my father was pleased with her management, I had nothing to object.

This state of things continued, without material variation, for several months. There were appearances in my father's deportment to Betty, which excited my reflections, but not my fears. The deference which was occasionally paid to the advice or the claims of this girl was accounted for by that feebleness of mind which degraded my father, in whatever scene he should be placed, to be the tool of others. I had no conception that her claims extended beyond a temporary or superficial gratification.

At length, however, a visible change took place in her

manners. A scornful affectation and awkward dignity began to be assumed. A greater attention was paid to dress, which was of gayer hues and more fashionable texture. I rallied her on these tokens of a sweetheart, and amused myself with expatiating to her on the qualifications of her lover. A clownish fellow was frequently her visitant. His attentions did not appear to be discouraged. He therefore was readily supposed to be the man. When pointed out as the favourite, great resentment was expressed, and obscure insinuations were made that her aim was not quite so low as that. These denials I supposed to be customary on such occasions, and considered the continuance of his visits as a sufficient confutation of them.

I frequently spoke of Betty, her newly-acquired dignity, and of the probable cause of her change of manners, to my father. When this theme was started, a certain coldness and reserve overspread his features. He dealt in monosyllables, and either laboured to change the subject or made some excuse for leaving me. This behaviour, though it occasioned surprise, was never very deeply reflected on. My father was old, and the mournful impressions which were made upon him by the death of his wife, the lapse of almost half a year seemed scarcely to have weakened. Betty had chosen her partner, and I was in daily expectation of receiving a summons to the wedding.

One afternoon this girl dressed herself in the gayest manner and seemed making preparations for some momentous ceremony. My father had directed me to put the horse to the chaise. On my inquiring whither he was going, he answered me, in general terms, that he had some business at a few miles' distance. I offered to go in his stead, but he said that was impossible. I was proceeding to ascertain the possibility of this when he left me to go to a field where his workmen were busy, directing me to inform him when the chaise was ready, to supply his place, while absent, in overlooking the workmen.

This office was performed; but before I called him from the field I exchanged a few words with the milk-maid, who sat on a bench, in all the primness of expectation, and decked with the most gaudy plumage. I rated her imaginary lover for his tardiness, and vowed eternal hatred to them both for not making me a bride's attendant. She listened to me with an air in which embarrassment was mingled sometimes with exultation and sometimes with malice. I left her at length, and returned to the house not till a late hour. As soon as I entered, my father presented Betty to me as his wife, and desired she might receive that treatment from me which was due to a mother.

It was not till after repeated and solemn declarations from both of them that I was prevailed upon to credit this event. Its effect upon my feelings may be easily conceived. I knew the woman to be rude, ignorant, and licentious. Had I suspected this event, I might have fortified my father's weakness and enabled him to shun the gulf to which he was tending; but my presumption had been careless of the danger. To think that such a one should take the place of my revered mother was intolerable.

To treat her in any way not squaring with her real merits; to hinder anger and scorn from rising at the sight of her in her new condition, was not in my power. To be degraded to the rank of her servant, to become the sport of her malice and her artifices, was not to be endured. I had no independent provision; but I was the only child of my father, and had reasonably hoped to succeed to his patrimony. On this hope I had built a thousand agreeable visions. I had meditated innumerable projects which the possession of this estate would enable me to execute. I had no wish beyond the trade of agriculture, and beyond the opulence which a hundred acres would give.

These visions were now at an end. No doubt her own interest would be, to this woman, the supreme law, and this would be considered as irreconcilably hostile to mine. My father would easily be moulded to her purpose, and that act easily extorted from him which should reduce me to beggary. She had a gross and perverse taste. She had a numerous kindred, indigent and hungry. On these his substance would speedily be lavished. Me she hated, because she was conscious of having injured me, because she knew that I held her in contempt, and because I had detected her in an illicit intercourse with the son of a neighbour.

The house in which I lived was no longer my own, nor even my father's. Hitherto I had thought and acted in it with the freedom of a master; but now I was become, in my own conceptions, an alien and an enemy to the roof under which I was born. Every tie which had bound me to it was dissolved or converted into something which repelled me to a distance from it. I was a guest whose presence was borne with anger and impatience.

I was fully impressed with the necessity of removal, but I knew not whither to go, or what kind of subsistence to seek. My father had been a Scottish emigrant, and had no kindred on this side of the ocean. My mother's family lived in New Hampshire, and long separation had extinguished all the rights of relationship in her offspring. Tilling the earth was my only profession, and, to profit by my skill in it, it would be necessary to become a day-labourer in the service of strangers; but this was a destiny to which I, who had so long enjoyed the pleasures of independence and command, could not suddenly reconcile myself. It occurred to me that the city might afford me an asylum. A short day's journey would transport me into it. I had been there twice or thrice in my life, but only for a few hours each time. I knew not a human face, and was a stranger to its modes and dangers. I was qualified for no employment, compatible with a town life, but that of the pen. This, indeed, had ever been a favourite tool with me; and, though it may appear somewhat strange, it is no less true that I had had nearly as much practice at the quill as at the mattock. But the sum of my skill lay in tracing distinct characters. I had used it merely to transcribe what others had written, or to give form to my own conceptions. Whether the city would afford me employment, as a mere copyist, sufficiently lucrative, was a point on which I possessed no means of information.

My determination was hastened by the conduct of my

new mother. My conjectures as to the course she would pursue with regard to me had not been erroneous. My father's deportment, in a short time, grew sullen and austere. Directions were given in a magisterial tone, and any remissness in the execution of his orders was rebuked with an air of authority. At length these rebukes were followed by certain intimations that I was now old enough to provide for myself; that it was time to think of some employment by which I might secure a livelihood; that it was a shame for me to spend my youth in idleness; that what he had gained was by his own labour; and I must be indebted for my living to the same source.

These hints were easily understood. At first, they excited indignation and grief. I knew the source whence they sprung, and was merely able to suppress the utterance of my feelings in her presence. My looks, however, were abundantly significant, and my company became hourly more insupportable. Abstracted from these considerations, my father's remonstrances were not destitute of weight. He gave me being, but sustenance ought surely to be my own gift. In the use of that for which he had been indebted to his own exertions, he might reasonably consult his own choice. He assumed no control over me; he merely did what he would with his own, and, so far from fettering my liberty, he exhorted me to use it for my own benefit, and to make provision for myself.

I now reflected that there were other manual occupations besides that of the plough. Among these none had fewer disadvantages than that of carpenter or cabinet-maker. I had no knowledge of this art; but neither custom, nor law, nor the impenetrableness of the mystery, required me to serve a seven years' apprenticeship to it. A master in this trade might possibly be persuaded to take me under his tuition; two or three years would suffice to give me the requisite skill. Meanwhile my father would, perhaps, consent to bear the cost of my maintenance. Nobody could live upon less than I was willing to do.

I mentioned these ideas to my father; but he merely commended my intentions without offering to assist me in the execution of them. He had full employment, he said, for all the profits of his ground. No doubt, if I would bind myself to serve four or five years, my master would be at the expense of my subsistence. Be that as it would, I must look for nothing from him. I had shown very little regard for his happiness; I had refused all marks of respect to a woman who was entitled to it from her relation to him. He did not see why he should treat as a son one who refused what was due to him as a father. He thought it right that I should henceforth maintain myself. He did not want my services on the farm, and the sooner I quitted his house the better.

I retired from this conference with a resolution to follow the advice that was given. I saw that henceforth I must be my own protector, and wondered at the folly that detained me so long under his roof. To leave it was now become indispensable, and there could be no reason for delaying my departure for a single hour. I determined to bend my course to the city. The scheme foremost in my mind was to apprentice myself to some mechanical trade. I did not overlook the evils of constraint and the dubiousness as to the character of the master I should choose. I was not without hopes that accident would suggest a different expedient, and enable me to procure an immediate subsistence without forfeiting my liberty.

I determined to commence my journey the next morning. No wonder the prospect of so considerable a change in my condition should deprive me of sleep. I spent the night ruminating on the future, and in painting to my fancy the adventures which I should be likely to meet. The foresight of man is in proportion to his knowledge. No wonder that, in my state of profound ignorance, not the faintest preconception should be formed of the events that really befell me. My temper was inquisitive, but there was nothing in the scene to which I was going from which my curiosity expected to derive gratification. Discords and evil smells, unsavoury food, unwholesome labour, and irksome companions, were, in my opinion, the unavoidable attendants of a city.

My best clothes were of the homeliest texture and shape. My whole stock of linen consisted of three check shirts. Part of my winter evenings' employment, since the death of my mother, consisted in knitting my own stockings. Of these I had three pair, one of which I put on, and the rest I formed, together with two shirts, into a bundle. Three quarter-dollar pieces composed my whole fortune in money.

CHAPTER III.

I ROSE at the dawn, and, without asking or bestowing a blessing, sallied forth into the highroad to the city, which passed near the house. I left nothing behind, the loss of which I regretted. I had purchased most of my own books with the product of my own separate industry, and, their number being, of course, small, I had, by incessant application, gotten the whole of them by rote. They had ceased, therefore, to be of any further use. I left them, without reluctance, to the fate for which I knew them to be reserved, that of affording food and habitation to mice.

I trod this unwonted path with all the fearlessness of youth. In spite of the motives to despondency and apprehension incident to my state, my heels were light and my heart joyous. "Now," said I, "I am mounted into man. I must build a name and a fortune for myself. Strange if this intellect and these hands will not supply me with an honest livelihood. I will try the city in the first place; but, if that should fail, resources are still left to me. I will resume my post in the cornfield and threshing-floor, to which I shall always have access, and where I shall always be happy."

I had proceeded some miles on my journey, when I began to feel the inroads of hunger. I might have stopped at any farm-house, and have breakfasted for nothing. It was prudent to husband, with the utmost care, my slender stock; but I felt reluctance to beg as long as I had the means of buying, and I imagined that coarse bread and a little milk would cost little even at a tavern, when any farmer was willing to bestow them for nothing. My resolution was further influenced by the appearance of a signpost. What excuse could I make for begging a breakfast with an inn at hand and silver in my pocket?

I stopped, accordingly, and breakfasted. The landlord was remarkably attentive and obliging, but his bread was stale, his milk sour, and his cheese the greenest imaginable. I disdained to animadvert on these defects, naturally supposing that his house could furnish no better.

Having finished my meal, I put, without speaking, one of my pieces into his hand. This deportment I conceived to be highly becoming, and to indicate a liberal and manly spirit. I always regarded with contempt a scrupulous maker of bargains. He received the money with a complaisant obeisance. "Right," said he. "*Just* the money, sir. You are on foot, sir. A pleasant way of travelling, sir. I wish you a good day, sir." So saying, he walked away.

This proceeding was wholly unexpected. I conceived myself entitled to at least three-fourths of it in change. The first impulse was to call him back, and contest the equity of his demand; but a moment's reflection showed me the absurdity of such conduct. I resumed my journey with spirits somewhat depressed. I have heard of voyagers and wanderers in deserts, who were willing to give a casket of gems for a cup of cold water. I had not supposed my own condition to be, in any respect, similar; yet I had just given one-third of my estate for a breakfast.

I stopped at noon at another inn. I counted on purchasing a dinner for the same price, since I meant to content myself with the same fare. A large company was just sitting down to a smoking banquet. The landlord invited me to join them. I took my place at the table, but was furnished with bread and milk. Being prepared to depart, I took him aside. "What is to pay?" said I.—"Did you drink any thing, sir?"—"Certainly. I drank the milk which was furnished."—"But any liquors, sir?"—"No."

He deliberated a moment, and then, assuming an air of disinterestedness, "'Tis our custom to charge dinner and club; but, as you drank nothing, we'll let the club go. A mere dinner is half a dollar, sir."

He had no leisure to attend to my fluctuations. After debating with myself on what was to be done, I concluded that compliance was best, and, leaving the money at the bar, resumed my way.

I had not performed more than half my journey, yet my purse was entirely exhausted. This was a specimen of the cost incurred by living at an inn. If I entered the city, a tavern must, at least for some time, be my abode; but I had not a farthing remaining to defray my charges. My father had formerly entertained a boarder for a dollar per week, and, in case of need, I was willing to subsist upon coarser fare and lie on a harder bed than those with which our guest had been supplied. These facts had been the foundation of my negligence on this occasion.

What was now to be done? To return to my paternal mansion was impossible. To relinquish my design of entering the city and to seek a temporary asylum, if not permanent employment, at some one of the plantations within view, was the most obvious expedient. These deliberations did not slacken my pace. I was almost unmindful of my way, when I found I had passed Schuylkill at the upper bridge. I was now within the precincts of the city, and night was hastening. It behooved me to come to a speedy decision.

Suddenly I recollected that I had not paid the customary toll at the bridge; neither had I money wherewith to pay it. A demand of payment would have suddenly arrested my progress; and so slight an incident would have precluded that wonderful destiny to which I was reserved. The obstacle that would have hindered my advance now prevented my return. Scrupulous honesty did not require me to turn back and awaken the vigilance of the toll-gatherer. I had nothing to pay, and by returning I should only double my debt. "Let it stand," said I, "where it does. All that honour enjoins is to pay when I am able."

I adhered to the crossways, till I reached Market Street. Night had fallen, and a triple row of lamps presented a spectacle enchanting and new. My personal cares were, for a time, lost in the tumultuous sensations with which I was now engrossed. I had never visited the city at this hour. When my last visit was paid, I was a mere child. The novelty which environed every object was, therefore, nearly absolute. I proceeded with more cautious steps, but was still absorbed in attention to passing objects. I reached the market-house, and, entering it, indulged myself in new delight and new wonder.

I need not remark that our ideas of magnificence and splendour are merely comparative; yet you may be prompted to smile when I tell you that, in walking through this avenue, I, for a moment, conceived myself transported to the hall "pendent with many a row of starry lamps and blazing crescents fed by naphtha and asphaltos." That this transition from my homely and quiet retreat had been effected in so few hours wore the aspect of miracle or magic.

I proceeded from one of these buildings to another, till I reached their termination in Front Street. Here my progress was checked, and I sought repose to my weary limbs by seating myself on a stall. No wonder some fatigue was felt by me, accustomed as I was to strenuous exertions, since, exclusive of the minutes spent at breakfast and dinner, I had travelled fifteen hours and forty-five miles.

I began now to reflect, with some earnestness, on my condition. I was a stranger, friendless and moneyless. I was unable to purchase food and shelter, and was wholly unused to the business of begging. Hunger was the only serious inconvenience to which I was immediately exposed. I had no objection to spend the night in the spot where I then sat. I had no fear that my visions would be troubled by the officers of police. It was no crime to be without a home; but how should I supply my present cravings and the cravings of to-morrow?

At length it occurred to me that one of our country neighbours was probably at this time in the city. He kept a store as well as cultivated a farm. He was a plain and well-meaning man, and, should I be so fortunate as to meet him, his superior knowledge of the city might be of essential benefit to me in my present forlorn circumstances. His generosity might likewise induce him to lend me so much as would purchase one meal. I had formed the resolution to leave the city next day, and was astonished at the folly that had led me into it; but, meanwhile, my physical wants must be supplied.

Where should I look for this man? In the course of conversation I recollected him to have referred to the place of his temporary abode. It was an inn; but the sign or the name of the keeper for some time withstood all my efforts to recall them.

At length I lighted on the last. It was Lesher's tavern. I immediately set out in search of it. After many inquiries, I at last arrived at the door. I was preparing to enter the house when I perceived that my bundle was gone. I had left it on the stall where I had been sitting. People were perpetually passing to and fro. It was scarcely possible not to have been noticed. No one that observed it would fail to make it his prey. Yet it was of too much value to me to allow me to be governed by a bare probability. I resolved to lose not a moment in returning.

With some difficulty I retraced my steps, but the bundle had disappeared. The clothes were, in themselves, of small value, but they constituted the whole of my wardrobe; and I now reflected that they were capable of being transmuted, by the pawn or sale of them, into food. There were other wretches as indigent as I was, and I consoled myself by thinking that my shirts and stockings might furnish a seasonable covering to their nakedness; but there was a relic concealed within this bundle, the loss of which could scarcely be endured by me. It was the portrait of a young man who died three years ago at my father's house, drawn by his own hand.

He was discovered one morning in the orchard with many marks of insanity upon him. His air and dress bespoke some elevation of rank and fortune. My mother's compassion was excited, and, as his singularities were harmless, an asylum was afforded him, though he was unable to pay for it. He was constantly declaiming, in an incoherent manner, about some mistress who had proved faithless. His speeches seemed, however, like the rantings of an actor, to be rehearsed by rote or for the sake of exercise. He was totally careless of his person and health, and, by repeated negligences of this kind, at last contracted a fever of which he speedily died. The name which he assumed was Clavering.

He gave no distinct account of his family, but stated, in loose terms, that they were residents in England, high-born and wealthy. That they had denied him the woman whom he loved and banished him to America, under penalty of death if he should dare to return, and that they had refused him all means of subsistence in a foreign land. He predicted, in his wild and declamatory way, his own death. He was very skilful at the pencil, and drew this portrait a short time before his dissolution, presented it to me, and charged me to preserve it in remembrance of him. My mother loved the youth because he was amiable and unfortunate, and chiefly because she fancied a very powerful resemblance between his countenance and mine. I was too young to build affection on any rational foundation. I loved him, for whatever reason, with an ardour unusual at my age, and which this portrait had contributed to prolong and to cherish.

In thus finally leaving my home, I was careful not to leave this picture behind. I wrapped it in paper in which a few elegiac stanzas were inscribed in my own hand, and with my utmost elegance of penmanship. I then placed it in a leathern case, which, for greater security, was deposited in the centre of my bundle. It will occur to you, perhaps, that it would be safer in some fold or pocket of the clothes which I wore. I was of a different opinion, and was now to endure the penalty of my error.

It was in vain to heap execrations on my negligence, or to consume the little strength left to me in regrets. I returned once more to the tavern and made inquiries for Mr. Capper, the person whom I have just mentioned as my father's neighbour. I was informed that Capper was now in town; that he had lodged, on the last night, at this house; that he had expected to do the same to-night, but a gentleman had called ten minutes ago, whose invitation to lodge with him to-night had been accepted. They had just gone out together. Who, I asked, was the gentleman? The landlord had no knowledge of him;

he knew neither his place of abode nor his name. Was Mr. Capper expected to return hither in the morning? No; he had heard the stranger propose to Mr. Capper to go with him into the country to-morrow, and Mr. Capper, he believed, had assented.

This disappointment was peculiarly severe. I had lost, by my own negligence, the only opportunity that would offer of meeting my friend. Had even the recollection of my loss been postponed for three minutes, I should have entered the house, and a meeting would have been secured. I could discover no other expedient to obviate the present evil. My heart began now, for the first time, to droop. I looked back, with nameless emotions, on the days of my infancy. I called up the image of my mother. I reflected on the infatuation of my surviving parent, and the usurpation of the detestable Betty, with horror. I viewed myself as the most calamitous and desolate of human beings.

At this time I was sitting in the common room. There were others in the same apartment, lounging, or whistling, or singing. I noticed them not, but, leaning my head upon my hand, I delivered myself up to painful and intense meditation. From this I was roused by some one placing himself on the bench near me and addressing me thus:—"Pray, sir, if you will excuse me, who was the person whom you were looking for just now? Perhaps I can give you the information you want. If I can, you will be very welcome to it." I fixed my eyes with some eagerness on the person that spoke. He was a young man, expensively and fashionably dressed, whose mien was considerably prepossessing, and whose countenance bespoke some portion of discernment. I described to him the man whom I sought. "I am in search of the same man myself," said he, "but I expect to meet him here. He may lodge elsewhere, but he promised to meet me here at half after nine. I have no doubt he will fulfil his promise, so that you will meet the gentleman."

I was highly gratified by this information, and thanked my informant with some degree of warmth. My gratitude he did not notice, but continued: "In order to beguile expectation, I have ordered supper; will you do me the favour to partake with me, unless indeed you have supped already?" I was obliged, somewhat awkwardly, to decline his invitation, conscious as I was that the means of payment were not in my power. He continued, however, to urge my compliance till at length it was, though reluctantly, yielded. My chief motive was the certainty of seeing Capper.

My new acquaintance was exceedingly conversible, but his conversation was chiefly characterized by frankness and good-humour. My reserve gradually diminished, and I ventured to inform him, in general terms, of my former condition and present views. He listened to my details with seeming attention, and commented on them with some judiciousness. His statements, however, tended to discourage me from remaining in the city.

Meanwhile the hour passed and Capper did not appear. I noticed this circumstance to him with no little solicitude. He said that possibly he might have forgotten or neglected his engagement. His affair was not of the highest importance, and might be readily postponed to a future opportunity. He perceived that my vivacity was greatly damped by this intelligence. He importuned me to disclose the cause. He made himself very merry with my distress, when it was at length discovered. As to the expense of supper, I had partaken of it at his invitation; he therefore should of course be charged with it. As to lodging, he had a chamber and a bed, which he would insist upon my sharing with him.

My faculties were thus kept upon the stretch of wonder. Every new act of kindness in this man surpassed the fondest expectation that I had formed. I saw no reason why I should be treated with benevolence. I should have acted in the same manner if placed in the same circumstances; yet it appeared incongruous and inexplicable. I know whence my ideas of human nature were derived. They certainly were not the offspring of my own feelings. These would have taught me that interest and duty were blended in every act of generosity.

I did not come into the world without my scruples and

suspicions. I was more apt to impute kindnesses to sinister and hidden than to obvious and laudable motives.

I paused to reflect upon the possible designs of this person. What end could be served by this behaviour? I was no subject of violence or fraud. I had neither trinket nor coin to stimulate the treachery of others. What was offered was merely lodging for the night. Was this an act of such transcendent disinterestedness as to be incredible? My garb was meaner than that of my companion, but my intellectual accomplishments were at least upon a level with his. Why should he be supposed to be insensible to my claims upon his kindness? I was a youth destitute of experience, money, and friends; but I was not devoid of all mental and personal endowments. That my merit should be discovered, even on such slender intercourse, had surely nothing in it that shocked belief.

While I was thus deliberating, my new friend was earnest in his solicitations for my company. He remarked my hesitation, but ascribed it to a wrong cause. "Come," said he, "I can guess your objections and can obviate them. You are afraid of being ushered into company; and people who have passed their lives like you have a wonderful antipathy to strange faces; but this is bedtime with our family, so that we can defer your introduction to them till to-morrow. We may go to our chamber without being seen by any but servants."

I had not been aware of this circumstance. My reluctance flowed from a different cause, but, now that the inconveniences of ceremony were mentioned, they appeared to me of considerable weight. I was well pleased that they should thus be avoided, and consented to go along with him.

We passed several streets and turned several corners. At last we turned into a kind of court which seemed to be chiefly occupied by stables. "We will go," said he, "by the back way into the house. We shall thus save ourselves the necessity of entering the parlour, where some of the family may still be."

My companion was as talkative as ever, but said nothing from which I could gather any knowledge of the number, character, and condition of his family.

CHAPTER IV.

WE arrived at a brick wall, through which we passed by a gate into an extensive court or yard. The darkness would allow me to see nothing but outlines. Compared with the pigmy dimensions of my father's wooden hovel, the buildings before me were of gigantic loftiness. The horses were here far more magnificently accommodated than I had been. By a large door we entered an elevated hall. "Stay here," said he, "just while I fetch a light."

He returned, bearing a candle, before I had time to ponder on my present situation.

We now ascended a staircase, covered with painted canvas. No one whose inexperience is less than mine can imagine to himself the impressions made upon me by surrounding objects. The height to which this stair ascended, its dimensions, and its ornaments, appeared to me a combination of all that was pompous and superb.

We stopped not till we had reached the third story. Here my companion unlocked and led the way into a chamber. "This," said he, "is my room; permit me to welcome you into it."

I had no time to examine this room before, by some accident, the candle was extinguished. "Curse upon my carelessness!" said he. "I must go down again and light the candle. I will return in a twinkling. Meanwhile you may undress yourself and go to bed." He went out, and, as I afterwards recollected, locked the door behind him.

I was not indisposed to follow his advice, but my curiosity would first be gratified by a survey of the room. Its height and spaciousness were imperfectly discernible by starlight, and by gleams from a street-lamp. The floor was covered with a carpet, the walls with brilliant hangings; the bed and windows were shrouded by curtains of a rich texture and glossy hues. Hitherto I had merely read of these things. I knew them to be the decorations of opulence; and yet, as I viewed them, and remembered where and what I was on the same hour the preceding day, I could scarcely believe myself awake, or that my senses were not beguiled by some spell.

"Where," said I, "will this adventure terminate? I rise on the morrow with the dawn and speed into the country. When this night is remembered, how like a vision will it appear! If I tell the tale by a kitchen-fire, my veracity will be disputed. I shall be ranked with the story-tellers of Shiraz and Bagdad."

Though busied in these reflections, I was not inattentive to the progress of time. Methought my companion was remarkably dilatory. He went merely to relight his candle, but certainly he might, during this time, have performed the operation ten times over. Some unforeseen accident might occasion his delay.

Another interval passed, and no tokens of his coming. I began now to grow uneasy. I was unable to account for his detention. Was not some treachery designed? I went to the door, and found that it was locked. This heightened my suspicions. I was alone, a stranger, in an upper room of the house. Should my conductor have disappeared, by design or by accident, and some one of the family should find me here, what would be the consequence? Should I not be arrested as a thief, and conveyed to prison? My transition from the street to this chamber would not be more rapid than my passage hence to a jail.

These ideas struck me with panic. I revolved them anew, but they only acquired greater plausibility. No doubt I had been the victim of malicious artifice. Inclination, however, conjured up opposite sentiments, and my fears began to subside. What motive, I asked, could induce a human being to inflict wanton injury? I could not account for his delay; but how numberless were the contingencies that might occasion it!

I was somewhat comforted by these reflections, but

the consolation they afforded was short-lived. I was listening with the utmost eagerness to catch the sound of a foot, when a noise was indeed heard, but totally unlike a step. It was human breath struggling, as it were, for passage. On the first effort of attention, it appeared like a groan. Whence it arose I could not tell. He that uttered it was near; perhaps in the room.

Presently the same noise was again heard, and now I perceived that it came from the bed. It was accompanied with a motion like some one changing his posture. What I at first conceived to be a groan appeared now to be nothing more than the expiration of a sleeping man. What should I infer from this incident? My companion did not apprize me that the apartment was inhabited. Was his imposture a jestful or a wicked one?

There was no need to deliberate. There were no means of concealment or escape. The person would some time awaken and detect me. The interval would only be fraught with agony, and it was wise to shorten it. Should I not withdraw the curtain, awake the person, and encounter at once all the consequences of my situation? I glided softly to the bed, when the thought occurred, May not the sleeper be a female?

I cannot describe the mixture of dread and of shame which glowed in my veins. The light in which such a visitant would be probably regarded by a woman's fears, the precipitate alarms that might be given, the injury which I might unknowingly inflict or undeservedly suffer, threw my thoughts into painful confusion. My presence might pollute a spotless reputation, or furnish fuel to jealousy.

Still, though it were a female, would not less injury be done by gently interrupting her slumber? But the question of sex still remained to be decided. For this end I once more approached the bed, and drew aside the silk. The sleeper was a babe. This I discovered by the glimmer of a street-lamp.

Part of my solicitudes were now removed. It was plain that this chamber belonged to a nurse or a mother. She had not yet come to bed. Perhaps it was a married pair, and their approach might be momently expected.

I pictured to myself their entrance and my own detection. I could imagine no consequence that was not disastrous and horrible, and from which I would not at any price escape. I again examined the door, and found that exit by this avenue was impossible. There were other doors in this room. Any practicable expedient in this extremity was to be pursued. One of these was bolted. I unfastened it and found a considerable space within. Should I immure myself in this closet? I saw no benefit that would finally result from it. I discovered that there was a bolt on the inside, which would somewhat contribute to security. This being drawn, no one could enter without breaking the door.

I had scarcely paused, when the long-expected sound of footsteps was heard in the entry. Was it my companion, or a stranger? If it were the latter, I had not yet mustered courage sufficient to meet him. I cannot applaud the magnanimity of my proceeding; but no one can expect intrepid or judicious measures from one in my circumstances. I stepped into the closet, and closed the door. Some one immediately after unlocked the chamber door. He was unattended with a light. The footsteps, as they moved along the carpet, could scarcely be heard.

I waited impatiently for some token by which I might be governed. I put my ear to the keyhole, and at length heard a voice, but not that of my companion, exclaim, somewhat above a whisper, "Smiling cherub! safe and sound, I see. Would to God my experiment may succeed, and that thou mayest find a mother where I have found a wife!" There he stopped. He appeared to kiss the babe, and, presently retiring, locked the door after him.

These words were capable of no consistent meaning. They served, at least, to assure me that I had been treacherously dealt with. This chamber, it was manifest, did not belong to my companion. I put up prayers to my Deity that he would deliver me from these toils. What a condition was mine! Immersed in palpable darkness! shut up in this unknown recess! lurking like a robber!

My meditations were disturbed by new sounds. The

door was unlocked, more than one person entered the apartment, and light streamed through the keyhole. I looked; but the aperture was too small and the figures passed too quickly to permit me the sight of them. I bent my ear, and this imparted some more authentic information.

The man, as I judged by the voice, was the same who had just departed. Rustling of silk denoted his companion to be female. Some words being uttered by the man, in too low a key to be overheard, the lady burst into a passion of tears. He strove to comfort her by soothing tones and tender appellations. "How can it be helped?" said he. "It is time to resume your courage. Your duty to yourself and to me requires you to subdue this unreasonable grief."

He spoke frequently in this strain, but all he said seemed to have little influence in pacifying the lady. At length, however, her sobs began to lessen in vehemence and frequency. He exhorted her to seek for some repose. Apparently she prepared to comply, and conversation was, for a few minutes, intermitted.

I could not but advert to the possibility that some occasion to examine the closet, in which I was immured, might occur. I knew not in what manner to demean myself if this should take place. I had no option at present. By withdrawing myself from view I had lost the privilege of an upright deportment. Yet the thought of spending the night in this spot was not to be endured.

Gradually I began to view the project of bursting from the closet, and trusting to the energy of truth and of an artless tale, with more complacency. More than once my hand was placed upon the bolt, but withdrawn by a sudden faltering of resolution. When one attempt failed, I recurred once more to such reflections as were adapted to renew my purpose.

I preconcerted the address which I should use. I resolved to be perfectly explicit; to withhold no particular of my adventures from the moment of my arrival. My description must necessarily suit some person within their knowledge. All I should want was liberty to depart; but, if this were not allowed, I might at least hope to escape any ill treatment, and to be confronted with my betrayer. In that case I did not fear to make him the attester of my innocence.

Influenced by these considerations, I once more touched the lock. At that moment the lady shrieked, and exclaimed, "Good God! What is here?" An interesting conversation ensued. The object that excited her astonishment was the child. I collected from what passed that the discovery was wholly unexpected by her. Her husband acted as if equally unaware of this event. He joined in all her exclamations of wonder and all her wild conjectures. When these were somewhat exhausted, he artfully insinuated the propriety of bestowing care upon the little foundling. I now found that her grief had been occasioned by the recent loss of her own offspring. She was, for some time, averse to her husband's proposal, but at length was persuaded to take the babe to her bosom and give it nourishment.

This incident had diverted my mind from its favourite project, and filled me with speculations on the nature of the scene. One explication was obvious, that the husband was the parent of this child, and had used this singular expedient to procure for it the maternal protection of his wife. It would soon claim from her all the fondness which she entertained for her own progeny. No suspicion probably had yet, or would hereafter, occur with regard to its true parent. If her character be distinguished by the usual attributes of women, the knowledge of this truth may convert her love into hatred. I reflected with amazement on the slightness of that thread by which human passions are led from their true direction. With no less amazement did I remark the complexity of incidents by which I had been empowered to communicate to her this truth. How baseless are the structures of falsehood, which we build in opposition to the system of eternal nature! If I should escape undetected from this recess, it will be true that I never saw the face of either of these persons, and yet I am acquainted with the most secret transaction of their lives.

My own situation was now more critical than before. The lights were extinguished, and the parties had sought repose. To issue from the closet now would be imminently dangerous. My councils were again at a stand and my designs frustrated. Meanwhile the persons did not drop their discourse, and I thought myself justified in listening. Many facts of the most secret and momentous nature were alluded to. Some allusions were unintelligible. To others I was able to affix a plausible meaning, and some were palpable enough. Every word that was uttered on that occasion is indelibly imprinted on my memory. Perhaps the singularity of my circumstances, and my previous ignorance of what was passing in the world, contributed to render me a greedy listener. Most that was said I shall overlook; but one part of the conversation it will be necessary to repeat.

A large company had assembled that evening at their house. They criticized the character and manners of several. At last the husband said, "What think you of the nabob? Especially when he talked about riches? How artfully he encourages the notion of his poverty! Yet not a soul believes him. I cannot for my part account for that scheme of his. I half suspect that his wealth flows from a bad source, since he is so studious of concealing it."

"Perhaps, after all," said the lady, "you are mistaken as to his wealth."

"Impossible," exclaimed the other. "Mark how he lives. Have I not seen his bank-account? His deposits, since he has been here, amount to no less than half a million."

"Heaven grant that it be so!" said the lady, with a sigh. "I shall think with less aversion of your scheme. If poor Tom's fortune be made, and he not the worse, or but little the worse on that account, I shall think it on the whole best."

"That," replied he, "is what reconciles me to the scheme. To him thirty thousand are nothing."

"But will he not suspect you of some hand in it?"

"How can he? Will I not appear to lose as well as himself? Tom is my brother, but who can be supposed to answer for a brother's integrity? but he cannot suspect either of us. Nothing less than a miracle can bring our plot to light. Besides, this man is not what he ought to be. He will, some time or other, come out to be a grand impostor. He makes money by other arts than bargain and sale. He has found his way, by some means, to the Portuguese treasury."

Here the conversation took a new direction, and, after some time, the silence of sleep ensued.

Who, thought I, is this nabob who counts his dollars by half-millions, and on whom it seems as if some fraud was intended to be practised? Amidst their wariness and subtlety, how little are they aware that their conversation has been overheard! By means as inscrutable as those which conducted me hither, I may hereafter be enabled to profit by this detection of a plot. But, meanwhile, what was I to do? How was I to effect my escape from this perilous asylum?

After much reflection, it occurred to me that to gain the street without exciting their notice was not utterly impossible. Sleep does not commonly end of itself, unless at a certain period. What impediments were there between me and liberty which I could not remove, and remove with so much caution as to escape notice? Motion and sound inevitably go together; but every sound is not attended to. The doors of the closet and the chamber did not creak upon their hinges. The latter might be locked. This I was able to ascertain only by experiment. If it were so, yet the key was probably in the lock, and might be used without much noise.

I waited till their slow and hoarser inspirations showed them to be both asleep. Just then, on changing my position, my head struck against some things which depended from the ceiling of the closet. They were implements of some kind which rattled against each other in consequence of this unlucky blow. I was fearful lest this noise should alarm, as the closet was little distant from the bed. The breathing of one instantly ceased, and a motion was made as if the head were lifted from the pillow. This motion, which was made by the husband, awaked his companion, who exclaimed, "What is the matter?"

"Something, I believe," replied he, "in the closet.

If I was not dreaming, I heard the pistols strike against each other as if some one was taking them down."

This intimation was well suited to alarm the lady. She besought him to ascertain the matter. This, to my utter dismay, he at first consented to do, but presently observed that probably his ears had misinformed him. It was hardly possible that the sound proceeded from them. It might be a rat, or his own fancy might have fashioned it. It is not easy to describe my trepidations while this conference was holding. I saw how easily their slumber was disturbed. The obstacles to my escape were less surmountable than I had imagined.

In a little time all was again still. I waited till the usual tokens of sleep were distinguishable. I once more resumed my attempt. The bolt was withdrawn with all possible slowness; but I could by no means prevent all sound. My state was full of inquietude and suspense; my attention being painfully divided between the bolt and the condition of the sleepers. The difficulty lay in giving that degree of force which was barely sufficient. Perhaps not less than fifteen minutes were consumed in this operation. At last it was happily effected, and the door was cautiously opened.

Emerging as I did from utter darkness, the light admitted into three windows produced, to my eyes, a considerable illumination. Objects which, on my first entrance into this apartment, were invisible, were now clearly discerned. The bed was shrouded by curtains, yet I shrunk back into my covert, fearful of being seen. To facilitate my escape, I put off my shoes. My mind was so full of objects of more urgent moment, that the propriety of taking them along with me never occurred. I left them in the closet.

I now glided across the apartment to the door. I was not a little discouraged by observing that the key was wanting. My whole hope depended on the omission to lock it. In my haste to ascertain this point, I made some noise which again roused one of the sleepers. He started, and cried, "Who is there?"

I now regarded my case as desperate, and detection as inevitable. My apprehensions, rather than my caution, kept me mute. I shrunk to the wall, and waited in a kind of agony for the moment that should decide my fate.

The lady was again roused. In answer to her inquiries, her husband said that some one, he believed, was at the door, but there was no danger of their entering, for he had locked it, and the key was in his pocket.

My courage was completely annihilated by this piece of intelligence. My resources were now at an end. I could only remain in this spot till the morning light, which could be at no great distance, should discover me. My inexperience disabled me from estimating all the perils of my situation. Perhaps I had no more than temporary inconveniences to dread. My intention was innocent, and I had been betrayed into my present situation, not by my own wickedness, but the wickedness of others.

I was deeply impressed with the ambiguousness which would necessarily rest upon my motives, and the scrutiny to which they would be subjected. I shuddered at the bare possibility of being ranked with thieves. These reflections again gave edge to my ingenuity in search of the means of escape. I had carefully attended to the circumstances of their entrance. Possibly the act of locking had been unnoticed; but was it not likewise possible that this person had been mistaken? The key was gone. Would this have been the case if the door were unlocked?

My fears, rather than my hopes, impelled me to make the experiment. I drew back the latch, and, to my unspeakable joy, the door opened.

I passed through and explored my way to the staircase. I descended till I reached the bottom. I could not recollect with accuracy the position of the door leading into the court, but, by carefully feeling along the wall with my hands, I at length discovered it. It was fastened by several bolts and a lock. The bolts were easily withdrawn, but the key was removed. I knew not where it was deposited. I thought I had reached the threshold of liberty, but here was an impediment that threatened to be insurmountable.

But, if doors could not be passed, windows might be unbarred. I remembered that my companion had gone into a door on the left hand, in search of a light. I searched for this door. Fortunately it was fastened only by a bolt. It admitted me into a room which I carefully explored till I reached a window. I will not dwell on my efforts to unbar this entrance. Suffice it to say that, after much exertion and frequent mistakes, I at length found my way into the yard, and thence passed into the court.

CHAPTER V.

Now I was once more on public ground. By so many anxious efforts had I disengaged myself from the perilous precincts of private property. As many stratagems as are usually made to enter a house had been employed by me to get out of it. I was urged to the use of them by my fears; yet, so far from carrying off spoil, I had escaped with the loss of an essential part of my dress.

I had now leisure to reflect. I seated myself on the ground and reviewed the scenes through which I had just passed. I began to think that my industry had been misemployed. Suppose I had met the person on his first entrance into his chamber? Was the truth so utterly wild as not to have found credit? Since the door was locked, and there was no other avenue, what other statement but the true one would account for my being found there? This deportment had been worthy of an honest purpose. My betrayer probably expected that this would be the issue of his jest. My rustic simplicity, he might think, would suggest no more ambiguous or elaborate expedient. He might likewise have predetermined to interfere if my safety had been really endangered.

On the morrow the two doors of the chamber and the window below would be found unclosed. They will suspect a design to pillage, but their searches will terminate in nothing but in the discovery of a pair of clumsy and dusty shoes in the closet. Now that I was safe I could not help smiling at the picture which my fancy drew of their anxiety and wonder. These thoughts, however, gave place to more momentous considerations.

I could not imagine to myself a more perfect example of indigence than I now exhibited. There was no being in the city on whose kindness I had any claim. Money I had none, and what I then wore comprised my whole stock of movables. I had just lost my shoes, and this loss rendered my stockings of no use. My dignity remonstrated against a barefoot pilgrimage, but to this, necessity now reconciled me. I threw my stockings between the bars of a stable-window, belonging, as I thought, to the mansion I had just left. These, together with my shoes, I left to pay the cost of my entertainment.

I saw that the city was no place for me. The end that I had had in view, of procuring some mechanical employment, could only be obtained by the use of means, but what means to pursue I knew not. This night's perils and deceptions gave me a distaste to a city life, and my ancient occupations rose to my view enhanced by a thousand imaginary charms. I resolved forthwith to strike into the country.

The day began now to dawn. It was Sunday, and I was desirous of eluding observation. I was somewhat recruited by rest, though the languors of sleeplessness oppressed me. I meant to throw myself on the first lap of verdure I should meet, and indulge in sleep that I so much wanted. I knew not the direction of the streets; but followed that which I first entered from the court, trusting that, by adhering steadily to one course, I should some time reach the fields. This street, as I afterwards found, tended to Schuylkill, and soon extricated me from houses. I could not cross this river without payment of toll. It was requisite to cross it in order to reach that part of the country whither I was desirous of going; but how should I effect my passage? I knew of no ford, and the smallest expense exceeded my capacity. Ten thousand guineas and a farthing were equally remote from nothing, and nothing was the portion allotted to me.

While my mind was thus occupied, I turned up one of the streets which tend northward. It was, for some length, uninhabited and unpaved. Presently I reached a pavement, and a painted fence, along which a row of poplars was planted. It bounded a garden into which a knot-hole permitted me to pry. The enclosure was a charming green, which I saw appended to a house of the loftiest and most stately order. It seemed like a recent erection, had all the gloss of novelty, and exhibited, to my unpractised eyes, the magnificence of palaces. My father's dwelling did not equal the height of one story, and might be easily comprised in one-fourth of those buildings which here were designed to accommodate the menials. My heart dictated the comparison between my own condition and that of the proprietors of this domain. How wide and how impassable was the gulf by which we were separated! This fair inheritance had fallen to one who, perhaps, would only abuse it to the purposes of luxury, while I, with intentions worthy of the friend of mankind, was doomed to wield the flail and the mattock.

I had been entirely unaccustomed to this strain of reflection. My books had taught me the dignity and safety of the middle path, and my darling writer abounded with encomiums on rural life. At a distance from luxury and pomp, I viewed them, perhaps, in a just light. A nearer scrutiny confirmed my early prepossessions; but, at the distance at which I now stood, the lofty edifices, the splendid furniture, and the copious accommodations of the rich excited my admiration and my envy.

I relinquished my station, and proceeded, in a heartless mood, along the fence. I now came to the mansion itself. The principal door was entered by a staircase of marble. I had never seen the stone of Carrara, and wildly supposed this to have been dug from Italian quarries. The beauty of the poplars, the coolness exhaled from the dew-besprent bricks, the commodiousness of the seat which these steps afforded, and the uncertainty into which I was plunged respecting my future conduct, all combined to make me pause. I sat down on the lower step and began to meditate.

By some transition it occurred to me that the supply of my most urgent wants might be found in some inhabitant of this house. I needed at present a few cents;

and what where a few cents to the tenant of a mansion like this? I had an invincible aversion to the calling of a beggar, but I regarded with still more antipathy the vocation of a thief; to this alternative, however, I was now reduced. I must either steal or beg; unless, indeed, assistance could be procured under the notion of a loan. Would a stranger refuse to lend the pittance that I wanted? Surely not, when the urgency of my wants was explained.

I recollected other obstacles. To summon the master of the house from his bed, perhaps, for the sake of such an application, would be preposterous. I should be in more danger of provoking his anger than exciting his benevolence. This request might, surely, with more propriety be preferred to a passenger. I should, probably, meet several before I should arrive at Schuylkill.

A servant just then appeared at the door, with bucket and brush. This obliged me, much sooner than I intended, to decamp. With some reluctance I rose and proceeded. This house occupied the corner of the street, and I now turned this corner towards the country. A person, at some distance before me, was approaching in an opposite direction.

"Why," said I, "may I not make my demand of the first man I meet? This person exhibits tokens of ability to lend. There is nothing chilling or austere in his demeanour."

The resolution to address this passenger was almost formed; but the nearer he advanced my resolves grew less firm. He noticed me not till he came within a few paces. He seemed busy in reflection; and, had not my figure caught his eye, or had he merely bestowed a passing glance upon me, I should not have been sufficiently courageous to have detained him. The event, however, was widely different.

He looked at me and started. For an instant, as it were, and till he had time to dart at me a second glance, he checked his pace. This behaviour decided mine, and he stopped on perceiving tokens of a desire to address him. I spoke, but my accents and air sufficiently denoted my embarrassments:—

"I am going to solicit a favour which my situation makes of the highest importance to me, and which I hope it will be easy for you, sir, to grant. It is not an alms, but a loan, that I seek; a loan that I will repay the moment I am able to do it. I am going to the country, but have not wherewith to pay my passage over Schuylkill, or to buy a morsel of bread. May I venture to request of you, sir, the loan of sixpence? As I told you, it is my intention to repay it."

I delivered this address, not without some faltering, but with great earnestness. I laid particular stress upon my intention to refund the money. He listened with a most inquisitive air. His eye perused me from head to foot.

After some pause, he said, in a very emphatic manner, "Why into the country? Have you family? Kindred? Friends?"

"No," answered I, "I have neither. I go in search of the means of subsistence. I have passed my life upon a farm, and propose to die in the same condition."

"Whence have you come?"

"I came yesterday from the country, with a view to earn my bread in some way, but have changed my plan and propose now to return."

"Why have you changed it? In what way are you capable of earning your bread?"

"I hardly know," said I. "I can, as yet, manage no tool, that can be managed in the city, but the pen. My habits have, in some small degree, qualified me for a writer. I would willingly accept employment of that kind."

He fixed his eyes upon the earth, and was silent for some minutes. At length, recovering himself, he said, "Follow me to my house. Perhaps something may be done for you. If not, I will lend you sixpence."

It may be supposed that I eagerly complied with the invitation. My companion said no more, his air bespeaking him to be absorbed by his own thoughts, till he reached his house, which proved to be that at the door of which I had been seated. We entered a parlour together.

Unless you can assume my ignorance and my simplicity, you will be unable to conceive the impressions that were made by the size and ornaments of this apartment. I shall omit these impressions, which, indeed, no description could adequately convey, and dwell on incidents of greater moment. He asked me to give him a specimen of my penmanship. I told you that I had bestowed very great attention upon this art. Implements were brought, and I sat down to the task. By some inexplicable connection a line in Shakspeare occurred to me, and I wrote,—

"My poverty, but not my will, consents."

The sentiment conveyed in this line powerfully affected him, but in a way which I could not then comprehend. I collected from subsequent events that the inference was not unfavourable to my understanding or my morals. He questioned me as to my history. I related my origin and my inducements to desert my father's house. With respect to last night's adventures I was silent. I saw no useful purpose that could be answered by disclosure, and I half suspected that my companion would refuse credit to my tale.

There were frequent intervals of abstraction and reflection between his questions. My examination lasted not much less than an hour. At length he said, "I want an amanuensis or copyist. On what terms will you live with me?"

I answered that I knew not how to estimate the value of my services. I knew not whether these services were agreeable or healthful. My life had hitherto been active. My constitution was predisposed to diseases of the lungs, and the change might be hurtful. I was willing, however, to try and to content myself for a month or a year, with so much as would furnish me with food, clothing, and lodging.

"'Tis well," said he. "You remain with me as long and no longer than both of us please. You shall lodge and eat in this house. I will supply you with clothing, and your task will be to write what I dictate. Your person, I see, has not shared much of your attention. It is in my power to equip you instantly in the manner which becomes a resident in this house. Come with me."

He led the way into the court behind and thence into a neat building, which contained large wooden vessels and a pump: "There," said he, "you may wash yourself; and, when that is done, I will conduct you to your chamber and your wardrobe."

This was speedily performed, and he accordingly led the way to the chamber. It was an apartment in the third story, finished and furnished in the same costly and superb style with the rest of the house. He opened closets and drawers which overflowed with clothes and linen of all and of the best kinds. "These are yours," said he, "as long as you stay with me. Dress yourself as likes you best. Here is every thing your nakedness requires. When dressed, you may descend to breakfast." With these words he left me.

The clothes were all in the French style, as I afterwards, by comparing my garb with that of others, discovered. They were fitted to my shape with the nicest precision. I bedecked myself with all my care. I remembered the style of dress used by my beloved Clavering. My locks were of shining auburn, flowing and smooth like his. Having wrung the wet from them, and combed, I tied them carelessly in a black riband. Thus equipped, I surveyed myself in a mirror.

You may imagine, if you can, the sensations which this instantaneous transformation produced. Appearances are wonderfully influenced by dress. Check shirt, buttoned at the neck, an awkward fustian coat, check trowsers and bare feet, were now supplanted by linen and muslin, nankeen coat striped with green, a white silk waistcoat elegantly needle-wrought, cassimere pantaloons, stockings of variegated silk, and shoes that in their softness, pliancy, and polished surface vied with satin. I could scarcely forbear looking back to see whether the image in the glass, so well proportioned, so gallant, and so graceful, did not belong to another. I could scarcely recognise any lineaments of my own. I walked to the window. "Twenty minutes ago," said I, "I was traversing that path a barefoot beggar; now I am thus." Again I surveyed myself. "Surely some insanity has fastened on my understanding. My senses are the sport of dreams.

Some magic that disdains the cumbrousness of nature's progress has wrought this change." I was roused from these doubts by a summons to breakfast, obsequiously delivered by a black servant.

I found Welbeck (for I shall henceforth call him by his true name) at the breakfast-table. A superb equipage of silver and china was before him. He was startled at my entrance. The change in my dress seemed for a moment to have deceived him. His eye was frequently fixed upon me with unusual steadfastness. At these times there was inquietude and wonder in his features.

I had now an opportunity of examining my host. There was nicety but no ornament in his dress. His form was of the middle height, spare, but vigorous and graceful. His face was cast, I thought, in a foreign mould. His forehead receded beyond the usual degree in visages which I had seen. His eyes large and prominent, but imparting no marks of benignity and habitual joy. The rest of his face forcibly suggested the idea of a convex edge. His whole figure impressed me with emotions of veneration and awe. A gravity that almost amounted to sadness invariably attended him when we were alone together.

He whispered the servant that waited, who immediately retired. He then said, turning to me, "A lady will enter presently, whom you are to treat with the respect due to my daughter. You must not notice any emotion she may betray at the sight of you, nor expect her to converse with you; for she does not understand your language." He had scarcely spoken when she entered. I was seized with certain misgivings and flutterings which a clownish education may account for. I so far conquered my timidity, however, as to snatch a look at her. I was not born to execute her portrait. Perhaps the turban that wreathed her head, the brilliant texture and inimitable folds of her drapery, and nymphlike port, more than the essential attributes of her person, gave splendour to the celestial vision. Perhaps it was her snowy hues, and the cast rather than the position of her features, that were so prolific of enchantment; or perhaps the wonder originated only in my own ignorance.

She did not immediately notice me. When she did

she almost shrieked with surprise. She held up her hands, and, gazing upon me, uttered various exclamations which I could not understand. I could only remark that her accents were thrillingly musical. Her perturbations refused to be stilled. It was with difficulty that she withdrew her regards from me. Much conversation passed between her and Welbeck, but I could comprehend no part of it. I was at liberty to animadvert on the visible part of their intercourse. I diverted some part of my attention from my own embarrassments, and fixed it on their looks.

In this art, as in most others, I was an unpractised simpleton. In the countenance of Welbeck, there was somewhat else than sympathy with the astonishment and distress of the lady; but I could not interpret these additional tokens. When her attention was engrossed by Welbeck, her eyes were frequently vagrant or downcast; her cheeks contracted a deeper hue; and her breathing was almost prolonged into a sigh. These were marks on which I made no comments at the time. My own situation was calculated to breed confusion in my thoughts and awkwardness in my gestures. Breakfast being finished, the lady, apparently at the request of Welbeck, sat down to a piano-forte.

Here again I must be silent. I was not wholly destitute of musical practice and musical taste. I had that degree of knowledge which enabled me to estimate the transcendent skill of this performer. As if the pathos of her touch were insufficient, I found after some time that the lawless jarrings of the keys were chastened by her own more liquid notes. She played without a book, and, though her bass might be preconcerted, it was plain that her right-hand notes were momentary and spontaneous inspirations. Meanwhile Welbeck stood, leaning his arms on the back of a chair near her, with his eyes fixed on her face. His features were fraught with a meaning which I was eager to interpret, but unable.

I have read of transitions effected by magic; I have read of palaces and deserts which were subject to the dominion of spells; poets may sport with their power, but I am certain that no transition was ever conceived more marvellous and more beyond the reach of foresight than that which I had just experienced. Heaths vexed by a midnight storm may be changed into a hall of choral nymphs and regal banqueting; forest glades may give sudden place to colonnades and carnivals; but he whose senses are deluded finds himself still on his natal earth. These miracles are contemptible when compared with that which placed me under this roof and gave me to partake in this audience. I know that my emotions are in danger of being regarded as ludicrous by those who cannot figure to themselves the consequences of a limited and rustic education.

CHAPTER VI.

In a short time the lady retired. I naturally expected that some comments would be made on her behaviour, and that the cause of her surprise and distress on seeing me would be explained; but Welbeck said nothing on that subject. When she had gone, he went to the window and stood for some time occupied, as it seemed, with his own thoughts. Then he turned to me, and, calling me by my name, desired me to accompany him up-stairs. There was neither cheerfulness nor mildness in his address, but neither was there any thing domineering or arrogant.

We entered an apartment on the same floor with my chamber, but separated from it by a spacious entry. It was supplied with bureaus, cabinets, and bookcases. "This," said he, "is your room and mine; but we must enter it and leave it together. I mean to act not as your master but your friend. My maimed hand" (so saying, he showed me his right hand, the forefinger of which was wanting) "will not allow me to write accurately or copiously. For this reason I have required your aid, in a work of some moment. Much haste will not be requisite, and, as to the hours and duration of employment, these will be seasonable and short.

"Your present situation is new to you, and we will

therefore defer entering on our business. Meanwhile you may amuse yourself in what manner you please. Consider this house as your home and make yourself familiar with it. Stay within or go out, be busy or be idle, as your fancy shall prompt: only you will conform to our domestic system as to eating and sleep; the servants will inform you of this. Next week we will enter on the task for which I designed you. You may now withdraw."

I obeyed this mandate with some awkwardness and hesitation. I went into my own chamber not displeased with an opportunity of loneliness. I threw myself on a chair and resigned myself to those thoughts which would naturally arise in this situation. I speculated on the character and views of Welbeck. I saw that he was embosomed in tranquillity and grandeur. Riches, therefore, were his; but in what did his opulence consist, and whence did it arise? What were the limits by which it was confined, and what its degree of permanence? I was unhabituated to ideas of floating or transferable wealth. The rent of houses and lands was the only species of property which was, as yet, perfectly intelligible. My previous ideas led me to regard Welbeck as the proprietor of this dwelling and of numerous houses and farms. By the same cause I was fain to suppose him enriched by inheritance, and that his life had been uniform.

I next adverted to his social condition. This mansion appeared to have but two inhabitants besides servants. Who was the nymph who had hovered for a moment in my sight? Had he not called her his daughter? The apparent difference in their ages would justify this relation; but her guise, her features, and her accents, were foreign. Her language I suspected strongly to be that of Italy. How should he be the father of an Italian? But were there not some foreign lineaments in his countenance?

This idea seemed to open a new world to my view. I had gained, from my books, confused ideas of European governments and manners. I knew that the present was a period of revolution and hostility. Might not these be illustrious fugitives from Provence or the Milanese?

Their portable wealth, which may reasonably be supposed to be great, they have transported hither. Thus may be explained the sorrow that veils their countenance. The loss of estates and honours; the untimely death of kindred, and perhaps of his wife, may furnish eternal food for regrets. Welbeck's utterance, though rapid and distinct, partook, as I conceived, in some very slight degree of a foreign idiom.

Such was the dream that haunted my undisciplined and unenlightened imagination. The more I revolved it, the more plausible it seemed. On due supposition every appearance that I had witnessed was easily solved,—unless it were their treatment of me. This, at first, was a source of hopeless perplexity. Gradually, however, a clue seemed to be afforded. Welbeck had betrayed astonishment on my first appearance. The lady's wonder was mingled with distress. Perhaps they discovered a remarkable resemblance between me and one who stood in the relation of son to Welbeck, and of brother to the lady. This youth might have perished on the scaffold or in war. These, no doubt, were his clothes. This chamber might have been reserved for him, but his death left it to be appropriated to another.

I had hitherto been unable to guess at the reason why all this kindness had been lavished on me. Will not this conjecture sufficiently account for it? No wonder that this resemblance was enhanced by assuming his dress.

Taking all circumstances into view, these ideas were not, perhaps, destitute of probability. Appearances naturally suggested them to me. They were, also, powerfully enforced by inclination. They threw me into transports of wonder and hope. When I dwelt upon the incidents of my past life, and traced the chain of events, from the death of my mother to the present moment, I almost acquiesced in the notion that some beneficent and ruling genius had prepared my path for me. Events which, when foreseen, would most ardently have been deprecated, and when they happened were accounted in the highest degree luckless, were now seen to be propitious. Hence I inferred the infatuation of despair, and the folly of precipitate conclusions.

But what was the fate reserved for me? Perhaps Welbeck would adopt me for his own son. Wealth has ever been capriciously distributed. The mere physical relation of birth is all that entitles us to manors and thrones. Identity itself frequently depends upon a casual likeness or an old nurse's imposture. Nations have risen in arms, as in the case of the Stuarts, in the cause of one the genuineness of whose birth has been denied and can never be proved. But if the cause be trivial and fallacious, the effects are momentous and solid. It ascertains our portion of felicity and usefulness, and fixes our lot among peasants or princes.

Something may depend upon my own deportment. Will it not behoove me to cultivate all my virtues and eradicate all my defects? I see that the abilities of this man are venerable. Perhaps he will not lightly or hastily decide in my favour. He will be governed by the proofs that I shall give of discernment and integrity. I had always been exempt from temptation, and was therefore undepraved; but this view of things had a wonderful tendency to invigorate my virtuous resolutions. All within me was exhilaration and joy.

There was but one thing wanting to exalt me to a dizzy height and give me place among the stars of heaven. My resemblance to her brother had forcibly affected this lady; but I was not her brother. I was raised to a level with her and made a tenant of the same mansion. Some intercourse would take place between us. Time would lay level impediments and establish familiarity, and this intercourse might foster love and terminate in—*marriage!*

These images were of a nature too glowing and expansive to allow me to be longer inactive. I sallied forth into the open air. This tumult of delicious thoughts in some time subsided, and gave way to images relative to my present situation. My curiosity was awake. As yet I had seen little of the city, and this opportunity for observation was not to be neglected. I therefore coursed through several streets, attentively examining the objects that successively presented themselves.

At length, it occurred to me to search out the house

in which I had lately been immured. I was not without hopes that at some future period I should be able to comprehend the allusions and brighten the obscurities that hung about the dialogue of last night.

The house was easily discovered. I reconnoitred the court and gate through which I had passed. The mansion was of the first order in magnitude and decoration. This was not the bound of my present discovery, for I was gifted with that confidence which would make me set on foot inquiries in the neighbourhood. I looked around for a suitable medium of intelligence. The opposite and adjoining houses were small, and apparently occupied by persons of an indigent class. At one of these was a sign denoting it to be the residence of a tailor. Seated on a bench at the door was a young man, with coarse uncombed locks, breeches knee-unbuttoned, stockings ungartered, shoes slipshod and unbuckled, and a face unwashed, gazing stupidly from hollow eyes. His aspect was embellished with good nature, though indicative of ignorance.

This was the only person in sight. He might be able to say something concerning his opulent neighbour. To him, therefore, I resolved to apply. I went up to him, and, pointing to the house in question, asked him who lived there.

He answered, "Mr. Matthews."

"What is his profession,—his way of life?"

"A gentleman. He does nothing but walk about."

"How long has he been married?"

"Married! He is not married as I know on. He never has been married. He is a bachelor."

This intelligence was unexpected. It made me pause to reflect whether I had not mistaken the house. This, however, seemed impossible. I renewed my questions.

"A bachelor, say you? Are you not mistaken?"

"No. It would be an odd thing if he was married. An old fellow, with one foot in the grave — Comical enough for him to *git* a *vife!*"

"An old man? Does he live alone? What is his family?"

"No, he does not live alone. He has a niece that

lives with him. She is married, and her husband lives there too."

"What is his name?"

"I don't know. I never heard it as I know on."

"What is his trade?"

"He's a marchant; he keeps a store somewhere or other; but I don't know where."

"How long has he been married?"

"About two years. They lost a child lately. The young woman was in a huge taking about it. They say she was quite crazy some days for the death of the child; and she is not quite out of *the dumps* yet. To-be-sure, the child was a sweet little thing; but they need not make such a rout about it. I'll war'n' they'll have enough of them before they die."

"What is the character of the young man? Where was he born and educated? Has he parents or brothers?"

My companion was incapable of answering these questions, and I left him with little essential addition to the knowledge I already possessed.

CHAPTER VII.

After viewing various parts of the city, intruding into churches, and diving into alleys, I returned. The rest of the day I spent chiefly in my chamber, reflecting on my new condition; surveying my apartment, its presses and closets; and conjecturing the causes of appearances.

At dinner and supper I was alone. Venturing to inquire of the servant where his master and mistress were, I was answered that they were engaged. I did not question him as to the nature of their engagement, though it was a fertile source of curiosity.

Next morning, at breakfast, I again met Welbeck and the lady. The incidents were nearly those of the preceding morning, if it were not that the lady exhibited tokens of somewhat greater uneasiness. When she left us, Welbeck sank into apparent meditation. I was at a loss whether to retire or remain where I was. At last, however, I was on the point of leaving the room, when he broke silence and began a conversation with me.

He put questions to me, the obvious scope of which was to know my sentiments on moral topics. I had no motives to conceal my opinions, and therefore delivered them with frankness. At length he introduced allusions to my own history, and made more particular inquiries on that head. Here I was not equally frank; yet I did not feign any thing, but merely dealt in generals. I had acquired notions of propriety on this head, perhaps somewhat fastidious. Minute details, respecting our own concerns, are apt to weary all but the narrator himself. I said thus much, and the truth of my remark was eagerly assented to.

With some marks of hesitation and after various preliminaries, my companion hinted that my own interest, as well as his, enjoined upon me silence to all but himself, on the subject of my birth and early adventures. It was not likely that, while in his service, my circle of acquaintance would be large or my intercourse with the world frequent; but in my communication with others he requested me to speak rather of others than of myself. This request, he said, might appear singular to me, but he had his reasons for making it, which it was not necessary, at present, to disclose, though, when I should know them, I should readily acknowledge their validity.

I scarcely knew what answer to make. I was willing to oblige him. I was far from expecting that any exigence would occur, making disclosure my duty. The employment was productive of pain more than of pleasure, and the curiosity that would uselessly seek a knowledge of my past life was no less impertinent than the loquacity that would uselessly communicate that knowledge. I readily promised, therefore, to adhere to his advice.

This assurance afforded him evident satisfaction; yet it did not seem to amount to quite as much as he wished. He repeated, in stronger terms, the necessity there was for caution. He was far from suspecting me to possess an impertinent and talkative disposition, or that, in my eagerness to expatiate on my own concerns, I should overstep the limits of politeness. But this was not enough. I was to govern myself by a persuasion that the interests of my friend and myself would be materially affected by my conduct.

Perhaps I ought to have allowed these insinuations to breed suspicion in my mind; but, conscious as I was of the benefits which I had received from this man; prone, from my inexperience, to rely upon professions and confide in appearances; and unaware that I could be placed in any condition in which mere silence respecting myself could be injurious or criminal, I made no scruple to promise compliance with his wishes. Nay, I went further than this; I desired to be accurately informed as to what it was proper to conceal. He answered that my silence might extend to every thing anterior to my arrival in the city and my being incorporated with his family. Here our conversation ended, and I retired to ruminate on what had passed.

I derived little satisfaction from my reflections. I began now to perceive inconveniences that might arise from this precipitate promise. Whatever should happen in consequence of my being immured in the chamber, and of the loss of my clothes and of the portrait of my friend, I had bound myself to silence. These inquietudes, however, were transient. I trusted that these events would operate auspiciously; but my curiosity was now awakened as to the motives which *Welbeck* could have for exacting from me this concealment. To act under the guidance of another, and to wander in the dark, ignorant whither my path tended and what effects might flow from my agency, was a new and irksome situation.

From these thoughts I was recalled by a message from Welbeck. He gave me a folded paper, which he requested me to carry to No. — South Fourth Street. "Inquire," said he, "for Mrs. Wentworth, in order merely to ascertain the house, for you need not ask to see her; merely give the letter to the servant and retire. Excuse me for imposing this service upon you. It is of too great moment to be trusted to a common messenger; I usually perform it myself, but am at present otherwise engaged."

I took the letter and set out to deliver it. This was a trifling circumstance, yet my mind was full of reflections on the consequences that might flow from it. I remembered the directions that were given, but construed them in a manner different, perhaps, from Welbeck's expectations or wishes. He had charged me to leave the billet with the servant who happened to answer my summons; but had he not said that the message was important, insomuch that it could not be intrusted to common hands? He had permitted, rather than enjoined, me to dispense with seeing the lady; and this permission I conceived to be dictated merely by regard to my convenience. It was incumbent on me, therefore, to take some pains to deliver the script into her own hands.

I arrived at the house and knocked. A female servant appeared. "Her mistress was up-stairs; she would tell her if I wished to see her," and meanwhile invited me to enter the parlour; I did so; and the girl retired to inform her mistress that one waited for her. I ought to mention that my departure from the directions which I had received was, in some degree, owing to an inquisitive temper; I was eager after knowledge, and was disposed to profit by every opportunity to survey the interior of dwellings and converse with their inhabitants.

I scanned the walls, the furniture, the pictures. Over the fireplace was a portrait in oil of a female. She was elderly and matron-like. Perhaps she was the mistress of this habitation, and the person to whom I should immediately be introduced. Was it a casual suggestion, or was there an actual resemblance between the strokes of the pencil which executed this portrait and that of Clavering? However that be, the sight of this picture revived the memory of my friend and called up a fugitive suspicion that this was the production of his skill.

I was busily revolving this idea when the lady herself entered. It was the same whose portrait I had been examining. She fixed scrutinizing and powerful eyes upon me. She looked at the superscription of the letter which I presented, and immediately resumed her examination of me. I was somewhat abashed by the closeness of her observation, and gave tokens of this state of mind which did not pass unobserved. They seemed instantly to remind her that she behaved with too little regard to civility. She recovered herself and began to peruse the letter. Having done this, her attention was once more fixed upon me. She was evidently desirous of entering into some conversation, but seemed at a loss in what manner to begin. This situation was new to me and was productive of no small embarrassment. I was preparing to take my leave when she spoke, though not without considerable hesitation:—

"This letter is from Mr. Welbeck—you are his friend —I presume—perhaps—a relation?"

I was conscious that I had no claim to either of these titles, and that I was no more than his servant. My pride would not allow me to acknowledge this, and I merely said, "I live with him at present, madam."

I imagined that this answer did not perfectly satisfy her; yet she received it with a certain air of acquiescence. She was silent for a few minutes, and then, rising, said, "Excuse me, sir, for a few minutes. I will write a few words to Mr. Welbeck." So saying, she withdrew.

I returned to the contemplation of the picture. From this, however, my attention was quickly diverted by a paper that lay on the mantel. A single glance was sufficient to put my blood into motion. I started and laid my hand upon the well-known packet. It was that which enclosed the portrait of Clavering!

I unfolded and examined it with eagerness. By what miracle came it hither? It was found, together with my bundle, two nights before. I had despaired of ever seeing it again, and yet here was the same portrait enclosed in the selfsame paper! I have forborne to dwell upon the regret, amounting to grief, with which I was affected in consequence of the loss of this precious relic. My joy on thus speedily and unexpectedly regaining it is not easily described.

For a time I did not reflect that to hold it thus in my hand was not sufficient to entitle me to repossession. I must acquaint this lady with the history of this picture, and convince her of my ownership. But how was this to be done? Was she connected in any way, by friendship or by consanguinity, with that unfortunate youth. If she were, some information as to his destiny would be anxiously sought. I did not, just then, perceive any impropriety in imparting it. If it came into her hands by accident, still, it will be necessary to relate the mode in which it was lost in order to prove my title to it.

I now heard her descending footsteps, and hastily replaced the picture on the mantel. She entered, and, presenting me a letter, desired me to deliver it to Mr. Welbeck. I had no pretext for deferring my departure, but was unwilling to go without obtaining possession of the portrait. An interval of silence and irresolution succeeded. I cast significant glances at the spot where it lay, and at length mustered up my strength of mind, and, pointing to the paper,—"Madam," said I, "*there* is something which I recognise to be mine: I know not how it came into your possession, but so lately as the day before yesterday it was in mine. I lost it by a strange accident, and, as I deem it of inestimable value, I hope you will have no objection to restore it."

During this speech the lady's countenance exhibited marks of the utmost perturbation. "Your picture!" she exclaimed; "you lost it! How? Where? Did you know that person? What has become of him?"

"I knew him well," said I. "That picture was executed by himself. He gave it to me with his own hands; and, till the moment I unfortunately lost it, it was my dear and perpetual companion."

"Good heaven!" she exclaimed, with increasing vehemence; "where did you meet with him? What has become of him? Is he dead, or alive?"

These appearances sufficiently showed me that Clavering and this lady were connected by some ties of tenderness. I answered that he was dead; that my mother and myself were his attendants and nurses, and that this portrait was his legacy to me.

This intelligence melted her into tears, and it was some time before she recovered strength enough to resume the conversation. She then inquired, "When and where was it that he died? How did you lose this portrait? It was found wrapped in some coarse clothes, lying in a stall in the market-house, on Saturday evening. Two negro women, servants of one of my friends, strolling through the market, found it and brought it to their mistress, who, recognising the portrait, sent it to me. To whom did that bundle belong? Was it yours?"

These questions reminded me of the painful predicament in which I now stood. I had promised Welbeck to conceal from every one my former condition; but to explain in what manner this bundle was lost, and how my intercourse with Clavering had taken place, was to violate this promise. It was possible, perhaps, to escape the confession of the truth by equivocation. Falsehoods were easily invented, and might lead her far away from my true condition; but I was wholly unused to equivocation. Never yet had a lie polluted my lips. I was not weak enough to be ashamed of my origin. This lady had an interest in the fate of Clavering, and might justly claim all the information which I was able to impart. Yet to forget the compact which I had so lately made, and an adherence to which might possibly be in the highest degree beneficial to me and to Welbeck; I was willing to adhere to it, provided falsehood could be avoided.

These thoughts rendered me silent. The pain of my embarrassment amounted almost to agony. I felt the keenest regret at my own precipitation in claiming the picture. Its value to me was altogether imaginary. The affection which this lady had borne the original, whatever was the source of that affection, would prompt her to cherish the copy, and, however precious it was in my eyes, I should cheerfully resign it to her.

In the confusion of my thoughts an expedient suggested itself sufficiently inartificial and bold. "It is true, madam, what I have said. I saw him breathe his last. This is his only legacy. If you wish it I willingly resign it; but this is all that I can now disclose. I am placed in circumstances which render it improper to say more."

These words were uttered not very distinctly, and the lady's vehemence hindered her from noticing them. She again repeated her interrogations, to which I returned the same answer.

At first she expressed the utmost surprise at my conduct. From this she descended to some degree of asperity. She made rapid allusions to the history of Clavering. He was the son of the gentleman who owned the house in which Welbeck resided. He was the object of immeasurable fondness and indulgence. He had sought permission to travel, and, this being refused by the absurd timidity of his parents, he had twice been frustrated in attempting to embark for Europe clandestinely. They ascribed his disappearance to a third and successful attempt of this kind, and had exercised anxious and unwearied diligence in endeavouring to trace his footsteps. All their efforts had failed. One motive for their returning to Europe was the hope of discovering some traces of him, as they entertained no doubt of his having crossed the ocean. The vehemence of Mrs. Wentworth's curiosity as to those particulars of his life and death may be easily conceived. My refusal only heightened this passion.

Finding me refractory to all her efforts, she at length dismissed me in anger.

CHAPTER VIII.

THIS extraordinary interview was now past. Pleasure as well as pain attended my reflections on it. I adhered to the promise I had improvidently given to Welbeck, but had excited displeasure, and perhaps suspicion, in the lady. She would find it hard to account for my silence. She would probably impute it to perverseness, or imagine it to flow from some incident connected with the death of Clavering, calculated to give a new edge to her curiosity.

It was plain that some connection subsisted between her

and Welbeck. Would she drop the subject at the point which it had now attained? Would she cease to exert herself to extract from me the desired information, or would she not rather make Welbeck a party in the cause, and prejudice my new friend against me? This was an evil proper, by all lawful means, to avoid. I knew of no other expedient than to confess to him the truth with regard to Clavering, and explain to him the dilemma in which my adherence to my promise had involved me.

I found him on my return home, and delivered him the letter with which I was charged. At the sight of it, surprise, mingled with some uneasiness, appeared in his looks. "What!" said he, in a tone of disappointment, "you then saw the lady?"

I now remembered his directions to leave my message at the door, and apologized for my neglecting them by telling my reasons. His chagrin vanished, but not without an apparent effort, and he said that all was well; the affair was of no moment.

After a pause of preparation, I entreated his attention to something which I had to relate. I then detailed the history of Clavering and of my late embarrassments. As I went on, his countenance betokened increasing solicitude. His emotion was particularly strong when I came to the interrogatories of Mrs. Wentworth in relation to Clavering; but this emotion gave way to profound surprise when I related the manner in which I had eluded her inquiries. I concluded with observing that, when I promised forbearance on the subject of my own adventures, I had not foreseen any exigence which would make an adherence to my promise difficult or inconvenient; that, if his interest was promoted by my silence, I was still willing to maintain it, and requested his directions how to conduct myself on this occasion.

He appeared to ponder deeply and with much perplexity on what I had said. When he spoke there was hesitation in his manner and circuity in his expressions, that proved him to have something in his thoughts which he knew not how to communicate. He frequently paused; but my answers and remarks, occasionally given, appeared to deter him from the revelation of his purpose. Our discourse ended, for the present, by his desiring me to persist in my present plan; I should suffer no inconveniences from it, since it would be my own fault if an interview again took place between the lady and me; meanwhile he should see her and effectually silence her inquiries.

I ruminated not superficially or briefly on this dialogue. By what means would he silence her inquiries? He surely meant not to mislead her by fallacious representations. Some inquietude now crept into my thoughts. I began to form conjectures as to the nature of the scheme to which my suppression of the truth was to be thus made subservient. It seemed as if I were walking in the dark and might rush into snares or drop into pits before I was aware of my danger. Each moment accumulated my doubts, and I cherished a secret foreboding that the event would prove my new situation to be far less fortunate than I had, at first, fondly believed. The question now occurred, with painful repetition, who and what was Welbeck? What was his relation to this foreign lady? What was the service for which I was to be employed?

I could not be contented without a solution of these mysteries. Why should I not lay my soul open before my new friend? Considering my situation, would he regard my fears and my surmises as criminal? I felt that they originated in laudable habits and views. My peace of mind depended on the favourable verdict which conscience should pass on my proceedings. I saw the emptiness of fame and luxury, when put in the balance against the recompense of virtue. Never would I purchase the blandishments of adulation and the glare of opulence at the price of my honesty.

Amidst these reflections the dinner-hour arrived. The lady and Welbeck were present. A new train of sentiments now occupied my mind. I regarded them both with inquisitive eyes. I cannot well account for the revolution which had taken place in my mind. Perhaps it was a proof of the capriciousness of my temper, or it was merely the fruit of my profound ignorance of life and manners. Whencesoever it arose, certain it is that I contemplated the scene before me with altered eyes. Its order and pomp was no longer the parent of tranquillity and awe. My wild reveries of inheriting this splendour and appropriating the affections of this nymph, I now regarded as lunatic hope and childish folly. Education and nature had qualified me for a different scene. This might be the mask of misery and the structure of vice.

My companions as well as myself were silent during the meal. The lady retired as soon as it was finished. My inexplicable melancholy increased. It did not pass unnoticed by Welbeck, who inquired, with an air of kindness, into the cause of my visible dejection. I am almost ashamed to relate to what extremes my folly transported me. Instead of answering him, I was weak enough to shed tears.

This excited afresh his surprise and his sympathy. He renewed his inquiries; my heart was full, but how to disburden it I knew not. At length, with some difficulty, I expressed my wishes to leave his house and return into the country.

What, he asked, had occurred to suggest this new plan? What motive could incite me to bury myself in rustic obscurity? How did I purpose to dispose of myself? Had some new friend sprung up more able or more willing to benefit me than he had been?

"No," I answered, "I have no relation who would own me, or friend who would protect. If I went into the country it would be to the toilsome occupations of a day-labourer; but even that was better than my present situation."

This opinion, he observed, must be newly formed. What was there irksome or offensive in my present mode of life?

That this man condescended to expostulate with me; to dissuade me from my new plan; and to enumerate the benefits which he was willing to confer, penetrated my heart with gratitude. I could not but acknowledge that leisure and literature, copious and elegant accommodation, were valuable for their own sake; that all the delights of sensation and refinements of intelligence were comprised within my present sphere, and would be nearly wanting in that to which I was going. I felt temporary compunction for my folly, and determined to adopt a different deportment. I could not prevail upon myself to unfold the true cause of my dejection, and permitted him therefore to ascribe it to a kind of homesickness; to inexperience; and to that ignorance which, on being ushered into a new scene, is oppressed with a sensation of forlornness. He remarked that these chimeras would vanish before the influence of time, and company, and occupation. On the next week he would furnish me with employment; meanwhile he would introduce me into company, where intelligence and vivacity would combine to dispel my glooms.

As soon as we separated, my disquietudes returned. I contended with them in vain, and finally resolved to abandon my present situation. When and how this purpose was to be effected I knew not. That was to be the theme of future deliberation.

Evening having arrived, Welbeck proposed to me to accompany me on a visit to one of his friends. I cheerfully accepted the invitation, and went with him to your friend Mr. Wortley's. A numerous party was assembled, chiefly of the female sex. I was introduced by Welbeck by the title of *a young friend of his*. Notwithstanding my embarrassment, I did not fail to attend to what passed on this occasion. I remarked that the utmost deference was paid to my companion, on whom his entrance into this company appeared to operate like magic. His eyes sparkled; his features expanded into a benign serenity; and his wonted reserve gave place to a torrent-like and overflowing elocution.

I marked this change in his deportment with the utmost astonishment. So great was it, that I could hardly persuade myself that it was the same person. A mind thus susceptible of new impressions must be, I conceived, of a wonderful texture. Nothing was further from my expectations than that this vivacity was mere dissimulation and would take its leave of him when he left the company; yet this I found to be the case. The door was no sooner closed after him than his accustomed solemnity returned. He spake little, and that little was delivered with emphatical and monosyllabic brevity.

We returned home at a late hour, and I immediately retired to my chamber, not so much from the desire of repose as in order to enjoy and pursue my own reflections without interruption.

The condition of my mind was considerably remote from happiness. I was placed in a scene that furnished fuel to my curiosity. This passion is a source of pleasure, provided its gratification be practicable. I had no reason, in my present circumstances, to despair of knowledge; yet suspicion and anxiety beset me. I thought upon the delay and toil which the removal of my ignorance would cost, and reaped only pain and fear from the reflection.

The air was remarkably sultry. Lifted sashes and lofty ceilings were insufficient to attemper it. The perturbation of my thoughts affected my body, and the heat which oppressed me was aggravated, by my restlessness, almost into fever. Some hours were thus painfully past, when I recollected that the bath, erected in the court below, contained a sufficient antidote to the scorching influence of the atmosphere.

I rose, and descended the stairs softly, that I might not alarm Welbeck and the lady, who occupied the two rooms on the second floor. I proceeded to the bath, and, filling the reservoir with water, speedily dissipated the heat that incommoded me. Of all species of sensual gratification, that was the most delicious; and I continued for a long time laving my limbs and moistening my hair. In the midst of this amusement, I noticed the approach of day, and immediately saw the propriety of returning to my chamber. I returned with the same caution which I had used in descending; my feet were bare, so that it was easy to proceed unattended by the smallest signal of my progress.

I had reached the carpeted staircase, and was slowly ascending, when I heard, within the chamber that was occupied by the lady, a noise, as of some one moving. Though not conscious of having acted improperly, yet I felt reluctance to be seen. There was no reason to suppose that this sound was connected with the detection of me in this situation; yet I acted as if this reason existed, and made haste to pass the door and gain the second flight of steps.

I was unable to accomplish my design, when the chamber door slowly opened, and Welbeck, with a light in his hand, came out. I was abashed and disconcerted at this interview. He started at seeing me; but, discovering in an instant who it was, his face assumed an expression in which shame and anger were powerfully blended. He seemed on the point of opening his mouth to rebuke me; but, suddenly checking himself, he said, in a tone of mildness, "How is this? Whence come you?"

His emotion seemed to communicate itself, with an electrical rapidity, to my heart. My tongue faltered while I made some answer. I said, "I had been seeking relief from the heat of the weather, in the bath." He heard my explanation in silence; and, after a moment's pause, passed into his own room, and shut himself in. I hastened to my chamber.

A different observer might have found in these circumstances no food for his suspicion or his wonder. To me, however, they suggested vague and tumultuous ideas.

As I strode across the room I repeated, "This woman is his daughter. What proof have I of that? He once asserted it; and has frequently uttered allusions and hints from which no other inference could be drawn. The chamber from which he came, in an hour devoted to sleep, was hers. For what end could a visit like this be paid? A parent may visit his child at all seasons, without a crime. On seeing me, methought his features indicated more than surprise. A keen interpreter would be apt to suspect a consciousness of wrong. What if this woman be not his child! How shall their relationship be ascertained?"

I was summoned at the customary hour to breakfast. My mind was full of ideas connected with this incident. I was not endowed with sufficient firmness to propose the cool and systematic observation of this man's deportment. I felt as if the state of my mind could not but be evident to him; and experienced in myself all the confusion which this discovery was calculated to produce in him. I would have willingly excused myself from meeting him; but that was impossible.

At breakfast, after the usual salutations, nothing was said. For a time I scarcely lifted my eyes from the table. Stealing a glance at Welbeck, I discovered in his features nothing but his wonted gravity. He appeared occupied with thoughts that had no relation to last night's adventure. This encouraged me; and I gradually recovered my composure. Their inattention to me allowed me occasionally to throw scrutinizing and comparing glances at the face of each.

The relationship of parent and child is commonly discovered in the visage; but the child may resemble either of its parents, yet have no feature in common with both. Here outlines, surfaces, and hues were in absolute contrariety. That kindred subsisted between them was possible, notwithstanding this dissimilitude; but this circumstance contributed to envenom my suspicions.

Breakfast being finished, Welbeck cast an eye of invitation to the piano-forte. The lady rose to comply with his request. My eye chanced to be, at that moment, fixed on her. In stepping to the instrument, some motion or appearance awakened a thought in my mind which affected my feelings like the shock of an earthquake.

I have too slight acquaintance with the history of the passions to truly explain the emotion which now throbbed in my veins. I had been a stranger to what is called love. From subsequent reflection, I have contracted a suspicion that the sentiment with which I regarded this lady was not untinctured from this source, and that hence arose the turbulence of my feelings on observing what I construed into marks of pregnancy. The evidence afforded me was slight; yet it exercised an absolute sway over my belief.

It was well that this suspicion had not been sooner excited. Now civility did not require my stay in the apartment, and nothing but flight could conceal the state of my mind. I hastened, therefore, to a distance, and shrouded myself in the friendly secrecy of my own chamber.

The constitution of my mind is doubtless singular and

perverse; yet that opinion, perhaps, is the fruit of my ignorance. It may by no means be uncommon for men to *fashion* their conclusions in opposition to evidence and *probability*, and so as to feed their malice and subvert their happiness. Thus it was, in an eminent degree, in my case. The simple fact was connected, in my mind, with a train of the most hateful consequences. The depravity of Welbeck was inferred from it. The charms of this angelic woman were tarnished and withered. I had formerly surveyed her as a precious and perfect monument, but now it was a scene of ruin and blast.

This had been a source of sufficient anguish; but this was not all. I recollected that the claims of a parent had been urged. Will you believe that these claims were now admitted, and that they heightened the iniquity of Welbeck into the blackest and most stupendous of all crimes? These ideas were necessarily transient. Conclusions more conformable to appearances succeeded. This lady might have been lately reduced to widowhood. The recent loss of a beloved companion would sufficiently account for her dejection, and make her present situation compatible with duty.

By this new train of ideas I was somewhat comforted. I saw the folly of precipitate inferences and the injustice of my atrocious imputations, and acquired some degree of patience in my present state of uncertainty. My heart was lightened of its wonted burden, and I laboured to invent some harmless explication of the scene that I had witnessed the preceding night.

At dinner Welbeck appeared as usual, but not the lady. I ascribed her absence to some casual indisposition, and ventured to inquire into the state of her health. My companion said she was well, but that she had left the city for a month or two, finding the heat of summer inconvenient where she was. This was no unplausible reason for retirement. A candid mind would have acquiesced in this representation, and found in it nothing inconsistent with a supposition respecting the cause of appearances favourable to her character; but otherwise was I affected. The uneasiness which had flown for a moment returned, and I sunk into gloomy silence.

From this I was roused by my patron, who requested me to deliver a billet, which he put into my hand, at the counting-house of Mr. Thetford, and to bring him an answer. This message was speedily performed. I entered a large building by the river-side. A spacious apartment presented itself, well furnished with pipes and hogsheads. In one corner was a smaller room, in which a gentleman was busy at writing. I advanced to the door of the room, but was there met by a young person, who received my paper and delivered it to him within. I stood still at the door; but was near enough to overhear what would pass between them.

The letter was laid upon the desk, and presently he that sat at it lifted his eyes and glanced at the superscription. He scarcely spoke above a whisper; but his words, nevertheless, were clearly distinguishable. I did not call to mind the sound of his voice, but his words called up a train of recollections.

"Lo!" said he, carelessly, "this from the *Nabob!*"

An incident so slight as this was sufficient to open a spacious scene of meditation. This little word, half whispered in a thoughtless mood, was a key to unlock an extensive cabinet of secrets. Thetford was probably indifferent whether his exclamation were overheard. Little did he think on the inferences which would be built upon it.

"The Nabob!" By this appellation had some one been denoted in the chamber dialogue of which I had been an unsuspected auditor. The man who pretended poverty, and yet gave proofs of inordinate wealth; whom it was pardonable to defraud of thirty thousand dollars; first, because the loss of that sum would be trivial to one opulent as he; and, secondly, because he was imagined to have acquired this opulence by other than honest methods. Instead of forthwith returning home, I wandered into the fields, to indulge myself in the new thoughts which were produced by this occurrence.

I entertained no doubt that the person alluded to was my patron. No new light was thrown upon his character; unless something were deducible from the charge vaguely made, that his wealth was the fruit of illicit practices. He was opulent, and the sources of his wealth were unknown, if not to the rest of the community, at least to Thetford. But here had a plot been laid. The fortune of Thetford's brother was to rise from the success of artifices of which the credulity of Welbeck was to be the victim. To detect and to counterwork this plot was obviously my duty. My interference might now indeed be too late to be useful; but this was at least to be ascertained by experiment.

How should my intention be effected? I had hitherto concealed from Welbeck my adventures at Thetford's house. These it was now necessary to disclose, and to mention the recent occurrence. My deductions, in consequence of my ignorance, might be erroneous; but of their truth his knowledge of his own affairs would enable him to judge. It was possible that Thetford and he whose chamber conversation I had overheard were different persons. I endeavoured in vain to ascertain their identity by a comparison of their voices. The words lately heard, my remembrance did not enable me certainly to pronounce to be uttered by the same organs.

This uncertainty was of little moment. It sufficed that Welbeck was designated by this appellation, and that therefore he was proved to be the subject of some fraudulent proceeding. The information that I possessed it was my duty to communicate as expeditiously as possible. I was resolved to employ the first opportunity that offered for this end.

My meditations had been ardently pursued, and, when I recalled my attention, I found myself bewildered among fields and fences. It was late before I extricated myself from unknown paths, and reached home.

I entered the parlour; but Welbeck was not there. A table, with tea-equipage for one person, was set; from which I inferred that Welbeck was engaged abroad. This belief was confirmed by the report of the servant. He could not inform me where his master was, but merely that he should not take tea at home. This incident was a source of vexation and impatience. I knew not but that delay would be of the utmost moment to the safety of my friend. Wholly unacquainted as I was with the nature of his contracts with Thetford, I could not decide whether a single hour would not avail to obviate the evils that threatened him. Had I known whither to trace his footsteps, I should certainly have sought an immediate interview; but, as it was, I was obliged to wait, with what patience I could collect, for his return to his own house.

I waited hour after hour in vain. The sun declined, and the shades of evening descended; but Welbeck was still at a distance.

CHAPTER IX.

WELBECK did not return, though hour succeeded hour till the clock struck ten. I inquired of the servants, who informed me that their master was not accustomed to stay out so late. I seated myself at a table, in a parlour, on which there stood a light, and listened for the signal of his coming, either by the sound of steps on the pavement without or by a peal from the bell. The silence was uninterrupted and profound, and each minute added to my sum of impatience and anxiety.

To relieve myself from the heat of the weather, which was aggravated by the condition of my thoughts, as well as to beguile this tormenting interval, it occurred to me to betake myself to the bath. I left the candle where it stood, and imagined that even in the bath I should hear the sound of the bell which would be rung upon his arrival at the door.

No such signal occurred, and, after taking this refreshment, I prepared to return to my post. The parlour was still unoccupied, but this was not all; the candle I had left upon the table was gone. This was an inexplicable circumstance. On my promise to wait for their master, the servants had retired to bed. No signal of any one's entrance had been given. The street door was locked, and the key hung at its customary place upon the wall. What was I to think? It was obvious to suppose that the candle had been removed by a domestic; but their footsteps could not be traced, and I was not sufficiently acquainted with the house to find the way, especially immersed in darkness, to their chamber. One measure, however, it was evidently proper to take, which was to supply myself, anew, with a light. This was instantly performed; but what was next to be done?

I was weary of the perplexities in which I was embroiled. I saw no avenue to escape from them but that which led me to the bosom of nature and to my ancient occupations. For a moment I was tempted to resume my rustic garb, and, on that very hour, to desert this habitation. One thing only detained me; the desire to apprize my patron of the treachery of Thetford. For this end I was anxious to obtain an interview; but now I reflected that this information could by other means be imparted. Was it not sufficient to write him briefly these particulars, and leave him to profit by the knowledge? Thus I might, likewise, acquaint him with my motives for thus abruptly and unseasonably deserting his service.

To the execution of this scheme pen and paper were necessary. The business of writing was performed in the chamber on the third story. I had been hitherto denied access to this room. In it was a show of papers and books. Here it was that the task, for which I had been retained, was to be performed; but I was to enter it and leave it only in company with Welbeck. For what reasons, I asked, was this procedure to be adopted?

The influence of prohibitions and an appearance of disguise in awakening curiosity is well known. My mind fastened upon the idea of this room with an unusual degree of intenseness. I had seen it but for a moment. Many of Welbeck's hours were spent in it. It was not to be inferred that they were consumed in idleness: what then was the nature of his employment over which a veil of such impenetrable secrecy was cast?

Will you wonder that the design of entering this recess was insensibly formed? Possibly it was locked, but its accessibleness was likewise possible. I meant not the commission of any crime. My principal purpose was to procure the implements of writing, which were elsewhere not to be found. I should neither unseal papers nor open drawers. I would merely take a survey of the volumes and attend to the objects that spontaneously presented themselves to my view. In this there surely was nothing criminal or blameworthy. Meanwhile I was not unmindful of the sudden disappearance of the candle. This incident filled my bosom with the inquietudes of fear and the perturbations of wonder.

Once more I paused to catch any sound that might arise from without. All was still. I seized the candle and prepared to mount the stairs. I had not reached the first landing when I called to mind my midnight meeting with Welbeck at the door of his daughter's chamber. The chamber was now desolate; perhaps it was accessible; if so, no injury was done by entering it. My curiosity was strong, but it pictured to itself no precise object. Three steps would bear me to the door. The trial, whether it was fastened, might be made in a moment; and I readily imagined that something might be found within to reward the trouble of examination. The door yielded to my hand, and I entered.

No remarkable object was discoverable. The apartment was supplied with the usual furniture. I bent my steps towards a table over which a mirror was suspended. My glances, which roved with swiftness from one object to another, shortly lighted on a miniature portrait that hung near. I scrutinized it with eagerness. It was impossible to overlook its resemblance to my own visage. This was so great that for a moment I imagined myself to have been the original from which it had been drawn. This flattering conception yielded place to a belief merely of similitude between me and the genuine original.

The thoughts which this opinion was fitted to produce were suspended by a new object. A small volume, that had, apparently, been much used, lay upon the toilet. I opened it, and found it to contain some of the Dramas of Apostolo Zeno. I turned over the leaves; a written paper saluted my sight. A single glance informed me that it was English. For the present I was insensible to all motives that would command me to forbear. I seized the paper with an intention to peruse it.

At that moment a stunning report was heard. It was

loud enough to shake the walls of the apartment, and abrupt enough to throw me into tremors. I dropped the book and yielded for a moment to confusion and surprise. From what quarter it came, I was unable accurately to determine; but there could be no doubt, from its loudness, that it was near, and even in the house. It was no less manifest that the sound arose from the discharge of a pistol. Some hand must have drawn the trigger. I recollected the disappearance of the candle from the room below. Instantly a supposition darted into my mind which made my hair rise and my teeth chatter.

"This," I said, "is the deed of Welbeck. He entered while I was absent from the room; he hied to his chamber; and, prompted by some unknown instigation, has inflicted on himself death!" This idea had a tendency to palsy my limbs and my thoughts. Some time passed in painful and tumultuous fluctuation. My aversion to this catastrophe, rather than a belief of being, by that means, able to prevent or repair the evil, induced me to attempt to enter his chamber. It was possible that my conjectures were erroneous.

The door of his room was locked. I knocked; I demanded entrance in a low voice; I put my eye and my ear to the keyhole and the crevices; nothing could be heard or seen. It was unavoidable to conclude that no one was within; yet the effluvia of gunpowder was perceptible.

Perhaps the room above had been the scene of this catastrophe. I ascended the second flight of stairs. I approached the door. No sound could be caught by my most vigilant attention. I put out the light that I carried, and was then able to perceive that there was light within the room. I scarcely knew how to act. For some minutes I paused at the door. I spoke, and requested permission to enter. My words were succeeded by a deathlike stillness. At length I ventured softly to withdraw the bolt, to open and to advance within the room. Nothing could exceed the horror of my expectation; yet I was startled by the scene that I beheld.

In a chair, whose back was placed against the front

wall, sat Welbeck. My entrance alarmed him not, nor roused him from the stupor into which he was plunged. He rested his hands upon his knees, and his eyes were riveted to something that lay, at the distance of a few feet before him, on the floor. A second glance was sufficient to inform me of what nature this object was. It was the body of a man, bleeding, ghastly, and still exhibiting the marks of convulsion and agony!

I shall omit to describe the shock which a spectacle like this communicated to my unpractised senses. I was nearly as panic-struck and powerless as Welbeck himself. I gazed, without power of speech, at one time, at Welbeck; then I fixed terrified eyes on the distorted features of the dead. At length, Welbeck, recovering from his reverie, looked up, as if to see who it was that had entered. No surprise, no alarm, was betrayed by him on seeing me. He manifested no desire or intention to interrupt the fearful silence.

My thoughts wandered in confusion and terror. The first impulse was to fly from the scene; but I could not be long insensible to the exigences of the moment. I saw that affairs must not be suffered to remain in their present situation. The insensibility or despair of Welbeck required consolation and succour. How to communicate my thoughts, or offer my assistance, I knew not. What led to this murderous catastrophe; who it was whose breathless corpse was before me; what concern Welbeck had in producing his death; were as yet unknown.

At length he rose from his seat, and strode at first with faltering, and then with more steadfast steps, across the floor. This motion seemed to put him in possession of himself. He seemed now, for the first time, to recognise my presence. He turned to me, and said, in a tone of severity,—

"How now? What brings you here?"

This rebuke was unexpected. I stammered out, in reply, that the report of the pistol had alarmed me, and that I came to discover the cause of it.

He noticed not my answer, but resumed his perturbed steps, and his anxious but abstracted looks. Suddenly he checked himself, and, glancing a furious eye at the corpse, he muttered, "Yes, the die is cast. This worthless and miserable scene shall last no longer. I will at once get rid of life and all its humiliations."

Here succeeded a new pause. The course of his thoughts seemed now to become once more tranquil. Sadness, rather than fury, overspread his features; and his accent, when he spoke to me, was not faltering, but solemn.

"Mervyn," said he, "you comprehend not this scene. Your youth and inexperience make you a stranger to a deceitful and flagitious world. You know me not. It is time that this ignorance should vanish. The knowledge of me and of my actions may be of use to you. It may teach you to avoid the shoals on which my virtue and my peace have been wrecked; but to the rest of mankind it can be of no use. The ruin of my fame is, perhaps, irretrievable; but the height of my iniquity need not be known. I perceive in you a rectitude and firmness worthy to be trusted; promise me, therefore, that not a syllable of what I tell you shall ever pass your lips."

I had lately experienced the inconvenience of a promise; but I was now confused, embarrassed, ardently inquisitive as to the nature of this scene, and unapprized of the motives that might afterwards occur, persuading or compelling me to disclosure. The promise which he exacted was given. He resumed:—

"I have detained you in my service, partly for your own benefit, but chiefly for mine. I intended to inflict upon you injury and to do you good. Neither of these ends can I now accomplish, unless the lessons which my example may inculcate shall inspire you with fortitude and arm you with caution.

"What it was that made me thus, I know not. I am not destitute of understanding. My thirst of knowledge, though irregular, is ardent. I can talk and can feel as virtue and justice prescribe; yet the tenor of my actions has been uniform. One tissue of iniquity and folly has been my life; while my thoughts have been familiar with enlightened and disinterested principles. Scorn and detestation I have heaped upon myself. Yesterday is remembered with remorse. To-morrow is contemplated with anguish and fear; yet every day is productive of the same crimes and of the same follies.

"I was left, by the insolvency of my father, (a trader of Liverpool,) without any means of support but such as labour should afford me. Whatever could generate pride, and the love of independence, was my portion. Whatever can incite to diligence was the growth of my condition; yet my indolence was a cureless disease; and there were no arts too sordid for me to practise.

"I was content to live on the bounty of a kinsman. His family was numerous, and his revenue small. He forbore to upbraid me, or even to insinuate the propriety of providing for myself; but he empowered me to pursue any liberal or mechanical profession which might suit my taste. I was insensible to every generous motive. I laboured to forget my dependent and disgraceful condition, because the remembrance was a source of anguish, without being able to inspire me with a steady resolution to change it.

"I contracted an acquaintance with a woman who was unchaste, perverse, and malignant. Me, however, she found it no difficult task to deceive. My uncle remonstrated against the union. He took infinite pains to unveil my error, and to convince me that wedlock was improper for one destitute, as I was, of the means of support, even if the object of my choice were personally unexceptionable.

"His representations were listened to with anger. That he thwarted my will in this respect, even by affectionate expostulation, cancelled all that debt of gratitude which I owed to him. I rewarded him for all his kindness by invective and disdain, and hastened to complete my ill-omened marriage. I had deceived the woman's father by assertions of possessing secret resources. To gratify my passion, I descended to dissimulation and falsehood. He admitted me into his family, as the husband of his child; but the character of my wife and the fallacy of my assertions were quickly discovered. He denied me accommodation under his roof, and I was turned forth to the world to endure the penalty of my rashness and my indolence.

"Temptation would have moulded me into any villanous shape. My virtuous theories and comprehensive erudition would not have saved me from the basest of crimes. Luckily for me, I was, for the present, exempted from temptation. I had formed an acquaintance with a young American captain. On being partially informed of my situation, he invited me to embark with him for his own country. My passage was gratuitous. I arrived, in a short time, at Charleston, which was the place of his abode.

"He introduced me to his family, every member of which was, like himself, imbued with affection and benevolence. I was treated like their son and brother. I was hospitably entertained until I should be able to select some path of lucrative industry. Such was my incurable depravity, that I made no haste to select my pursuit. An interval of inoccupation succeeded, which I applied to the worst purposes.

"My friend had a sister, who was married, but during the absence of her husband resided with her family. Hence originated our acquaintance. The purest of human hearts and the most vigorous understanding were hers. She idolized her husband, who well deserved to be the object of her adoration. Her affection for him, and her general principles, appeared to be confirmed beyond the power to be shaken. I sought her intercourse without illicit views; I delighted in the effusions of her candour and the flashes of her intelligence; I conformed, by a kind of instinctive hypocrisy, to her views; I spoke and felt from the influence of immediate and momentary conviction. She imagined she had found in me a friend worthy to partake in all her sympathies and forward all her wishes. We were mutually deceived. She was the victim of self-delusion; but I must charge myself with practising deceit both upon myself and her.

"I reflect with astonishment and horror on the steps which led to her degradation and to my calamity. In the high career of passion all consequences were overlooked. She was the dupe of the most audacious sophistry and the grossest delusion. I was the slave of sensual impulses and voluntary blindness. The effect may be easily conceived. Not till symptoms of pregnancy began to appear were our eyes opened to the ruin which impended over us.

"Then I began to revolve the consequences, which the mist of passion had hitherto concealed. I was tormented by the pangs of remorse, and pursued by the phantom of ingratitude. To complete my despair, this unfortunate lady was apprized of my marriage with another woman; a circumstance which I had anxiously concealed from her. She fled from her father's house at a time when her husband and brother were hourly expected. What became of her I knew not. She left behind her a letter to her father, in which the melancholy truth was told.

"Shame and remorse had no power over my life. To elude the storm of invective and upbraiding, to quiet the uproar of my mind, I did not betake myself to voluntary death. My pusillanimity still clung to this wretched existence. I abruptly retired from the scene, and, repairing to the port, embarked in the first vessel which appeared. The ship chanced to belong to Wilmington, in Delaware, and here I sought out an obscure and cheap abode.

"I possessed no means of subsistence. I was unknown to my neighbours, and desired to remain unknown. I was unqualified for manual labour by all the habits of my life; but there was no choice between penury and diligence,—between honest labour and criminal inactivity. I mused incessantly on the forlornness of my condition. Hour after hour passed, and the horrors of want began to encompass me. I sought with eagerness for an avenue by which I might escape from it. The perverseness of my nature led me on from one guilty thought to another. I took refuge in my customary sophistries, and reconciled myself at length to a scheme of—*forgery!*"

CHAPTER X.

"HAVING ascertained my purpose, it was requisite to search out the means by which I might effect it. These were not clearly or readily suggested. The more I contemplated my project, the more numerous and arduous its difficulties appeared. I had no associates in my undertaking. A due regard to my safety, and the unextinguished sense of honour, deterred me from seeking auxiliaries and co-agents. The esteem of mankind was the spring of all my activity, the parent of all my virtue and all my vice. To preserve this, it was necessary that my guilty projects should have neither witness nor partaker.

"I quickly discovered that to execute this scheme demanded time, application, and money, none of which my present situation would permit me to devote to it. At first it appeared that an attainable degree of skill and circumspection would enable me to arrive, by means of counterfeit bills, to the pinnacle of affluence and honour. My error was detected by a closer scrutiny, and I finally saw nothing in this path but enormous perils and insurmountable impediments.

"Yet what alternative was offered me? To maintain myself by the labour of my hands, to perform any toilsome or prescribed task, was incompatible with my nature. My habits debarred me from country occupations. My pride regarded as vile and ignominious drudgery any employment which the town could afford. Meanwhile, my wants were as urgent as ever, and my funds were exhausted.

"There are few, perhaps, whose external situation resembled mine, who would have found in it any thing but incitements to industry and invention. A thousand methods of subsistence, honest but laborious, were at my command, but to these I entertained an irreconcilable aversion. Ease and the respect attendant upon opulence I was willing to purchase at the price of ever-wakeful suspicion and eternal remorse; but, even at this price, the purchase was impossible.

"The desperateness of my condition became hourly more apparent. The further I extended my view, the darker grew the clouds which hung over futurity. Anguish and infamy appeared to be the inseparable conditions of my existence. There was one mode of evading the evils that impended. To free myself from self-upbraiding and to shun the persecutions of my fortune was possible only by shaking off life itself.

"One evening, as I traversed the bank of the creek, these dismal meditations were uncommonly intense. They at length terminated in a resolution to throw myself into the stream. The first impulse was to rush instantly to my death; but the remembrance of papers, lying at my lodgings, which might unfold more than I desired to the curiosity of survivors, induced me to postpone this catastrophe till the next morning.

"My purpose being formed, I found my heart lightened of its usual weight. By you it will be thought strange, but it is nevertheless true, that I derived from this new prospect not only tranquillity but cheerfulness. I hastened home. As soon as I entered, my landlord informed me that a person had been searching for me in my absence. This was an unexampled incident, and foreboded me no good. I was strongly persuaded that my visitant had been led hither not by friendly but hostile purposes. This persuasion was confirmed by the description of the stranger's guise and demeanour given by my landlord. My fears instantly recognised the image of Watson, the man by whom I had been so eminently benefited, and whose kindness I had compensated by the ruin of his sister and the confusion of his family.

"An interview with this man was less to be endured than to look upon the face of an avenging deity. I was determined to avoid this interview, and, for this end, to execute my fatal purpose within the hour. My papers were collected with a tremulous hand, and consigned to the flames. I then bade my landlord inform all visitants that I should not return till the next day, and once more hastened towards the river.

"My way led past the inn where one of the stages from Baltimore was accustomed to stop. I was not unaware that Watson had possibly been brought in the coach which had recently arrived, and which now stood before the door of the inn. The danger of my being descried or encountered by him as I passed did not fail to occur. This was to be eluded by deviating from the main street.

"Scarcely had I turned a corner for this purpose when I was accosted by a young man whom I knew to be an inhabitant of the town, but with whom I had hitherto had no intercourse but what consisted in a transient salutation. He apologized for the liberty of addressing me, and, at the same time, inquired if I understood the French language.

"Being answered in the affirmative, he proceeded to tell me that in the stage, just arrived, had come a passenger, a youth who appeared to be French, who was wholly unacquainted with our language, and who had been seized with a violent disease.

"My informant had felt compassion for the forlorn condition of the stranger, and had just been seeking me at my lodgings, in hope that my knowledge of French would enable me to converse with the sick man, and obtain from him a knowledge of his situation and views.

"The apprehensions I had precipitately formed were thus removed, and I readily consented to perform this service. The youth was, indeed, in a deplorable condition. Besides the pains of his disease, he was overpowered by dejection. The innkeeper was extremely anxious for the removal of his guest. He was by no means willing to sustain the trouble and expense of a sick or a dying man, for which it was scarcely probable that he should ever be reimbursed. The traveller had no baggage, and his dress betokened the pressure of many wants.

"My compassion for this stranger was powerfully awakened. I was in possession of a suitable apartment, for which I had no power to pay the rent that was accruing; but my inability in this respect was unknown, and I might enjoy my lodgings unmolested for some weeks. The fate of this youth would be speedily decided, and I should be left at liberty to execute my first intentions before my embarrassments should be visibly increased.

"After a moment's pause, I conducted the stranger to my home, placed him in my own bed, and became his nurse. His malady was such as is known in the tropical islands by the name of the yellow or malignant fever, and the physician who was called speedily pronounced his case desperate.

"It was my duty to warn him of the death that was hastening, and to promise the fulfilment of any of his wishes not inconsistent with my present situation. He received my intelligence with fortitude, and appeared anxious to communicate some information respecting his own state. His pangs and his weakness scarcely allowed him to be intelligible. From his feeble efforts and broken narrative I collected thus much concerning his family and fortune.

"His father's name was Vincentio Lodi. From a merchant at Leghorn, he had changed himself into a planter in the island of Guadaloupe. His son had been sent, at an early age, for the benefits of education, to Europe. The young Vincentio was, at length, informed by his father, that, being weary of his present mode of existence, he had determined to sell his property and transport himself to the United States. The son was directed to hasten home, that he might embark, with his father, on this voyage.

"The summons was cheerfully obeyed. The youth, on his arrival at the island, found preparation making for the funeral of his father. It appeared that the elder Lodi had flattered one of his slaves with the prospect of his freedom, but had, nevertheless, included this slave in the sale that he had made of his estate. Actuated by revenge, the slave assassinated Lodi in the open street, and resigned himself, without a struggle, to the punishment which the law had provided for such a deed.

"The property had been recently transferred, and the price was now presented to young Vincentio by the purchaser. He was by no means inclined to adopt his father's project, and was impatient to return with his inheritance to France. Before this could be done, the conduct of his father had rendered a voyage to the Continent indispensable.

"Lodi had a daughter, whom, a few weeks previous to his death, he had intrusted to an American captain for whom he had contracted a friendship. The vessel was bound to Philadelphia; but the conduct she was to pursue, and the abode she was to select, on her arrival, were known only to the father, whose untimely death involved the son in considerable uncertainty with regard to his sister's fate. His anxiety on this account induced him to seize the first conveyance that offered. In a short time he landed at Baltimore.

"As soon as he recovered from the fatigues of his voyage, he prepared to go to Philadelphia. Thither his baggage was immediately sent under the protection of a passenger and countryman. His money consisted in Portuguese gold, which, in pursuance of advice, he had changed into bank-notes. He besought me, in pathetic terms, to search out his sister, whose youth and poverty, and ignorance of the language and manners of the country, might expose her to innumerable hardships. At the same time, he put a pocket-book and small volume into my hand, indicating, by his countenance and gestures, his desire that I would deliver them to his sister.

"His obsequies being decently performed, I had leisure to reflect upon the change in my condition which this incident had produced. In the pocket-book were found bills to the amount of twenty thousand dollars. The volume proved to be a manuscript, written by the elder Lodi in Italian, and contained memoirs of the ducal house of Visconti, from whom the writer believed himself to have lineally descended.

"Thus had I arrived, by an avenue so much beyond my foresight, at the possession of wealth. The evil which impelled me to the brink of suicide, and which was the source, though not of all, yet of the larger portion, of my anguish, was now removed. What claims to honour or to ease were consequent on riches were, by an extraordinary fortune, now conferred upon me.

"Such, for a time, were my new-born but transitory raptures. I forgot that this money was not mine. That it had been received, under every sanction of fidelity, for another's use. To retain it was equivalent to robbery. The sister of the deceased was the rightful claimant; it was my duty to search her out, and perform my tacit but sacred obligations, by putting the whole into her possession.

"This conclusion was too adverse to my wishes not to be strenuously combated. I asked what it was that gave man the power of ascertaining the successor to his property. During his life, he might transfer the actual possession; but, if vacant at his death, he into whose hands accident should cast it was the genuine proprietor. It is true, that the law had sometimes otherwise decreed, but in law there was no validity further than it was able, by investigation and punishment, to enforce its decrees: but would the law extort this money from me?

"It was rather by gesture than by words that the will of Lodi was imparted. It was the topic of remote inferences and vague conjecture rather than of explicit and unerring declarations. Besides, if the lady were found, would not prudence dictate the reservation of her fortune to be administered by me, for her benefit? Of this her age and education had disqualified herself. It was sufficient for the maintenance of both. She would regard me as her benefactor and protector. By supplying all her wants and watching over her safety without apprizing her of the means by which I shall be enabled to do this, I shall lay irresistible claims to her love and her gratitude.

"Such were the sophistries by which reason was seduced and my integrity annihilated. I hastened away from my present abode. I easily traced the baggage of the deceased to an inn, and gained possession of it. It contained nothing but clothes and books. I then instituted the most diligent search after the young lady. For a time, my exertions were fruitless.

"Meanwhile, the possessor of this house thought proper to embark with his family for Europe. The sum which he demanded for his furniture, though enormous, was precipitately paid by me. His servants were continued in their former stations, and in the day at which he relinquished the mansion, I entered on possession.

"There was no difficulty in persuading the world that Welbeck was a personage of opulence and rank. My birth and previous adventures it was proper to conceal. The facility with which mankind are misled in their estimate of characters, their proneness to multiply inferences and conjectures, will not be readily conceived by one destitute of my experience. My sudden appearance on the stage, my stately reserve, my splendid habitation, and my circumspect deportment, were sufficient to entitle me to homage. The artifices that were used to unveil the truth, and the guesses that were current respecting me, were adapted to gratify my ruling passion.

"I did not remit my diligence to discover the retreat of Mademoiselle Lodi. I found her, at length, in the family of a kinsman of the captain under whose care she had come to America. Her situation was irksome and perilous. She had already experienced the evils of being protectorless and indigent, and my seasonable interference snatched her from impending and less supportable ills.

"I could safely unfold all that I knew of her brother's history, except the legacy which he had left. I ascribed the diligence with which I had sought her to his deathbed injunctions, and prevailed upon her to accept from me the treatment which she would have received from her brother if he had continued to live, and if his power to benefit had been equal to my own.

"Though less can be said in praise of the understanding than of the sensibilities of this woman, she is one whom no one could refrain from loving, though placed in situations far less favourable to the generation of that sentiment than mine. In habits of domestic and incessant intercourse, in the perpetual contemplation of features animated by boundless gratitude and ineffable sympathies, it could not be expected that either she or I should escape enchantment.

"The poison was too sweet not to be swallowed with avidity by me. Too late I remembered that I was already enslaved by inextricable obligations. It was easy to have hidden this impediment from the eyes of my companion, but here my integrity refused to yield. I can, indeed, lay claim to little merit on account of this forbearance. If there had been no alternative between deceit and the frustration of my hopes, I should doubtless have dissembled the truth with as little scruple on this as on a different occasion; but I could not be blind to the weakness of her with whom I had to contend.

CHAPTER XI.

"MEANWHILE large deductions had been made from my stock of money, and the remnant would be speedily consumed by my present mode of life. My expenses far exceeded my previous expectations. In no long time I should be reduced to my ancient poverty, which the luxurious existence that I now enjoyed, and the regard due to my beloved and helpless companion, would render more irksome than ever. Some scheme to rescue me from this fate was indispensable; but my aversion to labour, to any pursuit the end of which was merely gain, and which would require application and attention, continued undiminished.

"I was plunged anew into dejection and perplexity. From this I was somewhat relieved by a plan suggested by Mr. Thetford. I thought I had experience of his knowledge and integrity, and the scheme that he proposed seemed liable to no possibility of miscarriage. A ship was to be purchased, supplied with a suitable cargo, and despatched to a port in the West Indies. Loss from storms and enemies was to be precluded by insurance. Every hazard was to be enumerated, and the ship and cargo valued at the highest rate. Should the voyage be safely performed, the profits would be double the original expense. Should the ship be taken or wrecked, the insurers would have bound themselves to make ample, speedy, and certain indemnification. Thetford's brother, a wary and experienced trader, was to be the supercargo.

"All my money was laid out upon this scheme. Scarcely enough was reserved to supply domestic and personal wants. Large debts were likewise incurred. Our caution had, as we conceived, annihilated every chance of failure. Too much could not be expended on a project so infallible; and the vessel, amply fitted and freighted, departed on her voyage.

"An interval, not devoid of suspense and anxiety, succeeded. My mercantile inexperience made me distrust the clearness of my own discernment, and I could not but remember that my utter and irretrievable destruction was connected with the failure of my scheme. Time added to my distrust and apprehensions. The time at which tidings of the ship were to be expected elapsed without affording any information of her destiny. My anxieties, however, were to be carefully hidden from the world. I had taught mankind to believe that this project had been adopted more for amusement than gain; and the debts which I had contracted seemed to arise from willingness to adhere to established maxims, more than from the pressure of necessity.

"Month succeeded month, and intelligence was still withheld. The notes which I had given for one-third of the cargo, and for the premium of insurance, would shortly become due. For the payment of the former, and the cancelling of the latter, I had relied upon the expeditious return or the demonstrated loss of the vessel. Neither of these events had taken place.

"My cares were augmented from another quarter. My companion's situation now appeared to be such as, if our intercourse had been sanctified by wedlock, would have been regarded with delight. As it was, no symptoms were equally to be deplored. Consequences, as long as they were involved in uncertainty, were extenuated or overlooked; but now, when they became apparent and inevitable, were fertile of distress and upbraiding.

"Indefinable fears, and a desire to monopolize all the meditations and affections of this being, had induced me to perpetuate her ignorance of any but her native language, and debar her from all intercourse with the world. My friends were of course inquisitive respecting her character, adventures, and particularly her relation to me. The consciousness how much the truth redounded to my dishonour made me solicitous to lead conjecture astray. For this purpose I did not discountenance the conclusion that was adopted by some,—that she was my daughter. I reflected that all dangerous surmises would be effectually precluded by this belief.

"These precautions afforded me some consolation in my present difficulties. It was requisite to conceal the lady's condition from the world. If this should be ineffectual, it would not be difficult to divert suspicion from my person. The secrecy that I had practised would be justified, in the apprehension of those to whom the personal condition of Clemenza should be disclosed, by the feelings of a father.

"Meanwhile, it was an obvious expedient to remove the unhappy lady to a distance from impertinent observers. A rural retreat, lonely and sequestered, was easily procured, and hither she consented to repair. This arrangement being concerted, I had leisure to reflect upon the evils which every hour brought nearer, and which threatened to exterminate me.

"My inquietudes forbade me to sleep, and I was accustomed to rise before day and seek some respite in the fields. Returning from one of these unseasonable rambles, I chanced to meet you. Your resemblance to the deceased Lodi, in person and visage, is remarkable. When you first met my eye, this similitude startled me. Your subsequent appeal to my compassion was clothed in such terms as formed a powerful contrast with your dress, and prepossessed me greatly in favour of your education and capacity.

"In my present hopeless condition, every incident, however trivial, was attentively considered, with a view to extract from it some means of escaping from my difficulties. My love for the Italian girl, in spite of all my efforts to keep it alive, had begun to languish. Marriage was impossible; and had now, in some degree, ceased to be desirable. We are apt to judge of others by ourselves. The passion I now found myself disposed to ascribe chiefly to fortuitous circumstances; to the impulse of gratitude, and the exclusion of competitors; and believed that your resemblance to her brother, your age and personal accomplishments, might, after a certain time, and in consequence of suitable contrivances on my part, give a new direction to her feelings. To gain your concurrence, I relied upon your simplicity, your gratitude, and your susceptibility to the charms of this bewitching creature.

"I contemplated, likewise, another end. Mrs. Wentworth is rich. A youth who was once her favourite, and designed to inherit her fortunes, has disappeared, for some years, from the scene. His death is most probable, but of that there is no satisfactory information. The life of this person, whose name is Clavering, is an obstacle to some designs which had occurred to me in relation to this woman. My purposes were crude and scarcely formed. I need not swell the catalogue of my errors by expatiating upon them. Suffice it to say that the peculiar circumstances of your introduction to me led me to reflections on the use that might be made of your agency, in procuring this lady's acquiescence in my schemes. You were to be ultimately persuaded to confirm her in the belief that her nephew was dead. To this consummation it was indispensable to lead you by slow degrees and circuitous paths. Meanwhile, a profound silence, with regard to your genuine history, was to be observed; and to this forbearance your consent was obtained with more readiness than I expected.

"There was an additional motive for the treatment you received from me. My personal projects and cares had hitherto prevented me from reading Lodi's manuscript; a slight inspection, however, was sufficient to prove that the work was profound and eloquent. My ambition has panted, with equal avidity, after the reputation of literature and opulence. To claim the authorship of this work was too harmless and specious a stratagem not to be readily suggested. I meant to translate it into English, and to enlarge it by enterprising incidents of my own invention. My scruples to assume the merit of the original composer might thus be removed.

For this end, your assistance as an amanuensis would be necessary.

"You will perceive that all these projects depended on the seasonable arrival of intelligence from ——. The delay of another week would seal my destruction. The silence might arise from the foundering of the ship and the destruction of all on board. In this case, the insurance was not forfeited, but payment could not be obtained within a year. Meanwhile, the premium and other debts must be immediately discharged, and this was beyond my power. Meanwhile, I was to live in a manner that would not belie my pretensions; but my coffers were empty.

"I cannot adequately paint the anxieties with which I have been haunted. Each hour has added to the burden of my existence, till, in consequence of the events of this day, it has become altogether insupportable. Some hours ago, I was summoned by Thetford to his house. The messenger informed me that tidings had been received of my ship. In answer to my eager interrogations, he could give no other information than that she had been captured by the British. He was unable to relate particulars.

"News of her safe return would, indeed, have been far more acceptable; but even this information was a source of infinite congratulation. It precluded the demand of my insurers. The payment of other debts might be postponed for a month, and my situation be the same as before the adoption of this successless scheme. Hope and joy were reinstated in my bosom, and I hasted to Thetford's counting-house.

"He received me with an air of gloomy dissatisfaction. I accounted for his sadness by supposing him averse to communicate information which was less favourable than our wishes had dictated. He confirmed, with visible reluctance, the news of her capture. He had just received letters from his brother, acquainting him with all particulars, and containing the official documents of this transaction.

"This had no tendency to damp my satisfaction, and I proceeded to peruse with eagerness the papers which he put into my hand. I had not proceeded far, when my joyous hopes vanished. Two French mulattoes had, after much solicitation, and the most solemn promises to carry with them no articles which the laws of war decree to be contraband, obtained a passage in the vessel. She was speedily encountered by a privateer, by whom every receptacle was ransacked. In a chest, belonging to the Frenchmen, and which they had affirmed to contain nothing but their clothes, were found two sabres, and other accoutrements of an officer of cavalry. Under this pretence, the vessel was captured and condemned, and this was a cause of forfeiture which had not been provided against in the contract of insurance.

"By this untoward event my hopes were irreparably blasted. The utmost efforts were demanded to conceal my thoughts from my companion. The anguish that preyed upon my heart was endeavoured to be masked by looks of indifference. I pretended to have been previously informed by the messenger not only of the capture, but of the cause that led to it, and forbore to expatiate upon my loss, or to execrate the authors of my disappointment. My mind, however, was the theatre of discord and agony, and I waited with impatience for an opportunity to leave him.

"For want of other topics, I asked by whom this information had been brought. He answered, that the bearer was Captain Amos Watson, whose vessel had been forfeited, at the same time, under a different pretence. He added that, my name being mentioned accidentally to Watson, the latter had betrayed marks of great surprise, and been very earnest in his inquiries respecting my situation. Having obtained what knowledge Thetford was able to communicate, the captain had departed, avowing a former acquaintance with me, and declaring his intention of paying me a visit.

"These words operated on my frame like lightning. All within me was tumult and terror, and I rushed precipitately out of the house. I went forward with unequal steps, and at random. Some instinct led me into the fields, and I was not apprized of the direction of my steps, till, looking up, I found myself upon the shore of Schuylkill.

"Thus was I, a second time, overborne by hopeless and incurable evils. An interval of motley feelings, of specious artifice and contemptible imposture, had elapsed since my meeting with the stranger at Wilmington. Then my forlorn state had led me to the brink of suicide. A brief and feverish respite had been afforded me, but now was I transported to the verge of the same abyss.

"Amos Watson was the brother of the angel whom I had degraded and destroyed. What but fiery indignation and unappeasable vengeance could lead him into my presence? With what heart could I listen to his invectives? How could I endure to look upon the face of one whom I had loaded with such atrocious and intolerable injuries?

"I was acquainted with his loftiness of mind; his detestation of injustice, and the whirlwind passions that ingratitude and villany like mine were qualified to awaken in his bosom. I dreaded not his violence. The death that he might be prompted to inflict was no object of aversion. It was poverty and disgrace, the detection of my crimes, the looks and voice of malediction and upbraiding, from which my cowardice shrunk.

"Why should I live? I must vanish from that stage which I had lately trodden. My flight must be instant and precipitate. To be a fugitive from exasperated creditors, and from the industrious revenge of Watson, was an easy undertaking; but whither could I fly, where I should not be pursued by the phantoms of remorse, by the dread of hourly detection, by the necessities of hunger and thirst? In what scene should I be exempt from servitude and drudgery? Was my existence embellished with enjoyments that would justify my holding it, encumbered with hardships and immersed in obscurity?

"There was no room for hesitation. To rush into the stream before me, and put an end at once to my life and the miseries inseparably linked with it, was the only proceeding which fate had left to my choice. My muscles were already exerted for this end, when the helpless condition of Clemenza was remembered. What provision could I make against the evils that threatened her? Should I leave her utterly forlorn and friendless? Mrs. Wentworth's temper was forgiving and compassionate. Adversity had taught her to participate and her wealth enabled her to relieve distress. Who was there by whom such powerful claims to succour and protection could be urged as by this desolate girl? Might I not state her situation in a letter to this lady, and urge irresistible pleas for the extension of her kindness to this object?

"These thoughts made me suspend my steps. I determined to seek my habitation once more, and, having written and deposited this letter, to return to the execution of my fatal purpose. I had scarcely reached my own door, when some one approached along the pavement. The form, at first, was undistinguishable, but, by coming, at length, within the illumination of a lamp, it was perfectly recognised.

"To avoid this detested interview was now impossible. Watson approached and accosted me. In this conflict of tumultuous feelings I was still able to maintain an air of intrepidity. His demeanour was that of a man who struggles with his rage. His accents were hurried, and scarcely articulate. 'I have ten words to say to you,' said he; 'lead into the house, and to some private room. My business with you will be despatched in a breath.'

"I made him no answer, but led the way into my house, and to my study. On entering this room, I put the light upon the table, and, turning to my visitant, prepared silently to hear what he had to unfold. He struck his clenched hand against the table with violence. His motion was of that tempestuous kind as to overwhelm the power of utterance, and found it easier to vent itself in gesticulations than in words. At length he exclaimed,—

"'It is well. Now has the hour, so long and so impatiently demanded by my vengeance, arrived. Welbeck! Would that my first words could strike thee dead! They will so, if thou hast any title to the name of man.

"'My sister is dead; dead of anguish and a broken

heart. Remote from her friends; in a hovel; the abode of indigence and misery.

"'Her husband is no more. He returned after a long absence, a tedious navigation, and vicissitudes of hardships. He flew to the bosom of his love; of his wife. She was gone; lost to him, and to virtue. In a fit of desperation, he retired to his chamber and despatched himself. This is the instrument with which the deed was performed.'

"Saying this, Watson took a pistol from his pocket, and held it to my head. I lifted not my hand to turn aside the weapon. I did not shudder at the spectacle, or shrink from his approaching hand. With fingers clasped together, and eyes fixed upon the floor, I waited till his fury was exhausted. He continued:—

"'All passed in a few hours. The elopement of his daughter,—the death of his son. O my father! Most loved and most venerable of men! To see thee changed into a maniac! Haggard and wild! Deterred from outrage on thyself and those around thee by fetters and stripes! What was it that saved me from a like fate? To view this hideous ruin, and to think by whom it was occasioned! Yet not to become frantic like thee, my father; or not destroy myself like thee, my brother! My friend!—

"'No. For this hour was I reserved; to avenge your wrongs and mine in the blood of this ungrateful villain.

"'There,' continued he, producing a second pistol, and tendering it to me,—'there is thy defence. Take we opposite sides of this table, and fire at the same instant.'

"During this address I was motionless. He tendered the pistol, but I unclasped not my hands to receive it.

"'Why do you hesitate?' resumed he. 'Let the chance between us be equal, or fire you first.'

"'No,' said I, 'I am ready to die by your hand. I wish it. It will preclude the necessity of performing the office for myself. I have injured you, and merit all that your vengeance can inflict. I know your nature too well to believe that my death will be perfect expiation. When the gust of indignation is past, the remembrance of your deed will only add to your sum of misery; yet I do not love you well enough to wish that you would forbear. I desire to die, and to die by another's hand rather than my own.'

"'Coward!' exclaimed Watson, with augmented vehemence, 'you know me too well to believe me capable of assassination. Vile subterfuge! Contemptible plea! Take the pistol and defend yourself. You want not the power or the will; but, knowing that I spurn at murder, you think your safety will be found in passiveness. Your refusal will avail you little. Your fame, if not your life, is at my mercy. If you falter now, I will allow you to live, but only till I have stabbed your reputation.'

"I now fixed my eyes steadfastly upon him, and spoke:—'How much a stranger are you to the feelings of Welbeck! How poor a judge of his cowardice! I take your pistol, and consent to your conditions.'

"We took opposite sides of the table. 'Are you ready?' he cried; 'fire!'

"Both triggers were drawn at the same instant. Both pistols were discharged. Mine was negligently raised. Such is the untoward chance that presides over human affairs; such is the malignant destiny by which my steps have ever been pursued. The bullet whistled harmlessly by me,—levelled by an eye that never before failed, and with so small an interval between us. I escaped, but my blind and random shot took place in his heart.

"There is the fruit of this disastrous meeting. The catalogue of death is thus completed. Thou sleepest, Watson! Thy sister is at rest, and so art thou. Thy vows of vengeance are at an end. It was not reserved for thee to be thy own and thy sister's avenger. Welbeck's measure of transgressions is now full, and his own hand must execute the justice that is due to him."

CHAPTER XII.

SUCH was Welbeck's tale, listened to by me with an eagerness in which every faculty was absorbed. How adverse to my dreams were the incidents that had just been related! The curtain was lifted, and a scene of guilt and ignominy disclosed where my rash and inexperienced youth had suspected nothing but loftiness and magnanimity.

For a while the wondrousness of this tale kept me from contemplating the consequences that awaited us. My unfledged fancy had not hitherto soared to this pitch. All was astounding by its novelty, or terrific by its horror. The very scene of these offences partook, to my rustic apprehension, of fairy splendour and magical abruptness. My understanding was bemazed, and my senses were taught to distrust their own testimony.

From this musing state I was recalled by my companion, who said to me, in solemn accents, "Mervyn! I have but two requests to make. Assist me to bury these remains, and then accompany me across the river. I have no power to compel your silence on the acts that you have witnessed. I have meditated to benefit as well as to injure you; but I do not desire that your demeanour should conform to any other standard than justice. You have promised, and to that promise I trust.

"If you choose to fly from this scene, to withdraw yourself from what you may conceive to be a theatre of guilt or peril, the avenues are open; retire unmolested and in silence. If you have a manlike spirit, if you are grateful for the benefits bestowed upon you, if your discernment enables you to see that compliance with my request will entangle you in no guilt and betray you into no danger, stay, and aid me in hiding these remains from human scrutiny.

"Watson is beyond the reach of further injury. I never intended him harm, though I have torn from him his sister and friend, and have brought his life to an untimely close. To provide him a grave is a duty that I owe to the dead and to the living. I shall quickly place myself beyond the reach of inquisitors and judges, but would willingly rescue from molestation or suspicion those whom I shall leave behind."

What would have been the fruit of deliberation, if I had had the time or power to deliberate, I know not. My thoughts flowed with tumult and rapidity. To shut this spectacle from my view was the first impulse; but to desert this man, in a time of so much need, appeared a thankless and dastardly deportment. To remain where I was, to conform implicitly to his direction, required no effort. Some fear was connected with his presence, and with that of the dead; but, in the tremulous confusion of my present thoughts, solitude would conjure up a thousand phantoms.

I made no preparation to depart. I did not verbally assent to his proposal. He interpreted my silence into acquiescence. He wrapped the body in the carpet, and then, lifting one end, cast at me a look which indicated his expectations that I would aid him in lifting this ghastly burden. During this process, the silence was unbroken.

I knew not whither he intended to convey the corpse. He had talked of burial, but no receptacle had been provided. How far safety might depend upon his conduct in this particular, I was unable to estimate. I was in too heartless a mood to utter my doubts. I followed his example in raising the corpse from the floor.

He led the way into the passage and down-stairs. Having reached the first floor, he unbolted a door which led into the cellar. The stairs and passage were illuminated by lamps that hung from the ceiling and were accustomed to burn during the night. Now, however, we were entering darksome and murky recesses.

"Return," said he, in a tone of command, "and fetch the light. I will wait for you."

I obeyed. As I returned with the light, a suspicion stole into my mind, that Welbeck had taken this opportunity to fly; and that, on regaining the foot of the stairs, I should find the spot deserted by all but the dead. My blood was chilled by this image. The momentary resolution it inspired was to follow the example of the fugitive, and leave the persons whom the ensuing day might convene on this spot, to form their own conjectures as to the cause of this catastrophe.

Meanwhile, I cast anxious eyes forward. Welbeck was discovered in the same place and posture in which he had been left. Lifting the corpse and its shroud in his arms, he directed me to follow him. The vaults beneath were lofty and spacious. He passed from one to the other till we reached a small and remote cell. Here he cast his burden on the ground. In the fall, the face of Watson chanced to be disengaged from its covering. Its closed eyes and sunken muscles were rendered in a tenfold degree ghastly and rueful by the feeble light which the candle shed upon it.

This object did not escape the attention of Welbeck. He leaned against the wall, and, folding his arms, resigned himself to reverie. He gazed upon the countenance of Watson, but his looks denoted his attention to be elsewhere employed.

As to me, my state will not be easily described. My eye roved fearfully from one object to another. By turns it was fixed upon the murdered person and the murderer. The narrow cell in which we stood, its rudely-fashioned walls and arches, destitute of communication with the external air, and its palpable dark scarcely penetrated by the rays of a solitary candle, added to the silence which was deep and universal, produced an impression on my fancy which no time will obliterate.

Perhaps my imagination was distempered by terror. The incident which I am going to relate may appear to have existed only in my fancy. Be that as it may, I experienced all the effects which the fullest belief is adapted to produce. Glancing vaguely at the countenance of Watson, my attention was arrested by a convulsive motion in the eyelids. This motion increased, till at length the eyes opened, and a glance, languid but wild, was thrown around. Instantly they closed, and the tremulous appearance vanished.

I started from my place and was on the point of uttering some involuntary exclamation. At the same moment, Welbeck seemed to recover from his reverie.

"How is this?" said he. "Why do we linger here? Every moment is precious. We cannot dig for him a grave with our hands. Wait here, while I go in search of a spade."

Saying this, he snatched the candle from my hand, and hasted away. My eye followed the light as its gleams shifted their place upon the walls and ceilings, and, gradually vanishing, gave place to unrespited gloom. This proceeding was so unexpected and abrupt, that I had no time to remonstrate against it. Before I retrieved the power of reflection, the light had disappeared and the footsteps were no longer to be heard.

I was not, on ordinary occasions, destitute of equanimity; but perhaps the imagination of man is naturally abhorrent of death, until tutored into indifference by habit. Every circumstance combined to fill me with shuddering and panic. For a while, I was enabled to endure my situation by the exertions of my reason. That the lifeless remains of a human being are powerless to injure or benefit, I was thoroughly persuaded. I summoned this belief to my aid, and was able, if not to subdue, yet to curb, my fears. I listened to catch the sound of the returning footsteps of Welbeck, and hoped that every new moment would terminate my solitude.

No signal of his coming was afforded. At length it occurred to me that Welbeck had gone with no intention to return; that his malice had seduced me hither to encounter the consequences of his deed. He had fled and barred every door behind him. This suspicion may well be supposed to overpower my courage, and to call forth desperate efforts for my deliverance.

I extended my hands and went forward. I had been too little attentive to the situation and direction of these vaults and passages, to go forward with undeviating accuracy. My fears likewise tended to confuse my perceptions and bewilder my steps. Notwithstanding the danger of encountering obstructions, I rushed towards the entrance with precipitation.

My temerity was quickly punished. In a moment, I

was repelled by a jutting angle of the wall, with such force that I staggered backward and fell. The blow was stunning, and, when I recovered my senses, I perceived that a torrent of blood was gushing from my nostrils. My clothes were moistened with this unwelcome effusion, and I could not but reflect on the hazard which I should incur by being detected in this recess, covered by these accusing stains.

This reflection once more set me on my feet and incited my exertions. I now proceeded with greater wariness and caution. I had lost all distinct notions of my way. My motions were at random. All my labour was to shun obstructions and to advance whenever the vacuity would permit. By this means, the entrance was at length found, and, after various efforts, I arrived, beyond my hopes, at the foot of the staircase.

I ascended, but quickly encountered an insuperable impediment. The door at the stair-head was closed and barred. My utmost strength was exerted in vain, to break the lock or the hinges. Thus were my direst apprehensions fulfilled. Welbeck had left me to sustain the charge of murder; to obviate suspicions the most atrocious and plausible that the course of human events is capable of producing.

Here I must remain till the morrow; till some one can be made to overhear my calls and come to my deliverance. What effects will my appearance produce on the spectator? Terrified by phantoms and stained with blood, shall I not exhibit the tokens of a maniac as well as an assassin?

The corpse of Watson will quickly be discovered. If, previous to this disclosure, I should change my blood-stained garments and withdraw into the country, shall I not be pursued by the most vehement suspicions, and, perhaps, hunted to my obscurest retreat by the ministers of justice? I am innocent; but my tale, however circumstantial or true, will scarcely suffice for my vindication. My flight will be construed into a proof of incontestable guilt.

While harassed by these thoughts, my attention was attracted by a faint gleam cast upon the bottom of the staircase. It grew stronger, hovered for a moment in my sight, and then disappeared. That it proceeded from a lamp or candle, borne by some one along the passages, was no untenable opinion, but was far less probable than that the effulgence was meteorous. I confided in the latter supposition, and fortified myself anew against the dread of preternatural dangers. My thoughts reverted to the contemplation of the hazards and suspicions which flowed from my continuance in this spot.

In the midst of my perturbed musing, my attention was again recalled by an illumination like the former. Instead of hovering and vanishing, it was permanent. No ray could be more feeble; but the tangible obscurity to which it succeeded rendered it conspicuous as an electrical flash. For a while I eyed it without moving from my place, and in momentary expectation of its disappearance.

Remarking its stability, the propriety of scrutinizing it more nearly, and of ascertaining the source whence it flowed, was at length suggested. Hope, as well as curiosity, was the parent of my conduct. Though utterly at a loss to assign the cause of this appearance, I was willing to believe some connection between that cause and the means of my deliverance.

I had scarcely formed the resolution of descending the stair, when my hope was extinguished by the recollection that the cellar had narrow and grated windows, through which light from the street might possibly have found access. A second recollection supplanted this belief, for in my way to this staircase my attention would have been solicited, and my steps, in some degree, been guided, by light coming through these avenues.

Having returned to the bottom of the stair, I perceived every part of the long-drawn passage illuminated. I threw a glance forward to the quarter whence the rays seemed to proceed, and beheld, at a considerable distance, Welbeck in the cell which I had left, turning up the earth with a spade.

After a pause of astonishment, the nature of the error which I had committed rushed upon my apprehension.

I now perceived that the darkness had misled me to a different staircase from that which I had originally descended. It was apparent that Welbeck intended me no evil, but had really gone in search of the instrument which he had mentioned.

This discovery overwhelmed me with contrition and shame, though it freed me from the terrors of imprisonment and accusation. To return to the cell which I had left, and where Welbeck was employed in his disastrous office, was the expedient which regard to my own safety unavoidably suggested.

Welbeck paused at my approach, and betrayed a momentary consternation at the sight of my ensanguined visage. The blood, by some inexplicable process of nature, perhaps by the counteracting influence of fear, had quickly ceased to flow. Whether the cause of my evasion, and of my flux of blood, was guessed, or whether his attention was withdrawn, by more momentous objects, from my condition, he proceeded in his task in silence.

A shallow bed and a slight covering of clay were provided for the hapless Watson. Welbeck's movements were hurried and tremulous. His countenance betokened a mind engrossed by a single purpose, in some degree foreign to the scene before him. An intensity and fixedness of features were conspicuous, that led me to suspect the subversion of his reason.

Having finished the task, he threw aside his implement. He then put into my hand a pocket-book, saying it belonged to Watson, and might contain something serviceable to the living. I might make what use of it I thought proper. He then remounted the stairs, and, placing the candle on a table in the hall, opened the principal door and went forth. I was driven, by a sort of mechanical impulse, in his footsteps. I followed him because it was agreeable to him and because I knew not whither else to direct my steps.

The streets were desolate and silent. The watchman's call, remotely and faintly heard, added to the general solemnity. I followed my companion in a state of mind not easily described. I had no spirit even to inquire whither he was going. It was not till we arrived at the water's edge that I persuaded myself to break silence. I then began to reflect on the degree in which his present schemes might endanger Welbeck or myself. I had acted long enough a servile and mechanical part; and been guided by blind and foreign impulses. It was time to lay aside my fetters, and demand to know whither the path tended in which I was importuned to walk.

Meanwhile I found myself entangled among boats and shipping. I am unable to describe the spot by any indisputable tokens. I know merely that it was the termination of one of the principal streets. Here Welbeck selected a boat and prepared to enter it. For a moment I hesitated to comply with his apparent invitation. I stammered out an interrogation:—"Why is this? Why should we cross the river? What service can I do for you? I ought to know the purpose of my voyage before I enter it."

He checked himself and surveyed me for a minute in silence. "What do you fear?" said he. "Have I not explained my wishes? Merely cross the river with me, for I cannot navigate a boat by myself. Is there any thing arduous or mysterious in this undertaking? we part on the Jersey shore, and I shall leave you to your destiny. All I shall ask from you will be silence, and to hide from mankind what you know concerning me."

He now entered the boat and urged me to follow his example. I reluctantly complied. I perceived that the boat contained but one oar, and that was a small one. He seemed startled and thrown into great perplexity by this discovery. "It will be impossible," said he, in a tone of panic and vexation, "to procure another at this hour: what is to be done?"

This impediment was by no means insuperable. I had sinewy arms, and knew well how to use an oar for the double purpose of oar and rudder. I took my station at the stern, and quickly extricated the boat from its neighbours and from the wharves. I was wholly unacquainted with the river. The bar by which it was encumbered I knew to exist, but in what direction and to what extent it existed, and how it might be avoided in the present state of the tide, I knew not. It was probable, therefore, unknowing as I was of the proper track, that our boat would speedily have grounded.

My attention, meanwhile, was fixed upon the oar. My companion sat at the prow, and was in a considerable degree unnoticed. I cast my eyes occasionally at the scene which I had left. Its novelty, joined with the incidents of my condition, threw me into a state of suspense and wonder which frequently slackened my hand and left the vessel to be driven by the downward current. Lights were sparingly seen, and these were perpetually fluctuating, as masts, yards, and hulls were interposed, and passed before them. In proportion as we receded from the shore, the clamours seemed to multiply, and the suggestion that the city was involved in confusion and uproar did not easily give way to maturer thoughts. *Twelve* was the hour cried, and this ascended at once from all quarters, and was mingled with the baying of dogs, so as to produce trepidation and alarm.

From this state of magnificent and awful feeling I was suddenly called by the conduct of Welbeck. We had scarcely moved two hundred yards from the shore, when he plunged into the water. The first conception was that some implement or part of the boat had fallen overboard. I looked back and perceived that his seat was vacant. In my first astonishment I loosened my hold of the oar, and it floated away. The surface was smooth as glass, and the eddy occasioned by his sinking was scarcely visible. I had not time to determine whether this was designed or accidental. Its suddenness deprived me of the power to exert myself for his succour. I wildly gazed around me, in hopes of seeing him rise. After some time my attention was drawn, by the sound of agitation in the water, to a considerable distance.

It was too dark for any thing to be distinctly seen. There was no cry for help. The noise was like that of one vigorously struggling for a moment, and then sinking to the bottom. I listened with painful eagerness, but was unable to distinguish a third signal. He sunk to rise no more.

I was for a time inattentive to my own situation. The dreadfulness and unexpectedness of this catastrophe occupied me wholly. The quick motion of the lights upon the shore showed me that I was borne rapidly along with the tide. How to help myself, how to impede my course or to regain either shore, since I had lost the oar, I was unable to tell. I was no less at a loss to conjecture whither the current, if suffered to control my vehicle, would finally transport me.

The disappearance of lights and buildings, and the diminution of the noises, acquainted me that I had passed the town. It was impossible longer to hesitate. The shore was to be regained by one way only, which was swimming. To any exploit of this kind, my strength and my skill were adequate. I threw away my loose gown; put the pocket-book of the unfortunate Watson in my mouth, to preserve it from being injured by moisture; and committed myself to the stream.

I landed in a spot incommoded with mud and reeds. I sunk knee-deep into the former, and was exhausted by the fatigue of extricating myself. At length I recovered firm ground, and threw myself on the turf to repair my wasted strength, and to reflect on the measures which my future welfare enjoined me to pursue.

What condition was ever parallel to mine? The transactions of the last three days resembled the monstrous creations of delirium. They were painted with vivid hues on my memory; but so rapid and incongruous were these transitions, that I almost denied belief to their reality. They exercised a bewildering and stupefying influence on my mind, from which the meditations of an hour were scarcely sufficient to relieve me. Gradually I recovered the power of arranging my ideas and forming conclusions.

Welbeck was dead. His property was swallowed up, and his creditors left to wonder at his disappearance. All that was left was the furniture of his house, to which Mrs. Wentworth would lay claim, in discharge of the unpaid rent. What now was the destiny that awaited the lost and friendless Mademoiselle Lodi? Where was she concealed? Welbeck had dropped no intimation by which I might be led to suspect the place of her abode. If my power, in other respects, could have contributed aught to her relief, my ignorance of her asylum had utterly disabled me.

But what of the murdered person? He had suddenly vanished from the face of the earth. His fate and the place of his interment would probably be suspected and ascertained. Was I sure to escape from the consequences of this deed? Watson had relatives and friends. What influence on their state and happiness his untimely and mysterious fate would possess, it was obvious to inquire. This idea led me to the recollection of his pocket-book. Some papers might be there explanatory of his situation.

I resumed my feet. I knew not where to direct my steps. I was dropping with wet, and shivering with the cold. I was destitute of habitation and friend. I had neither money nor any valuable thing in my possession. I moved forward mechanically and at random. Where I landed was at no great distance from the verge of the town. In a short time I discovered the glimmering of a distant lamp. To this I directed my steps, and here I paused to examine the contents of the pocket-book.

I found three bank-notes, each of fifty dollars, enclosed in a piece of blank paper. Besides these were three letters, apparently written by his wife, and dated at Baltimore. They were brief, but composed in a strain of great tenderness, and containing affecting allusions to their child. I could gather, from their date and tenor, that they were received during his absence on his recent voyage; that her condition was considerably necessitous, and surrounded by wants which their prolonged separation had increased.

The fourth letter was open, and seemed to have been very lately written. It was directed to Mrs. Mary Watson. He informed her in it of his arrival at Philadelphia from St. Domingo; of the loss of his ship and cargo; and of his intention to hasten home with all possible expedition. He told her that all was lost but one hundred and fifty dollars, the greater part of which he should bring with him, to relieve her more pressing wants. The letter was signed, and folded, and superscribed, but unsealed.

A little consideration showed me in what manner it became me, on this occasion, to demean myself. I put the bank-notes in the letter, and sealed it with a wafer; a few of which were found in the pocket-book. I hesitated some time whether I should add any thing to the information which the letter contained, by means of a pencil which offered itself to my view; but I concluded to forbear. I could select no suitable terms in which to communicate the mournful truth. I resolved to deposit this letter at the post-office, where I knew letters could be left at all hours.

My reflections at length reverted to my own condition. What was the fate reserved for me? How far my safety might be affected by remaining in the city, in consequence of the disappearance of Welbeck, and my known connection with the fugitive, it was impossible to foresee. My fears readily suggested innumerable embarrassments and inconveniences which would flow from this source. Besides, on what pretence should I remain? To whom could I apply for protection or employment? All avenues, even to subsistence, were shut against me. The country was my sole asylum. Here, in exchange for my labour, I could at least purchase food, safety, and repose. But, if my choice pointed to the country, there was no reason for a moment's delay. It would be prudent to regain the fields, and be far from this detested city before the rising of the sun.

Meanwhile I was chilled and chafed by the clothes that I wore. To change them for others was absolutely necessary to my ease. The clothes which I wore were not my own, and were extremely unsuitable to my new condition. My rustic and homely garb was deposited in my chamber at Welbeck's. These thoughts suggested the design of returning thither. I considered that, probably, the servants had not been alarmed. That the door was unfastened, and the house was accessible. It would be easy to enter and retire without notice; and this, not without some waverings and misgivings, I presently determined to do.

Having deposited my letter at the office, I proceeded to my late abode. I approached, and lifted the latch with caution. There were no appearances of any one having been disturbed. I procured a light in the kitchen, and hied softly and with dubious footsteps to my chamber. There I disrobed, and resumed my check shirt, and trowsers, and fustian coat. This change being accomplished, nothing remained but that I should strike into the country with the utmost expedition.

In a momentary review which I took of the past, the design for which Welbeck professed to have originally detained me in his service occurred to my mind. I knew the danger of reasoning loosely on the subject of property. To any trinket or piece of furniture in this house I did not allow myself to question the right of Mrs. Wentworth; a right accruing to her in consequence of Welbeck's failure in the payment of his rent; but there was one thing which I felt an irresistible desire, and no scruples which should forbid me, to possess, and that was, the manuscript to which Welbeck had alluded, as having been written by the deceased Lodi.

I was well instructed in Latin, and knew the Tuscan language to be nearly akin to it. I despaired not of being at some time able to cultivate this language, and believed that the possession of this manuscript might essentially contribute to this end, as well as to many others equally beneficial. It was easy to conjecture that the volume was to be found among his printed books, and it was scarcely less easy to ascertain the truth of this conjecture. I entered, not without tremulous sensations, into the apartment which had been the scene of the disastrous interview between Watson and Welbeck. At every step I almost dreaded to behold the spectre of the former rise before me.

Numerous and splendid volumes were arranged on mahogany shelves, and screened by doors of glass. I ran swiftly over their names, and was at length so fortunate as to light upon the book of which I was in search. I immediately secured it, and, leaving the candle extinguished on a table in the parlour, I once more issued forth into the street. With light steps and palpitating heart I turned my face towards the country. My necessitous condition I believed would justify me in passing without payment the Schuylkill bridge, and the eastern sky began to brighten with the dawn of morning not till I had gained the distance of nine miles from the city.

Such is the tale which I proposed to relate to you. Such are the memorable incidents of five days of my life; from which I have gathered more instruction than from the whole tissue of my previous existence. Such are the particulars of my knowledge respecting the crimes and misfortunes of Welbeck; which the insinuations of Wortley, and my desire to retain your good opinion, have induced me to unfold.

CHAPTER XIII.

MERVYN'S pause allowed his auditors to reflect on the particulars of his narration, and to compare them with the facts with a knowledge of which their own observation had supplied them. My profession introduced me to the friendship of Mrs. Wentworth, by whom, after the disappearance of Welbeck, many circumstances respecting him had been mentioned. She particularly dwelt upon the deportment and appearance of this youth, at the single interview which took place between them, and her representations were perfectly conformable to those which Mervyn had himself delivered.

Previously to this interview, Welbeck had insinuated to her that a recent event had put him in possession of the truth respecting the destiny of Clavering. A kinsman of his had arrived from Portugal, by whom this intelligence had been brought. He dexterously eluded her entreaties to be furnished with minuter information, or to introduce this kinsman to her acquaintance. As soon as Mervyn was ushered into her presence, she suspected him to be the person to whom Welbeck had alluded, and this suspicion his conversation had confirmed. She was at a loss to comprehend the reasons of the silence which he so pertinaciously maintained.

Her uneasiness, however, prompted her to renew her

solicitations. On the day subsequent to the catastrophe related by Mervyn, she sent a messenger to Welbeck, with a request to see him. Gabriel, the black servant, informed the messenger that his master had gone into the country for a week. At the end of the week, a messenger was again despatched with the same errand. He called and knocked, but no one answered his signals. He examined the entrance by the kitchen, but every avenue was closed. It appeared that the house was wholly deserted.

These appearances naturally gave birth to curiosity and suspicion. The house was repeatedly examined, but the solitude and silence within continued the same. The creditors of Welbeck were alarmed by these appearances, and their claims to the property remaining in the house were precluded by Mrs. Wentworth, who, as owner of the mansion, was legally entitled to the furniture, in place of the rent which Welbeck had suffered to accumulate.

On examining the dwelling, all that was valuable and portable, particularly linen and plate, was removed. The remainder was distrained, but the tumults of pestilence succeeded and hindered it from being sold. Things were allowed to continue in their former situation, and the house was carefully secured. We had no leisure to form conjectures on the causes of this desertion. An explanation was afforded us by the narrative of this youth. It is probable that the servants, finding their master's absence continue, had pillaged the house and fled.

Meanwhile, though our curiosity with regard to Welbeck was appeased, it was obvious to inquire by what series of inducements and events Mervyn was reconducted to the city and led to the spot where I first met with him. We intimated our wishes in this respect, and our young friend readily consented to take up the thread of his story and bring it down to the point that was desired. For this purpose, the ensuing evening was selected. Having, at an early hour, shut ourselves up from all intruders and visitors, he continued as follows.

I have mentioned that, by sunrise, I had gained the distance of many miles from the city. My purpose was to stop at the first farm-house, and seek employment as a day-labourer. The first person whom I observed was a man of placid mien and plain garb. Habitual benevolence was apparent amidst the wrinkles of age. He was traversing his buckwheat-field, and measuring, as it seemed, the harvest that was now nearly ripe.

I accosted him with diffidence, and explained my wishes. He listened to my tale with complacency, inquired into my name and family, and into my qualifications for the office to which I aspired. My answers were candid and full.

"Why," said he, "I believe thou and I can make a bargain. We will, at least, try each other for a week or two. If it does not suit our mutual convenience, we can change. The morning is damp and cool, and thy plight does not appear the most comfortable that can be imagined. Come to the house and eat some breakfast."

The behaviour of this good man filled me with gratitude and joy. Methought I could embrace him as a father, and entrance into his house appeared like return to a long-lost and much-loved home. My desolate and lonely condition appeared to be changed for paternal regards and the tenderness of friendship.

These emotions were confirmed and heightened by every object that presented itself under this roof. The family consisted of Mrs. Hadwin, two simple and affectionate girls, his daughters, and servants. The manners of this family, quiet, artless, and cordial, the occupations allotted me, the land by which the dwelling was surrounded, its pure airs, romantic walks, and exhaustless fertility, constituted a powerful contrast to the scenes which I had left behind, and were congenial with every dictate of my understanding and every sentiment that glowed in my heart.

My youth, mental cultivation, and circumspect deportment, entitled me to deference and confidence. Each hour confirmed me in the good opinion of Mr. Hadwin, and in the affections of his daughters. In the mind of my employer, the simplicity of the husbandman and the devotion of the Quaker were blended with humanity and intelligence. The sisters, Susan and Eliza, were unacquainted with calamity and vice through the medium of either observation or books. They were strangers to the benefits of an elaborate education, but they were endowed with curiosity and discernment, and had not suffered their slender means of instruction to remain unimproved.

The sedateness of the elder formed an amusing contrast with the laughing eye and untamable vivacity of the younger; but they smiled and they wept in unison. They thought and acted in different but not discordant keys. On all momentous occasions, they reasoned and felt alike. In ordinary cases, they separated, as it were, into different tracks; but this diversity was productive not of jarring, but of harmony.

A romantic and untutored disposition like mine may be supposed liable to strong impressions from perpetual converse with persons of their age and sex. The elder was soon discovered to have already disposed of her affections. The younger was free, and somewhat that is more easily conceived than named stole insensibly upon my heart. The images that haunted me at home and abroad, in her absence and her presence, gradually coalesced into one shape, and gave birth to an incessant train of latent palpitations and indefinable hopes. My days were little else than uninterrupted reveries, and night only called up phantoms more vivid and equally enchanting.

The memorable incidents which had lately happened scarcely counterpoised my new sensations or diverted my contemplations from the present. My views were gradually led to rest upon futurity, and in that I quickly found cause of circumspection and dread. My present labours were light, and were sufficient for my subsistence in a single state; but wedlock was the parent of new wants and of new cares. Mr. Hadwin's possessions were adequate to his own frugal maintenance, but, divided between his children, would be too scanty for either. Besides, this division could only take place at his death, and that was an event whose speedy occurrence was neither desirable nor probable.

Another obstacle was now remembered. Hadwin was the conscientious member of a sect which forbade the marriage of its votaries with those of a different communion. I had been trained in an opposite creed, and imagined it impossible that I should ever become a proselyte to Quakerism. It only remained for me to feign conversion, or to root out the opinions of my friend and win her consent to a secret marriage. Whether hypocrisy was eligible was no subject of deliberation. If the possession of all that ambition can conceive were added to the transports of union with Eliza Hadwin, and offered as the price of dissimulation, it would have been instantly rejected. My external goods were not abundant nor numerous, but the consciousness of rectitude was mine; and, in competition with this, the luxury of the heart and of the senses, the gratifications of boundless ambition and inexhaustible wealth, were contemptible and frivolous.

The conquest of Eliza's errors was easy; but to introduce discord and sorrow into this family was an act of the utmost ingratitude and profligacy. It was only requisite for my understanding clearly to discern, to be convinced of the insuperability of this obstacle. It was manifest, therefore, that the point to which my wishes tended was placed beyond my reach.

To foster my passion was to foster a disease destructive either of my integrity or my existence. It was indispensable to fix my thoughts upon a different object, and to debar myself even from her intercourse. To ponder on themes foreign to my darling image, and to seclude myself from her society, at hours which had usually been spent with her, were difficult tasks. The latter was the least practicable. I had to contend with eyes which alternately wondered at and upbraided me for my unkindness. She was wholly unaware of the nature of her own feelings, and this ignorance made her less scrupulous in the expression of her sentiments.

Hitherto I had needed not employment beyond myself and my companions. Now my new motives made me eager to discover some means of controlling and beguiling my thoughts. In this state, the manuscript of Lodi occurred to me. In my way hither, I had resolved to make the study of the language of this book, and the translation of its contents into English, the business and solace of my leisure. Now this resolution was revived with new force.

My project was perhaps singular. The ancient language of Italy possessed a strong affinity with the modern. My knowledge of the former was my only means of gaining the latter. I had no grammar or vocabulary to explain how far the meanings and inflections of Tuscan words varied from the Roman dialect. I was to ponder on each sentence and phrase; to select among different conjectures the most plausible, and to ascertain the true by patient and repeated scrutiny.

This undertaking, fantastic and impracticable as it may seem, proved, upon experiment, to be within the compass of my powers. The detail of my progress would be curious and instructive. What impediments, in the attainment of a darling purpose, human ingenuity and patience are able to surmount; how much may be done by strenuous and solitary efforts; how the mind, unassisted, may draw forth the principles of inflection and arrangement; may profit by remote, analogous, and latent similitudes, would be forcibly illustrated by my example; but the theme, however attractive, must, for the present, be omitted.

My progress was slow; but the perception of hourly improvement afforded me unspeakable pleasure. Having arrived near the last pages, I was able to pursue, with little interruption, the thread of an eloquent narration. The triumph of a leader of outlaws over the popular enthusiasm of the Milanese and the claims of neighbouring potentates was about to be depicted. The *Condottiero* Sforza had taken refuge from his enemies in a tomb, accidentally discovered amidst the ruins of a Roman fortress in the Apennines. He had sought this recess for the sake of concealment, but found in it a treasure by which he would be enabled to secure the wavering and venal faith of that crew of ruffians that followed his standard, provided he fell not into the hands of the enemies who were now in search of him.

My tumultuous curiosity was suddenly checked by the following leaves being glued together at the edges. To dissever them without injury to the written spaces was by no means easy. I proceeded to the task, not without precipitation. The edges were torn away, and the leaves parted.

It may be thought that I took up the thread where it had been broken; but no. The object that my eyes encountered, and which the cemented leaves had so long concealed, was beyond the power of the most capricious or lawless fancy to have prefigured; yet it bore a shadowy resemblance to the images with which my imagination was previously occupied. I opened, and beheld—*a bank-note!*

To the first transports of surprise, the conjecture succeeded, that the remaining leaves, cemented together in the same manner, might enclose similar bills. They were hastily separated, and the conjecture was verified. My sensations at this discovery were of an inexplicable kind. I gazed at the notes in silence. I moved my finger over them; held them in different positions; read and reread the name of each sum, and the signature; added them together, and repeated to myself—"*Twenty thousand dollars!* They are mine, and by such means!"

This sum would have redeemed the fallen fortunes of Welbeck. The dying Lodi was unable to communicate all the contents of this inestimable volume. He had divided his treasure, with a view to its greater safety, between this volume and his pocket-book. Death hasted upon him too suddenly to allow him to explain his precautions. Welbeck had placed the book in his collection, purposing some time to peruse it; but, deterred by anxieties which the perusal would have dissipated, he rushed to desperation and suicide, from which some evanescent contingency, by unfolding this treasure to his view, would have effectually rescued him.

But was this event to be regretted? This sum, like the former, would probably have been expended in the same pernicious prodigality. His career would have continued some time longer; but his inveterate habits would have finally conducted his existence to the same criminal and ignominious close.

But the destiny of Welbeck was accomplished. The money was placed, without guilt or artifice, in my possession. My fortune had been thus unexpectedly and wondrously propitious. How was I to profit by her favour? Would not this sum enable me to gather round me all the instruments of pleasure? Equipage, and palace, and a multitude of servants; polished mirrors, splendid hangings, banquets, and flatterers, were equally abhorrent to my taste and my principles. The accumulation of knowledge, and the diffusion of happiness, in which riches may be rendered eminently instrumental, were the only precepts of duty, and the only avenues to genuine felicity.

"But what," said I, "is my title to this money? By retaining it, shall I not be as culpable as Welbeck? It came into his possession, as it came into mine, without a crime; but my knowledge of the true proprietor is equally certain, and the claims of the unfortunate stranger are as valid as ever. Indeed, if utility, and not law, be the measure of justice, her claim, desolate and indigent as she is, unfitted, by her past life, by the softness and the prejudices of her education, for contending with calamity, is incontestable.

"As to me, health and diligence will give me, not only the competence which I seek, but the power of enjoying it. If my present condition be unchangeable, I shall not be unhappy. My occupations are salutary and meritorious; I am a stranger to the cares as well as to the enjoyment of riches; abundant means of knowledge are possessed by me, as long as I have eyes to gaze at man and at nature, as they are exhibited in their original forms or in books. The precepts of my duty cannot be mistaken. The lady must be sought and the money restored to her."

Certain obstacles existed to the immediate execution of this scheme. How should I conduct my search? What apology should I make for withdrawing thus abruptly, and contrary to the terms of an agreement into which I had lately entered, from the family and service of my friend and benefactor Hadwin?

My thoughts were called away from pursuing these inquiries by a rumour, which had gradually swelled to formidable dimensions; and which, at length, reached us in our quiet retreats. The city, we were told, was involved in confusion and panic, for a pestilential disease had begun its destructive progress. Magistrates and citizens were flying to the country. The numbers of the sick multiplied beyond all example; even in the pest-affected cities of the Levant. The malady was malignant and unsparing.

The usual occupations and amusements of life were at an end. Terror had exterminated all the sentiments of nature. Wives were deserted by husbands, and children by parents. Some had shut themselves in their houses, and debarred themselves from all communication with the rest of mankind. The consternation of others had destroyed their understanding, and their misguided steps hurried them into the midst of the danger which they had previously laboured to shun. Men were seized by this disease in the streets; passengers fled from them; entrance into their own dwellings was denied to them; they perished in the public ways.

The chambers of disease were deserted, and the sick left to die of negligence. None could be found to remove the lifeless bodies. Their remains, suffered to decay by piecemeal, filled the air with deadly exhalations, and added tenfold to the devastation.

Such was the tale, distorted and diversified a thousand ways by the credulity and exaggeration of the tellers. At first I listened to the story with indifference or mirth. Methought it was confuted by its own extravagance. The enormity and variety of such an evil made it unworthy to be believed. I expected that every new day would detect the absurdity and fallacy of such representations. Every new day, however, added to the number of witnesses and the consistency of the tale, till, at length, it was not possible to withhold my faith.

CHAPTER XIV.

THIS rumour was of a nature to absorb and suspend the whole soul. A certain sublimity is connected with enormous dangers that imparts to our consternation or our pity a tincture of the pleasing. This, at least, may be experienced by those who are beyond the verge of peril. My own person was exposed to no hazard. I had leisure to conjure up terrific images, and to personate the witnesses and sufferers of this calamity. This employment was not enjoined upon me by necessity, but was ardently pursued, and must therefore have been recommended by some nameless charm.

Others were very differently affected. As often as the tale was embellished with new incidents or enforced by new testimony, the hearer grew pale, his breath was stifled by inquietudes, his blood was chilled, and his stomach was bereaved of its usual energies. A temporary indisposition was produced in many. Some were haunted by a melancholy bordering upon madness, and some, in consequence of sleepless panics, for which no cause could be assigned, and for which no opiates could be found, were attacked by lingering or mortal diseases.

Mr. Hadwin was superior to groundless apprehensions. His daughters, however, partook in all the consternation which surrounded them. The eldest had, indeed, abundant reason for her terror. The youth to whom she was betrothed resided in the city. A year previous to this, he had left the house of Mr. Hadwin, who was his uncle, and had removed to Philadelphia in pursuit of fortune.

He made himself clerk to a merchant, and, by some mercantile adventures in which he had successfully engaged, began to flatter himself with being able, in no long time, to support a family. Meanwhile, a tender and constant correspondence was maintained between him and his beloved Susan. This girl was a soft enthusiast, in whose bosom devotion and love glowed with an ardour that has seldom been exceeded.

The first tidings of the *yellow fever* was heard by her with unspeakable perturbation. Wallace was interrogated, by letter, respecting its truth. For a time, he treated it as a vague report. At length, a confession was extorted from him that there existed a pestilential disease in the city; but he added that it was hitherto confined to one quarter, distant from the place of his abode.

The most pathetic entreaties were urged by her that he would withdraw into the country. He declared his resolution to comply when the street in which he lived should become infected and his stay should be attended with real danger. He stated how much his interests depended upon the favour of his present employer, who had used the most powerful arguments to detain him, but declared that, when his situation should become, in the least degree, perilous, he would slight every consideration of gratitude and interest, and fly to *Malverton.* Meanwhile, he promised to communicate tidings of his safety by every opportunity.

Belding, Mr. Hadwin's next neighbour, though not uninfected by the general panic, persisted to visit the city daily with his *market-cart.* He set out by sunrise, and usually returned by noon. By him a letter was punctually received by Susan. As the hour of Belding's return approached, her impatience and anxiety increased. The daily epistle was received and read, in a transport of eagerness. For a while her emotion subsided, but returned with augmented vehemence at noon on the ensuing day.

These agitations were too vehement for a feeble constitution like hers. She renewed her supplications to Wallace to quit the city. He repeated his assertions of being, hitherto, secure, and his promise of coming when the danger should be imminent. When Belding returned, and, instead of being accompanied by Wallace, merely brought a letter from him, the unhappy Susan would sink into fits of lamentation and weeping, and repel every effort to console her with an obstinacy that partook of madness. It was, at length, manifest that Wallace's delays would be fatally injurious to the health of his mistress.

Mr. Hadwin had hitherto been passive. He conceived that the entreaties and remonstrances of his daughter were more likely to influence the conduct of Wallace than any representations which he could make. Now, however, he wrote the contumacious Wallace a letter, in which he laid his commands upon him to return in company with Belding, and declared that by a longer delay the youth would forfeit his favour.

The malady had, at this time, made considerable progress. Belding's interest at length yielded to his fears, and this was the last journey which he proposed to make. Hence our impatience for the return of Wallace was augmented; since, if this opportunity were lost, no suitable conveyance might again be offered him.

Belding set out, as usual, at the dawn of day. The customary interval between his departure and return was spent by Susan in a tumult of hopes and fears. As noon approached, her suspense arose to a pitch of wildness and agony. She could scarcely be restrained from running along the road, many miles, towards the city; that she might, by meeting Belding half-way, the sooner ascertain the fate of her lover. She stationed herself at a window which overlooked the road along which Belding was to pass.

Her sister and her father, though less impatient, marked, with painful eagerness, the first sound of the approaching vehicle. They snatched a look at it as soon as it appeared in sight. Belding was without a companion.

This confirmation of her fears overwhelmed the unhappy Susan. She sunk into a fit, from which, for a long time, her recovery was hopeless. This was succeeded by paroxysms of a furious insanity, in which she attempted to snatch any pointed implement which lay within her reach, with a view to destroy herself. These being carefully removed, or forcibly wrested from her, she resigned herself to sobs and exclamations.

Having interrogated Belding, he informed us that he occupied his usual post in the market-place; that heretofore Wallace had duly sought him out, and exchanged letters; but that, on this morning, the young man had not made his appearance, though Belding had been induced, by his wish to see him, to prolong his stay in the city much beyond the usual period.

That some other cause than sickness had occasioned this omission was barely possible. There was scarcely room for the most sanguine temper to indulge a hope. Wallace was without kindred, and probably without friends, in the city. The merchant in whose service he had placed himself was connected with him by no considerations but that of interest. What then must be his situation when seized with a malady which all believed to be contagious, and the fear of which was able to dissolve the strongest ties that bind human beings together?

I was personally a stranger to this youth. I had seen his letters, and they bespoke, not indeed any great refinement or elevation of intelligence, but a frank and generous spirit, to which I could not refuse my esteem; but his chief claim to my affection consisted in his consanguinity to Mr. Hadwin, and his place in the affections of Susan. His welfare was essential to the happiness of those whose happiness had become essential to mine. I witnessed the outrages of despair in the daughter, and the symptoms of a deep but less violent grief in the sister and parent. Was it not possible for me to alleviate their pangs? Could not the fate of Wallace be ascertained?

This disease assailed men with different degrees of malignity. In its worst form perhaps it was incurable; but, in some of its modes, it was doubtless conquerable by the skill of physicians and the fidelity of nurses. In its least formidable symptoms, negligence and solitude would render it fatal.

Wallace might, perhaps, experience this pest in its most lenient degree; but the desertion of all mankind, the want not only of medicines but of food, would irrevocably seal his doom. My imagination was incessantly pursued by the image of this youth, perishing alone, and in obscurity; calling on the name of distant friends, or invoking, ineffectually, the succour of those who were near.

Hitherto distress had been contemplated at a distance, and through the medium of a fancy delighting to be startled by the wonderful, or transported by sublimity. Now the calamity had entered my own doors, imaginary evils were supplanted by real, and my heart was the seat of commiseration and horror.

I found myself unfit for recreation or employment. I shrouded myself in the gloom of the neighbouring forest, or lost myself in the maze of rocks and dells. I endeavoured, in vain, to shut out the phantoms of the dying Wallace, and to forget the spectacle of domestic woes. At length it occurred to me to ask, May not this evil be obviated, and the felicity of the Hadwins re-established? Wallace is friendless and succourless; but cannot I supply to him the place of protector and nurse? Why not hasten to the city, search out his abode, and ascertain whether he be living or dead? If he still retain life, may I not, by consolation and attendance, contribute to the restoration of his health, and conduct him once more to the bosom of his family?

With what transports will his arrival be hailed! How amply will their impatience and their sorrow be compensated by his return! In the spectacle of their joys, how rapturous and pure will be my delight! Do the benefits which I have received from the Hadwins demand a less retribution than this?

It is true that my own life will be endangered; but my danger will be proportioned to the duration of my stay in this seat of infection. The death or the flight of Wallace may absolve me from the necessity of spending one night in the city. The rustics who daily frequent the market are, as experience proves, exempt from this disease; in consequence, perhaps, of limiting their continuance in the city to a few hours. May I not, in this respect, conform to their example, and enjoy a similar exemption?

My stay, however, may be longer than the day. I may be condemned to share in the common destiny. What then? Life is dependent on a thousand contingencies, not to be computed or foreseen. The seeds of an early and lingering death are sown in my constitution. It is in vain to hope to escape the malady by which my mother and my brothers have died. We are a race whose existence some inherent property has limited to the short space of twenty years. We are exposed, in common with the rest of mankind, to innumerable casualties; but, if these be shunned, we are unalterably fated to perish by *consumption*. Why then should I scruple to lay down my life in the cause of virtue and humanity? It is better to die in the consciousness of having offered an heroic sacrifice, to die by a speedy stroke, than by the perverseness of nature, in ignominious inactivity and lingering agonies.

These considerations determined me to hasten to the city. To mention my purpose to the Hadwins would be useless or pernicious. It would only augment the sum of their present anxieties. I should meet with a thousand obstacles in the tenderness and terror of Eliza, and in the prudent affection of her father. Their arguments I should be condemned to hear, but should not be able to confute; and should only load myself with imputations of perverseness and temerity.

But how else should I explain my absence? I had hitherto preserved my lips untainted by prevarication or falsehood. Perhaps there was no occasion which would justify an untruth; but here, at least, it was superfluous or hurtful. My disappearance, if effected without notice or warning, will give birth to speculation and conjecture; but my true motives will never be suspected, and therefore will excite no fears. My conduct will not be charged with guilt. It will merely be thought upon with some regret, which will be alleviated by the opinion of my safety, and the daily expectation of my return.

But, since my purpose was to search out Wallace, I must be previously furnished with directions to the place of his abode, and a description of his person. Satisfaction on this head was easily obtained from Mr. Hadwin; who was prevented from suspecting the motives of my curiosity, by my questions being put in a manner apparently casual. He mentioned the street, and the number of the house.

I listened with surprise. It was a house with which I was already familiar. He resided, it seems, with a merchant. Was it possible for me to be mistaken?

What, I asked, was the merchant's name?

Thetford.

This was a confirmation of my first conjecture. I recollected the extraordinary means by which I had gained access to the house and bedchamber of this gentleman. I recalled the person and appearance of the youth by whose artifices I had been entangled in the snare. These artifices implied some domestic or confidential connection between Thetford and my guide. Wallace was a member of the family. Could it be he by whom I was betrayed?

Suitable questions easily obtained from Hadwin a description of the person and carriage of his nephew. Every circumstance evinced the identity of their persons. Wallace, then, was the engaging and sprightly youth whom I had encountered at Lesher's; and who, for purposes not hitherto discoverable, had led me into a situation so romantic and perilous.

I was far from suspecting that these purposes were criminal. It was easy to infer that his conduct proceeded from juvenile wantonness and a love of sport. My resolution was unaltered by this disclosure; and, having obtained all the information which I needed, I secretly began my journey.

My reflections, on the way, were sufficiently employed in tracing the consequences of my project; in computing the inconveniences and dangers to which I was preparing to subject myself; in fortifying my courage against the influence of rueful sights and abrupt transitions; and in imagining the measures which it would be proper to pursue in every emergency.

Connected as these views were with the family and character of Thetford, I could not but sometimes advert to those incidents which formerly happened. The mercantile alliance between him and Welbeck was remembered; the allusions which were made to the condition of the latter in the chamber-conversation of which I was an unsuspected auditor; and the relation which these allusions might possess with subsequent occurrences. Welbeck's property was forfeited. It had been confided to the care of Thetford's brother. Had the cause of this forfeiture been truly or thoroughly explained? Might not contraband articles have been admitted through the management or under the connivance of the brothers? and might not the younger Thetford be furnished with the means of purchasing the captured vessel and her cargo,—which, as usual, would be sold by auction at a fifth or tenth of its real value?

Welbeck was not alive to profit by the detection of this artifice, admitting these conclusions to be just. My knowledge will be useless to the world; for by what motives can I be influenced to publish the truth? or by whom will my single testimony be believed, in opposition to that plausible exterior, and, perhaps, to that general integrity, which Thetford has maintained? To myself it will not be unprofitable. It is a lesson on the principles of human nature; on the delusiveness of appearances; on the perviousness of fraud; and on the power with which nature has invested human beings over the thoughts and actions of each other.

Thetford and his frauds were dismissed from my thoughts, to give place to considerations relative to Clemenza Lodi, and the money which chance had thrown into my possession. Time had only confirmed my purpose to restore these bills to the rightful proprietor, and heightened my impatience to discover her retreat. I reflected, that the means of doing this were more likely to suggest themselves at the place to which I was going than elsewhere. I might, indeed, perish before my views, in this respect, could be accomplished. Against these evils I had at present no power to provide. While I lived, I would bear perpetually about me the volume and its precious contents. If I died, a superior power must direct the course of this as of all other events.

CHAPTER XV.

THESE meditations did not enfeeble my resolution, or slacken my pace. In proportion as I drew near the city, the tokens of its calamitous condition became more apparent. Every farm-house was filled with supernumerary tenants, fugitives from home, and haunting the skirts of the road, eager to detain every passenger with inquiries after news. The passengers were numerous; for the tide of emigration was by no means exhausted. Some were on foot, bearing in their countenances the tokens of their recent terror, and filled with mournful reflections on the forlornness of their state. Few had secured to themselves an asylum; some were without the means of paying for victuals or lodging for the coming night; others, who were not thus destitute, yet knew not whither to apply for entertainment, every house being already overstocked with inhabitants, or barring its inhospitable doors at their approach.

Families of weeping mothers and dismayed children, attended with a few pieces of indispensable furniture, were carried in vehicles of every form. The parent or husband had perished; and the price of some movable, or the pittance handed forth by public charity, had been expended to purchase the means of retiring from this theatre of disasters, though uncertain and hopeless of accommodation in the neighbouring districts.

Between these and the fugitives whom curiosity had led to the road, dialogues frequently took place, to which I was suffered to listen. From every mouth the tale of sorrow was repeated with new aggravations. Pictures of their own distress, or of that of their neighbours, were exhibited in all the hues which imagination can annex to pestilence and poverty.

My preconceptions of the evil now appeared to have fallen short of the truth. The dangers into which I was rushing seemed more numerous and imminent than I had previously imagined. I wavered not in my purpose. A panic crept to my heart, which more vehement exertions were necessary to subdue or control; but I harboured not a momentary doubt that the course which I had taken was prescribed by duty. There was no difficulty or reluctance in proceeding. All for which my efforts were demanded was to walk in this path without tumult or alarm.

Various circumstances had hindered me from setting out upon this journey as early as was proper. My frequent pauses to listen to the narratives of travellers contributed likewise to procrastination. The sun had nearly set before I reached the precincts of the city. I pursued the track which I had formerly taken, and entered High Street after nightfall. Instead of equipages and a throng of passengers, the voice of levity and glee, which I had formerly observed, and which the mildness of the season would, at other times, have produced, I found nothing but a dreary solitude.

The market-place, and each side of this magnificent avenue, were illuminated, as before, by lamps; but between the verge of Schuylkill and the heart of the city I met not more than a dozen figures; and these were ghost-like, wrapped in cloaks, from behind which they cast upon me glances of wonder and suspicion, and, as I approached, changed their course, to avoid touching me. Their clothes were sprinkled with vinegar, and their nostrils defended from contagion by some powerful perfume.

I cast a look upon the houses, which I recollected to have formerly been, at this hour, brilliant with lights, resounding with lively voices, and thronged with busy faces. Now they were closed, above and below; dark, and without tokens of being inhabited. From the upper windows of some, a gleam sometimes fell upon the pavement I was traversing, and showed that their tenants had not fled, but were secluded or disabled.

These tokens were new, and awakened all my panics. Death seemed to hover over this scene, and I dreaded that the floating pestilence had already lighted on my frame. I had scarcely overcome these tremors, when I approached a house the door of which was opened, and before which stood a vehicle, which I presently recognised to be a *hearse*.

The driver was seated on it. I stood still to mark his visage, and to observe the course which he proposed to take. Presently a coffin, borne by two men, issued from the house. The driver was a negro; but his companions were white. Their features were marked by ferocious indifference to danger or pity. One of them, as he assisted in thrusting the coffin into the cavity provided for it, said, "I'll be damned if I think the poor dog was quite dead. It wasn't the *fever* that ailed him, but the sight of the girl and her mother on the floor. I wonder how they all got into that room. What carried them there?"

The other surlily muttered, "Their legs, to-be-sure."

"But what should they hug together in one room for?"

"To save us trouble, to-be-sure."

"And I thank them with all my heart; but, damn it, it wasn't right to put him in his coffin before the breath was fairly gone. I thought the last look he gave me told me to stay a few minutes."

"Pshaw! He could not live. The sooner dead the better for him; as well as for us. Did you mark how he eyed us when we carried away his wife and daughter? I never cried in my life, since I was knee-high, but curse me if I ever felt in better tune for the business than just then. Hey!" continued he, looking up, and observing me standing a few paces distant, and listening to their discourse; "what's wanted? Anybody dead?"

I stayed not to answer or parley, but hurried forward. My joints trembled, and cold drops stood on my forehead. I was ashamed of my own infirmity; and, by vigorous efforts of my reason, regained some degree of composure. The evening had now advanced, and it behooved me to procure accommodation at some of the inns.

These were easily distinguished by their *signs*, but many were without inhabitants. At length I lighted upon one, the hall of which was open and the windows lifted. After knocking for some time, a young girl appeared, with many marks of distress. In answer to my question, she answered that both her parents were sick, and that they could receive no one. I inquired, in vain, for any other tavern at which strangers might be accommodated. She knew of none such, and left me, on some one's calling to her from above, in the midst of my embarrassment. After a moment's pause, I returned, discomfited and perplexed, to the street.

I proceeded, in a considerable degree, at random. At length I reached a spacious building in Fourth Street, which the sign-post showed me to be an inn. I knocked loudly and often at the door. At length a female opened the window of the second story, and, in a tone of peevishness, demanded what I wanted. I told her that I wanted lodging.

"Go hunt for it somewhere else," said she; "you'll find none here." I began to expostulate; but she shut the window with quickness, and left me to my own reflections.

I began now to feel some regret at the journey I had taken. Never, in the depth of caverns or forests, was I equally conscious of loneliness. I was surrounded by the habitations of men; but I was destitute of associate or friend. I had money, but a horse-shelter, or a morsel of food, could not be purchased. I came for the purpose of relieving others, but stood in the utmost need myself. Even in health my condition was helpless and forlorn; but what would become of me should this fatal malady be contracted? To hope that an asylum would be afforded to a sick man, which was denied to one in health, was unreasonable.

The first impulse which flowed from these reflections was to hasten back to *Malverton;* which, with sufficient diligence, I might hope to regain before the morning light. I could not, methought, return upon my steps with too much speed. I was prompted to run, as if the pest was rushing upon me and could be eluded only by the most precipitate flight.

This impulse was quickly counteracted by new ideas. I thought with indignation and shame on the imbecility of my proceeding. I called up the images of Susan Hadwin, and of Wallace. I reviewed the motives which had led me to the undertaking of this journey. Time had, by no means, diminished their force. I had, indeed, nearly arrived at the accomplishment of what I had intended. A few steps would carry me to Thetford's habitation. This might be the critical moment when succour was most needed and would be most efficacious.

I had previously concluded to defer going thither till the ensuing morning; but why should I allow myself a moment's delay? I might at least gain an external view of the house, and circumstances might arise which would absolve me from the obligation of remaining an hour longer in the city. All for which I came might be performed; the destiny of Wallace be ascertained; and I be once more safe within the precincts of *Malverton* before the return of day.

I immediately directed my steps towards the habitation of Thetford. Carriages bearing the dead were frequently discovered. A few passengers likewise occurred, whose hasty and perturbed steps denoted their participation in the common distress. The house of which I was in quest quickly appeared. Light from an upper window indicated that it was still inhabited.

I paused a moment to reflect in what manner it became me to proceed. To ascertain the existence and condition of Wallace was the purpose of my journey. He had inhabited this house; and whether he remained in it was now to be known. I felt repugnance to enter, since my safety might, by entering, be unawares and uselessly endangered. Most of the neigbouring houses were apparently deserted. In some there were various tokens of people being within. Might I not inquire, at one of these, respecting the condition of Thetford's family? Yet why should I disturb them by inquiries so impertinent at this unseasonable hour? To knock at Thetford's door, and put my questions to him who should obey the signal, was the obvious method.

I knocked dubiously and lightly. No one came. I knocked again, and more loudly; I likewise drew the bell. I distinctly heard its distant peals. If any were within, my signal could not fail to be noticed. I paused, and listened, but neither voice nor footsteps could be heard. The light, though obscured by window-curtains, which seemed to be drawn close, was still perceptible.

I ruminated on the causes that might hinder my summons from being obeyed. I figured to myself nothing but the helplessness of disease, or the insensibility of death. These images only urged me to persist in endeavouring to obtain admission. Without weighing the consequences of my act, I involuntarily lifted the latch. The door yielded to my hand, and I put my feet within the passage.

Once more I paused. The passage was of considerable extent, and at the end of it I perceived light as from a lamp or candle. This impelled me to go forward, till I reached the foot of a staircase. A candle stood upon the lowest step.

This was a new proof that the house was not deserted. I struck my heel against the floor with some violence; but this, like my former signals, was unnoticed. Having proceeded thus far, it would have been absurd to retire with my purpose uneffected. Taking the candle in my hand, I opened a door that was near. It led into a spacious parlour, furnished with profusion and splendour. I walked to and fro, gazing at the objects which presented themselves; and, involved in perplexity, I knocked with my heel louder than ever; but no less ineffectually.

Notwithstanding the lights which I had seen, it was possible that the house was uninhabited. This I was resolved to ascertain, by proceeding to the chamber which I had observed, from without, to be illuminated. This chamber, as far as the comparison of circumstances would permit me to decide, I believed to be the same in which I had passed the first night of my late abode in the city. Now was I, a second time, in almost equal ignorance of my situation, and of the consequences which impended, exploring my way to the same recess.

I mounted the stair. As I approached the door of which I was in search, a vapour, infectious and deadly, assailed my senses. It resembled nothing of which I had ever before been sensible. Many odours had been met with, even since my arrival in the city, less supportable than this. I seemed not so much to smell as to taste the element that now encompassed me. I felt as if I had inhaled a poisonous and subtle fluid, whose power instantly bereft my stomach of all vigour. Some fatal influence appeared to seize upon my vitals, and the work of corrosion and decomposition to be busily begun.

For a moment, I doubted whether imagination had not some share in producing my sensation; but I had not been previously panic-struck; and even now I attended to my own sensations without mental discomposure. That I had imbibed this disease was not to be questioned. So far the chances in my favour were annihilated. The lot of sickness was drawn.

Whether my case would be lenient or malignant, whether I should recover or perish, was to be left to the decision of the future. This incident, instead of appalling me, tended rather to invigorate my courage. The danger which I feared had come. I might enter with indifference on this theatre of pestilence. I might execute, without faltering, the duties that my circumstances might create. My state was no longer hazardous; and my destiny would be totally uninfluenced by my future conduct.

The pang with which I was first seized, and the momentary inclination to vomit, which it produced, presently subsided. My wholesome feelings, indeed, did not revisit me, but strength to proceed was restored to me. The effluvia became more sensible as I approached the door of the chamber. The door was ajar; and the light within was perceived. My belief that those within were dead was presently confuted by sound, which I first supposed to be that of steps moving quickly and timorously across the floor. This ceased, and was succeeded by sounds of different but inexplicable import.

Having entered the apartment, I saw a candle on the hearth. A table was covered with vials and other apparatus of a sick-chamber. A bed stood on one side, the curtain of which was dropped at the foot, so as to conceal any one within. I fixed my eyes upon this object. There were sufficient tokens that some one lay upon the bed. Breath, drawn at long intervals; mutterings scarcely audible; and a tremulous motion in the bedstead, were fearful and intelligible indications.

If my heart faltered, it must not be supposed that my trepidations arose from any selfish considerations. Wallace only, the object of my search, was present to my fancy. Pervaded with remembrance of the Hadwins; of the agonies which they had already endured; of the despair which would overwhelm the unhappy Susan when the death of her lover should be ascertained; observant of the lonely condition of this house, whence I could only infer that the sick had been denied suitable attendance; and reminded, by the symptoms that appeared, that this being was struggling with the agonies of death; a sickness of the heart, more insupportable than that which I had just experienced, stole upon me.

My fancy readily depicted the progress and completion of this tragedy. Wallace was the first of the family on whom the pestilence had seized. Thetford had fled from his habitation. Perhaps as a father and husband, to shun the danger attending his stay was the injunction of his duty. It was questionless the conduct which selfish regards would dictate. Wallace was left to perish alone; or, perhaps, (which, indeed, was a supposition somewhat justified by appearances,) he had been left to the tendance of mercenary wretches; by whom, at this desperate moment, he had been abandoned.

I was not mindless of the possibility that these forebodings, specious as they were, might be false. The dying person might be some other than Wallace. The whispers of my hope were, indeed, faint; but they, at least, prompted me to snatch a look at the expiring man. For this purpose I advanced and thrust my head within the curtain.

CHAPTER XVI.

The features of one whom I had seen so transiently as Wallace may be imagined to be not easily recognised, especially when those features were tremulous and deathful. Here, however, the differences were too conspicuous to mislead me. I beheld one in whom I could recollect none that bore resemblance. Though ghastly and livid, the traces of intelligence and beauty were undefaced. The life of Wallace was of more value to a feeble individual; but surely the being that was stretched before me, and who was hastening to his last breath, was preciou to thousands.

Was he not one in whose place I would willingly have died? The offering was too late. His extremities were already cold. A vapour, noisome and contagious, hovered over him. The flutterings of his pulse had ceased. His existence was about to close amidst convulsion and pangs.

I withdrew my gaze from this object, and walked to a table. I was nearly unconscious of my movements. My thoughts were occupied with contemplations of the train of horrors and disasters that pursue the race of man. My musings were quickly interrupted by the sight of a small cabinet, the hinges of which were broken and the lid half raised. In the present state of my thoughts, I was prone to suspect the worst. Here were traces of pillage. Some casual or mercenary attendant had not only contributed to hasten the death of the patient, but had rifled his property and fled.

This suspicion would, perhaps, have yielded to mature reflections, if I had been suffered to reflect. A moment scarcely elapsed, when some appearance in the mirror, which hung over the table, called my attention. It was a human figure. Nothing could be briefer than the glance that I fixed upon this apparition; yet there was room enough for the vague conception to suggest itself, that the dying man had started from his bed and was approaching me. This belief was, at the same instant, confuted, by the survey of his form and garb. One eye, a scar upon his cheek, a tawny skin, a form grotesquely misproportioned, brawny as Hercules, and habited in livery, composed, as it were, the parts of one view.

To perceive, to fear, and to confront this apparition were blended into one sentiment. I turned towards him with the swiftness of lightning; but my speed was useless to my safety. A blow upon my temple was succeeded by an utter oblivion of thought and of feeling. I sunk upon the floor prostrate and senseless.

My insensibility might be mistaken by observers for death, yet some part of this interval was haunted by a fearful dream. I conceived myself lying on the brink of a pit, whose bottom the eye could not reach. My hands and legs were fettered, so as to disable me from resisting two grim and gigantic figures who stooped to lift me from the earth. Their purpose, methought, was to cast me into this abyss. My terrors were unspeakable, and I struggled with such force, that my bonds snapped and I found myself at liberty. At this moment my senses returned, and I opened my eyes.

The memory of recent events was, for a time, effaced by my visionary horrors. I was conscious of transition from one state of being to another; but my imagination was still filled with images of danger. The bottomless gulf and my gigantic persecutors were still dreaded. I looked up with eagerness. Beside me I discovered three figures, whose character or office was explained by a coffin of pine boards which lay upon the floor. One stood with hammer and nails in his hand, as ready to replace and fasten the lid of the coffin as soon as its burden should be received.

I attempted to rise from the floor, but my head was dizzy and my sight confused. Perceiving me revive, one of the men assisted me to regain my feet. The mist and confusion presently vanished, so as to allow me to stand unsupported and to move. I once more gazed at my attendants, and recognised the three men whom I had met in High Street, and whose conversation I have mentioned that I overheard. I looked again upon the coffin. A wavering recollection of the incidents that led me hither, and of the stunning blow which I had received, occurred to me. I saw into what error appearances had misled these men, and shuddered to reflect by what hairbreadth means I had escaped being buried alive.

Before the men had time to interrogate me, or to comment upon my situation, one entered the apartment, whose habit and mien tended to encourage me. The stranger was characterized by an aspect full of composure and benignity, a face in which the serious lines of age were blended with the ruddiness and smoothness of youth, and a garb that bespoke that religious profession with whose benevolent doctrines the example of Hadwin had rendered me familiar.

On observing me on my feet, he betrayed marks of surprise and satisfaction. He addressed me in a tone of mildness:—

"Young man," said he, "what is thy condition? Art thou sick? If thou art, thou must consent to receive the best treatment which the times will afford. These men will convey thee to the hospital at Bush Hill."

The mention of that contagious and abhorred receptacle inspired me with some degree of energy. "No," said I, "I am not sick; a violent blow reduced me to this situation. I shall presently recover strength enough to leave this spot without assistance."

He looked at me with an incredulous but compassionate air:—"I fear thou dost deceive thyself or me. The necessity of going to the hospital is much to be regretted, but, on the whole, it is best. Perhaps, indeed, thou hast kindred or friends who will take care of thee?"

"No," said I; "neither kindred nor friends. I am a stranger in the city. I do not even know a single being."

"Alas!" returned the stranger, with a sigh, "thy state is sorrowful. But how camest thou hither?" continued he, looking around him; "and whence comest thou?"

"I came from the country. I reached the city a few hours ago. I was in search of a friend who lived in this house."

"Thy undertaking was strangely hazardous and rash; but who is the friend thou seekest? Was it he who died in that bed, and whose corpse has just been removed?"

The men now betrayed some impatience; and inquired of the last comer, whom they called Mr. Estwick, what they were to do. He turned to me, and asked if I were willing to be conducted to the hospital.

I assured him that I was free from disease, and stood in no need of assistance; adding, that my feebleness was owing to a stunning blow received from a ruffian on my temple. The marks of this blow were conspicuous, and after some hesitation he dismissed the men; who, lifting the empty coffin on their shoulders, disappeared.

He now invited me to descend into the parlour; "for," said he, "the air of this room is deadly. I feel already as if I should have reason to repent of having entered it."

He now inquired into the cause of those appearances

which he had witnessed. I explained my situation as clearly and succinctly as I was able.

After pondering, in silence, on my story,—"I see how it is," said he; "the person whom thou sawest in the agonies of death was a stranger. He was attended by his servant and a hired nurse. His master's death being certain, the nurse was despatched by the servant to procure a coffin. He probably chose that opportunity to rifle his master's trunk, that stood upon the table. Thy unseasonable entrance interrupted him; and he designed, by the blow which he gave thee, to secure his retreat before the arrival of a hearse. I know the man, and the apparition thou hast so well described was his. Thou sayest that a friend of thine lived in this house: thou hast come too late to be of service. The whole family have perished. Not one was suffered to escape."

This intelligence was fatal to my hopes. It required some efforts to subdue my rising emotions. Compassion not only for Wallace, but for Thetford, his father, his wife and his child, caused a passionate effusion of tears. I was ashamed of this useless and childlike sensibility; and attempted to apologize to my companion. The sympathy, however, had proved contagious, and the stranger turned away his face to hide his own tears.

"Nay," said he, in answer to my excuses, "there is no need to be ashamed of thy emotion. Merely to have known this family, and to have witnessed their deplorable fate, is sufficient to melt the most obdurate heart. I suspect that thou wast united to some one of this family by ties of tenderness like those which led the unfortunate *Maravegli* hither."

This suggestion was attended, in relation to myself, with some degree of obscurity; but my curiosity was somewhat excited by the name that he had mentioned. I inquired into the character and situation of this person, and particularly respecting his connection with this family.

"Maravegli," answered he, "was the lover of the eldest daughter, and already betrothed to her. The whole family, consisting of helpless females, had placed themselves under his peculiar guardianship. Mary Walpole and her children enjoyed in him a husband and a father."

The name of Walpole, to which I was a stranger, suggested doubts which I hastened to communicate. "I am in search," said I, "not of a female friend, though not devoid of interest in the welfare of Thetford and his family. My principal concern is for a youth, by name Wallace."

He looked at me with surprise. "Thetford! this is not his abode. He changed his habitation some weeks previous to the *fever*. Those who last dwelt under this roof were an Englishwoman and seven daughters."

This detection of my error somewhat consoled me. It was still possible that Wallace was alive and in safety. I eagerly inquired whither Thetford had removed, and whether he had any knowledge of his present condition.

They had removed to No. —, in Market Street. Concerning their state he knew nothing. His acquaintance with Thetford was imperfect. Whether he had left the city or had remained, he was wholly uninformed.

It became me to ascertain the truth in these respects. I was preparing to offer my parting thanks to the person by whom I had been so highly benefited; since, as he now informed me, it was by his interposition that I was hindered from being enclosed alive in a coffin. He was dubious of my true condition, and peremptorily commanded the followers of the hearse to desist. A delay of twenty minutes, and some medical application, would, he believed, determine whether my life was extinguished or suspended. At the end of this time, happily, my senses were recovered.

Seeing my intention to depart, he inquired why, and whither I was going. Having heard my answer,—"Thy design," resumed he, "is highly indiscreet and rash. Nothing will sooner generate this fever than fatigue and anxiety. Thou hast scarcely recovered from the blow so lately received. Instead of being useful to others, this precipitation will only disable thyself. Instead of roaming the streets and inhaling this unwholesome air, thou hadst better betake thyself to bed and try to obtain some sleep. In the morning, thou wilt be better qualified to ascertain the fate of thy friend, and afford him the relief which he shall want."

I could not but admit the reasonableness of these remonstrances; but where should a chamber and bed be sought? It was not likely that a new attempt to procure accommodation at the inns would succeed better than the former.

"Thy state," replied he, "is sorrowful. I have no house to which I can lead thee. I divide my chamber, and even my bed, with another, and my landlady could not be prevailed upon to admit a stranger. What thou wilt do, I know not. This house has no one to defend it. It was purchased and furnished by the last possessor; but the whole family, including mistress, children, and servants, were cut off in a single week. Perhaps no one in America can claim the property. Meanwhile, plunderers are numerous and active. A house thus totally deserted, and replenished with valuable furniture, will, I fear, become their prey. To-night nothing can be done towards rendering it secure, but staying in it. Art thou willing to remain here till the morrow?

"Every bed in the house has probably sustained a dead person. It would not be proper, therefore, to lie in any one of them. Perhaps thou mayest find some repose upon this carpet. It is, at least, better than the harder pavement and the open air."

This proposal, after some hesitation, I embraced. He was preparing to leave me, promising, if life were spared to him, to return early in the morning. My curiosity respecting the person whose dying agonies I had witnessed prompted me to detain him a few minutes.

"Ah!" said he, "this, perhaps, is the only one of many victims to this pestilence whose loss the remotest generations may have reason to deplore. He was the only descendant of an illustrious house of Venice. He has been devoted from his childhood to the acquisition of knowledge and the practice of virtue. He came hither as an enlightened observer; and, after traversing the country, conversing with all the men in it eminent for their talents or their office, and collecting a fund of observations whose solidity and justice have seldom been paralleled, he embarked, three months ago, for Europe.

"Previously to his departure, he formed a tender connection with the eldest daughter of this family. The mother and her children had recently arrived from England. So many faultless women, both mentally and personally considered, it was not my fortune to meet with before. This youth well deserved to be adopted into this family. He proposed to return with the utmost expedition to his native country, and, after the settlement of his affairs, to hasten back to America and ratify his contract with Fanny Walpole.

"The ship in which he embarked had scarcely gone twenty leagues to sea, before she was disabled by a storm, and obliged to return to port. He posted to New York, to gain a passage in a packet shortly to sail. Meanwhile this malady prevailed among us. Mary Walpole was hindered by her ignorance of the nature of that evil which assailed us, and the counsel of injudicious friends, from taking the due precautions for her safety. She hesitated to fly till flight was rendered impracticable. Her death added to the helplessness and distraction of the family. They were successively seized and destroyed by the same pest.

"Maravegli was apprized of their danger. He allowed the packet to depart without him, and hastened to rescue the Walpoles from the perils which encompassed them. He arrived in this city time enough to witness the interment of the last survivor. In the same hour he was seized himself by this disease: the catastrophe is known to thee.

"I will now leave thee to thy repose. Sleep is no less needful to myself than to thee; for this is the second night which has passed without it." Saying this, my companion took his leave.

I now enjoyed leisure to review my situation. I experienced no inclination to sleep. I lay down for a moment, but my comfortless sensations and restless contemplations would not permit me to rest. Before I entered this house, I was tormented with hunger; but my craving had given place to inquietude and loathing. I paced, in thoughtful and anxious mood, across the floor of the apartment.

I mused upon the incidents related by Estwick, upon the exterminating nature of this pestilence, and on the horrors of which it was productive. I compared the experience of the last hours with those pictures which my imagination had drawn in the retirements of *Malverton.* I wondered at the contrariety that exists between the scenes of the city and the country; and fostered, with more zeal than ever, the resolution to avoid those seats of depravity and danger.

Concerning my own destiny, however, I entertained no doubt. My new sensations assured me that my stomach had received this corrosive poison. Whether I should die or live was easily decided. The sickness which assiduous attendance and powerful prescriptions might remove would, by negligence and solitude, be rendered fatal; but from whom could I expect medical or friendly treatment?

I had indeed a roof over my head. I should not perish in the public way; but what was my ground for hoping to continue under this roof? My sickness being suspected, I should be dragged in a cart to the hospital; where I should, indeed, die, but not with the consolation of loneliness and silence. Dying groans were the only music, and livid corpses were the only spectacle, to which I should there be introduced.

Immured in these dreary meditations, the night passed away. The light glancing through the window awakened in my bosom a gleam of cheerfulness. Contrary to my expectations, my feelings were not more distempered, notwithstanding my want of sleep, than on the last evening. This was a token that my state was far from being so desperate as I suspected. It was possible, I thought, that this was the worst indisposition to which I was liable.

Meanwhile, the coming of Estwick was impatiently expected. The sun arose, and the morning advanced, but he came not. I remembered that he talked of having reason to repent his visit to this house. Perhaps he, likewise, was sick, and this was the cause of his delay. This man's kindness had even my love. If I had known the way to his dwelling, I should have hastened thither, to inquire into his condition, and to perform for him every office that humanity might enjoin; but he had not afforded me any information on that head.

CHAPTER XVII.

It was now incumbent on me to seek the habitation of Thetford. To leave this house accessible to every passenger appeared to be imprudent. I had no key by which I might lock the principal door. I therefore bolted it on the inside, and passed through a window, the shutters of which I closed, though I could not fasten after me. This led me into a spacious court, at the end of which was a brick wall, over which I leaped into the street. This was the means by which I had formerly escaped from the same precincts.

The streets, as I passed, were desolate and silent. The largest computation made the number of fugitives two-thirds of the whole people; yet, judging by the universal desolation, it seemed as if the solitude were nearly absolute. That so many of the houses were closed, I was obliged to ascribe to the cessation of traffic, which made the opening of their windows useless, and the terror of infection, which made the inhabitants seclude themselves from the observation of each other.

I proceeded to search out the house to which Estwick had directed me as the abode of Thetford. What was my consternation when I found it to be the same at the door of which the conversation took place of which I had been an auditor on the last evening!

I recalled the scene of which a rude sketch had been given by the *hearse-men*. If such were the fate of the master of the family, abounding with money and friends, what could be hoped for the moneyless and friendless Wallace? The house appeared to be vacant and silent; but these tokens might deceive. There was little room for hope; but certainty was wanting, and might, perhaps, be obtained by entering the house. In some of the upper rooms a wretched being might be immured; by whom the information, so earnestly desired, might be imparted, and to whom my presence might bring relief, not only from pestilence, but famine. For a moment, I forgot my own necessitous condition, and reflected not that abstinence had already undermined my strength.

I proceeded to knock at the door. That my signal was unnoticed produced no surprise. The door was unlocked, and I opened. At this moment my attention was attracted by the opening of another door near me. I looked, and perceived a man issuing forth from a house at a small distance.

It now occurred to me, that the information which I sought might possibly be gained from one of Thetford's neighbours. This person was aged, but seemed to have lost neither cheerfulness nor vigour. He had an air of intrepidity and calmness. It soon appeared that I was the object of his curiosity. He had, probably, marked my deportment through some window of his dwelling, and had come forth to make inquiries into the motives of my conduct.

He courteously saluted me. "You seem," said he, "to be in search of some one. If I can afford you the information you want, you will be welcome to it."

Encouraged by this address, I mentioned the name of Thetford; and added my fears that he had not escaped the general calamity.

"It is true," said he. "Yesterday himself, his wife, and his child, were in a hopeless condition. I saw them in the evening, and expected not to find them alive this morning. As soon as it was light, however, I visited the house again; but found it empty. I suppose they must have died, and been removed in the night."

Though anxious to ascertain the destiny of Wallace, I was unwilling to put direct questions. I shuddered, while I longed to know the truth.

"Why," said I, falteringly, "did he not seasonably withdraw from the city? Surely he had the means of purchasing an asylum in the country."

"I can scarcely tell you," he answered. "Some infatuation appeared to have seized him. No one was more timorous; but he seemed to think himself safe as long as he avoided contact with infected persons. He was likewise, I believe, detained by a regard to his interest. His flight would not have been more injurious to his affairs than it was to those of others; but gain was, in his eyes, the supreme good. He intended ultimately to withdraw; but his escape to-day, gave him new courage to encounter the perils of to-morrow. He deferred his departure from day to day, till it ceased to be practicable."

"His family," said I, "was numerous. It consisted of more than his wife and children. Perhaps these retired in sufficient season."

"Yes," said he; "his father left the house at an early period. One or two of the servants likewise forsook him. One girl, more faithful and heroic than the rest, resisted the remonstrances of her parents and friends, and resolved to adhere to him in every fortune. She was anxious that the family should fly from danger, and would willingly have fled in their company; but while they stayed, it was her immovable resolution not to abandon them.

"Alas, poor girl! She knew not of what stuff the heart of Thetford was made. Unhappily, she was the first to become sick. I question much whether her disease was pestilential. It was, probably, a slight indisposition, which, in a few days, would have vanished of itself, or have readily yielded to suitable treatment.

"Thetford was transfixed with terror. Instead of summoning a physician, to ascertain the nature of her symptoms, he called a negro and his cart from Bush Hill. In vain the neighbours interceded for this unhappy victim. In vain she implored his clemency, and asserted the lightness of her indisposition. She besought him to allow her to send to her mother, who resided a few miles in the country, who would hasten to her succour, and relieve him and his family from the danger and trouble of nursing her.

"The man was lunatic with apprehension. He rejected her entreaties, though urged in a manner that would have subdued a heart of flint. The girl was innocent, and amiable, and courageous, but entertained an unconquerable dread of the hospital. Finding entreaties ineffectual, she exerted all her strength in opposition to the man who lifted her into the cart.

"Finding that her struggles availed nothing, she resigned herself to despair. In going to the hospital, she believed herself led to certain death, and to the sufferance of every evil which the known inhumanity of its attendants could inflict. This state of mind, added to exposure to a noonday sun, in an open vehicle, moving, for a mile, over a rugged pavement, was sufficient to destroy her. I was not surprised to hear that she died the next day.

"This proceeding was sufficiently iniquitous; yet it was not the worst act of this man. The rank and education of the young woman might be some apology for negligence; but his clerk, a youth who seemed to enjoy his confidence, and to be treated by his family on the footing of a brother or son, fell sick on the next night, and was treated in the same manner."

These tidings struck me to the heart. A burst of indignation and sorrow filled my eyes. I could scarcely stifle my emotions sufficiently to ask, "Of whom, sir, do you speak? Was the name of the youth—his name—was——"

"His name was Wallace. I see that you have some interest in his fate. He was one whom I loved. I would have given half my fortune to procure him accommodation under some hospitable roof. His attack was violent; but, still, his recovery, if he had been suitably attended, was possible. That he should survive removal to the hospital, and the treatment he must receive when there, was not to be hoped.

"The conduct of Thetford was as absurd as it was wicked. To imagine this disease to be contagious was the height of folly; to suppose himself secure, merely by not permitting a sick man to remain under his roof, was no less stupid; but Thetford's fears had subverted his understanding. He did not listen to arguments or supplications. His attention was incapable of straying from one object. To influence him by words was equivalent to reasoning with the deaf.

"Perhaps the wretch was more to be pitied than hated. The victims of his implacable caution could scarcely have endured agonies greater than those which his pusillanimity inflicted on himself. Whatever be the amount of his guilt, the retribution has been adequate. He witnessed the death of his wife and child, and last night was the close of his own existence. Their sole attendant was a black woman; whom, by frequent visits, I endeavoured, with little success, to make diligent in the performance of her duty."

Such, then, was the catastrophe of Wallace. The end for which I journeyed hither was accomplished. His destiny was ascertained; and all that remained was to fulfil the gloomy predictions of the lovely but unhappy Susan. To tell them all the truth would be needlessly to exasperate her sorrow. Time, aided by the tenderness and sympathy of friendship, may banish her despair, and relieve her from all but the witcheries of melancholy.

Having disengaged my mind from these reflections, I explained to my companion, in general terms, my reasons for visiting the city, and my curiosity respecting Thetford. He inquired into the particulars of my journey, and the time of my arrival. When informed that I had come in the preceding evening, and had passed the subsequent hours without sleep or food, he expressed astonishment and compassion.

"Your undertaking," said he, "has certainly been hazardous. There is poison in every breath which you draw, but this hazard has been greatly increased by abstaining from food and sleep. My advice is to hasten back into the country; but you must first take some repose and some victuals. If you pass Schuylkill before nightfall, it will be sufficient."

I mentioned the difficulty of procuring accommodation on the road. It would be most prudent to set out upon my journey so as to reach *Malverton* at night. As to food and sleep, they were not to be purchased in this city.

"True," answered my companion, with quickness, "they are not to be bought; but I will furnish you with as much as you desire of both, for nothing. That is my abode," continued he, pointing to the house which he had lately left. "I reside with a widow lady and her daughter, who took my counsel, and fled in due season. I remain to moralize upon the scene, with only a faithful black, who makes my bed, prepares my coffee, and bakes my loaf. If I am sick, all that a physician can do, I will do for myself, and all that a nurse can perform, I expect to be performed by *Austin*.

"Come with me, drink some coffee, rest a while on my mattress, and then fly, with my benedictions on your head."

These words were accompanied by features disembarrassed and benevolent. My temper is alive to social impulses, and I accepted his invitation, not so much because I wished to eat or to sleep, but because I felt reluctance to part so soon with a being who possessed so much fortitude and virtue.

He was surrounded by neatness and plenty. Austin added dexterity to submissiveness. My companion, whose name I now found to be Medlicote, was prone to converse, and commented on the state of the city like one whose reading had been extensive and experience large. He combated an opinion which I had casually formed respecting the origin of this epidemic, and imputed it, not to infected substances imported from the East or West, but to a morbid constitution of the atmosphere, owing wholly or in part to filthy streets, airless habitations, and squalid persons.

As I talked with this man, the sense of danger was obliterated, I felt confidence revive in my heart, and energy revisit my stomach. Though far from my wonted health, my sensation grew less comfortless, and I found myself to stand in no need of repose.

Breakfast being finished, my friend pleaded his daily engagements as reasons for leaving me. He counselled me to strive for some repose, but I was conscious of incapacity to sleep. I was desirous of escaping, as soon as possible, from this tainted atmosphere, and reflected whether any thing remained to be done respecting Wallace.

It now occurred to me that this youth must have left some clothes and papers, and, perhaps, books. The property of these was now vested in the Hadwins. I might deem myself, without presumption, their representative or agent. Might I not take some measures for obtaining possession, or at least for the security, of these articles?

The house and its furniture were tenantless and unprotected. It was liable to be ransacked and pillaged by those desperate ruffians of whom many were said to be hunting for spoil even at a time like this. If these should overlook this dwelling, Thetford's unknown successor or heir might appropriate the whole. Numberless accidents might happen to occasion the destruction or embezzlement of what belonged to Wallace, which might be prevented by the conduct which I should now pursue.

Immersed in these perplexities, I remained bewildered and motionless. I was at length roused by some one knocking at the door. Austin obeyed the signal, and instantly returned, leading in—Mr. Hadwin!

I know not whether this unlooked-for interview excited on my part most grief or surprise. The motive of his coming was easily divined. His journey was on two accounts superfluous. He whom he sought was dead. The duty of ascertaining his condition I had assigned to myself.

I now perceived and deplored the error of which I had been guilty, in concealing my intended journey from my patron. Ignorant of the part I had acted, he had rushed into the jaws of this pest, and endangered a life unspeakably valuable to his children and friends. I should doubtless have obtained his grateful consent to the project which I had conceived; but my wretched policy had led me into this clandestine path. Secrecy may seldom be a crime. A virtuous intention may produce it; but surely it is always erroneous and pernicious.

My friend's astonishment at the sight of me was not inferior to my own. The causes which led to this unexpected interview were mutually explained. To soothe the agonies of his child, he consented to approach the city, and endeavour to procure intelligence of Wallace. When he left his house, he intended to stop in the environs, and hire some emissary, whom an ample reward might tempt to enter the city, and procure the information which was needed.

No one could be prevailed upon to execute so dangerous a service. Averse to return without performing his commission, he concluded to examine for himself. Thetford's removal to this street was known to him; but, being ignorant of my purpose, he had not mentioned this circumstance to me, during our last conversation.

I was sensible of the danger which Hadwin had incurred by entering the city. Perhaps my knowledge of the inexpressible importance of his life to the happiness of his daughters made me aggravate his danger. I knew that the longer he lingered in this tainted air, the hazard was increased. A moment's delay was unnecessary. Neither Wallace nor myself were capable of being benefited by his presence.

I mentioned the death of his nephew as a reason for hastening his departure. I urged him in the most vehement terms to remount his horse and to fly; I endeavoured to preclude all inquiries respecting myself or Wallace; promising to follow him immediately, and answer all his questions at *Malverton.* My importunities were enforced by his own fears, and, after a moment's hesitation, he rode away.

The emotions produced by this incident were, in the present critical state of my frame, eminently hurtful. My morbid indications suddenly returned. I had reason to ascribe my condition to my visit to the chamber of Maravegli; but this and its consequences to myself, as well as the journey of Hadwin, were the fruits of my unhappy secrecy.

I had always been accustomed to perform my journeys on foot. This, on ordinary occasions, was the preferable method, but now I ought to have adopted the easiest and swiftest means. If Hadwin had been acquainted with my purpose he would not only have approved, but would have allowed me, the use of a horse. These reflections were rendered less pungent by the recollection that my motives were benevolent, and that I had endeavoured the benefit of others by means which appeared to me most suitable.

Meanwhile, how was I to proceed? What hindered me from pursuing the footsteps of Hadwin with all the expedition which my uneasiness, of brain and stomach, would allow? I conceived that to leave any thing undone, with regard to Wallace, would be absurd. His property might be put under the care of my new friend. But how was it to be distinguished from the property of others? It was, probably, contained in trunks, which were designated by some label or mark. I was unacquainted with his chamber, but, by passing from one to the other, I might finally discover it. Some token, directing my footsteps, might occur, though at present unforeseen.

Actuated by these considerations, I once more entered Thetford's habitation. I regretted that I had not procured the counsel or attendance of my new friend; but some engagements, the nature of which he did not explain, occasioned him to leave me as soon as breakfast was finished.

CHAPTER XVIII.

I WANDERED over this deserted mansion, in a considerable degree, at random. Effluvia of a pestilential nature assailed me from every corner. In the front room of the second story, I imagined that I discovered vestiges of that catastrophe which the past night had produced. The bed appeared as if some one had recently been dragged from it. The sheets were tinged with yellow, and with that substance which is said to be characteristic of this disease, the gangrenous or black vomit. The floor exhibited similar stains.

There are many who will regard my conduct as the last refinement of temerity, or of heroism. Nothing, indeed, more perplexes me than a review of my own conduct. Not, indeed, that death is an object always to be dreaded, or that my motive did not justify my actions; but of all dangers, those allied to pestilence, by being mysterious and unseen, are the most formidable. To disarm them of their terrors requires the longest familiarity. Nurses and physicians soonest become intrepid or indifferent; but the rest of mankind recoil from the scene with unconquerable loathing.

I was sustained, not by confidence of safety, and a belief of exemption from this malady, or by the influence of habit, which inures us to all that is detestable or perilous, but by a belief that this was as eligible an avenue to death as any other; and that life is a trivial sacrifice in the cause of duty.

I passed from one room to the other. A portmanteau, marked with the initials of Wallace's name, at length attracted my notice. From this circumstance I inferred that this apartment had been occupied by him. The room was neatly arranged, and appeared as if no one had lately used it. There were trunks and drawers. That which I have mentioned was the only one that bore marks of Wallace's ownership. This I lifted in my arms with a view to remove it to Medlicote's house.

At that moment, methought I heard a footstep slowly and lingeringly ascending the stair. I was disconcerted at this incident. The footstep had in it a ghost-like solemnity and tardiness. This phantom vanished in a moment, and yielded place to more humble conjectures. A human being approached, whose office and commission were inscrutable. That we were strangers to each other was easily imagined; but how would my appearance, in this remote chamber, and loaded with another's property, be interpreted? Did he enter the house after me, or was he the tenant of some chamber hitherto unvisited; whom my entrance had awakened from his trance and called from his couch?

In the confusion of my mind, I still held my burden uplifted. To have placed it on the floor, and encountered this visitant, without this equivocal token about me, was the obvious proceeding. Indeed, time only could decide whether these footsteps tended to this, or to some other apartment.

My doubts were quickly dispelled. The door opened, and a figure glided in. The portmanteau dropped from my arms, and my heart's blood was chilled. If an apparition of the dead were possible, (and that possibility I could not deny,) this was such an apparition. A hue, yellowish and livid; bones, uncovered with flesh; eyes, ghastly, hollow, woe-begone, and fixed in an agony of wonder upon me; and locks, matted and negligent, constituted the image which I now beheld. My belief of somewhat preternatural in this appearance was confirmed by recollection of resemblances between these features and those of one who was dead. In this shape and visage, shadowy and death-like as they were, the lineaments of Wallace, of him who had misled my rustic simplicity on my first visit to this city, and whose death I had conceived to be incontestably ascertained, were forcibly recognised.

This recognition, which at first alarmed my superstition, speedily led to more rational inferences. Wallace had been dragged to the hospital. Nothing was less to be suspected than that he would return alive from that hideous receptacle, but this was by no means impossible. The figure that stood before me had just risen from the bed of sickness, and from the brink of the grave. The crisis of his malady had passed, and he was once more entitled to be ranked among the living.

This event, and the consequences which my imagination connected with it, filled me with the liveliest joy. I thought not of his ignorance of the causes of my satisfaction, of the doubts to which the circumstances of our interview would give birth, respecting the integrity of my purpose. I forgot the artifices by which I had formerly been betrayed, and the embarrassments which a meeting with the victim of his artifices would excite in him; I thought only of the happiness which his recovery would confer upon his uncle and his cousins.

I advanced towards him with an air of congratulation, and offered him my hand. He shrunk back, and exclaimed, in a feeble voice, "Who are you? What business have you here?"

"I am the friend of Wallace, if he will allow me to

be so. I am a messenger from your uncle and cousins at *Malverton*. I came to know the cause of your silence, and to afford you any assistance in my power."

He continued to regard me with an air of suspicion and doubt. These I endeavoured to remove by explaining the motives that led me hither. It was with difficulty that he seemed to credit my representations. When thoroughly convinced of the truth of my assertions, he inquired with great anxiety and tenderness concerning his relations; and expressed his hope that they were ignorant of what had befallen him.

I could not encourage his hopes. I regretted my own precipitation in adopting the belief of his death. This belief had been uttered with confidence, and without stating my reasons for embracing it, to Mr. Hadwin. These tidings would be borne to his daughters, and their grief would be exasperated to a deplorable and perhaps to a fatal degree.

There was but one method of repairing or eluding this mischief. Intelligence ought to be conveyed to them of his recovery. But where was the messenger to be found? No one's attention could be found disengaged from his own concerns. Those who were able or willing to leave the city had sufficient motives for departure, in relation to themselves. If vehicle or horse were procurable for money, ought it not to be secured for the use of Wallace himself, whose health required the easiest and speediest conveyance from this theatre of death?

My companion was powerless in mind as in limbs. He seemed unable to consult upon the means of escaping from the inconveniences by which he was surrounded. As soon as sufficient strength was regained, he had left the hospital. To repair to *Malverton* was the measure which prudence obviously dictated; but he was hopeless of effecting it. The city was close at hand; this was his usual home; and hither his tottering and almost involuntary steps conducted him.

He listened to my representations and counsels, and acknowledged their propriety. He put himself under my protection and guidance, and promised to conform implicitly to my directions. His strength had sufficed to bring him thus far, but was now utterly exhausted. The task of searching for a carriage and horse devolved upon me.

In effecting this purpose, I was obliged to rely upon my own ingenuity and diligence. Wallace, though so long a resident in the city, knew not to whom I could apply, or by whom carriages were let to hire. My own reflections taught me, that this accommodation was most likely to be furnished by innkeepers, or that some of those might at least inform me of the best measures to be taken. I resolved to set out immediately on this search. Meanwhile, Wallace was persuaded to take refuge in Medlicote's apartments; and to make, by the assistance of Austin, the necessary preparation for his journey.

The morning had now advanced. The rays of a sultry sun had a sickening and enfeebling influence beyond any which I had ever experienced. The drought of unusual duration had bereft the air and the earth of every particle of moisture. The element which I breathed appeared to have stagnated into noxiousness and putrefaction. I was astonished at observing the enormous diminution of my strength. My brows were heavy, my intellects benumbed, my sinews enfeebled, and my sensations universally unquiet.

These prognostics were easily interpreted. What I chiefly dreaded was, that they would disable me from executing the task which I had undertaken. I summoned up all my resolution, and cherished a disdain of yielding to this ignoble destiny. I reflected that the source of all energy, and even of life, is seated in thought; that nothing is arduous to human efforts; that the external frame will seldom languish, while actuated by an unconquerable soul.

I fought against my dreary feelings, which pulled me to the earth. I quickened my pace, raised my drooping eyelids, and hummed a cheerful and favourite air. For all that I accomplished during this day, I believe myself indebted to the strenuousness and ardour of my resolutions.

I went from one tavern to another. One was deserted; in another the people were sick, and their attendants refused to hearken to my inquiries or offers; at a third, their horses were engaged. I was determined to prosecute my search as long as an inn or a livery-stable remained unexamined, and my strength would permit.

To detail the events of this expedition, the arguments and supplications which I used to overcome the dictates of avarice and fear, the fluctuation of my hopes and my incessant disappointments, would be useless. Having exhausted all my expedients ineffectually, I was compelled to turn my weary steps once more to Medlicote's lodgings.

My meditations were deeply engaged by the present circumstances of my situation. Since the means which were first suggested were impracticable, I endeavoured to investigate others. Wallace's debility made it impossible for him to perform this journey on foot; but would not his strength and his resolution suffice to carry him beyond Schuylkill? A carriage or horse, though not to be obtained in the city, could, without difficulty, be procured in the country. Every farmer had beasts for burden and draught. One of these might be hired, at no immoderate expense, for half a day.

This project appeared so practicable and so specious, that I deeply regretted the time and the efforts which had already been so fruitlessly expended. If my project, however, had been mischievous, to review it with regret was only to prolong and to multiply its mischiefs. I trusted that time and strength would not be wanting to the execution of this new design.

On entering Medlicote's house, my looks, which, in spite of my languors, were sprightly and confident, flattered Wallace with the belief that my exertions had succeeded. When acquainted with their failure, he sunk as quickly into hopelessness. My new expedient was heard by him with no marks of satisfaction. It was impossible, he said, to move from this spot by his own strength. All his powers were exhausted by his walk from Bush Hill.

I endeavoured, by arguments and railleries, to revive

his courage. The pure air of the country would exhilarate him into new life. He might stop at every fifty yards, and rest upon the green sod. If overtaken by the night, we would procure a lodging, by address and importunity; but, if every door should be shut against us, we should at least enjoy the shelter of some barn, and might diet wholesomely upon the new-laid eggs that we should find there. The worst treatment we could meet with was better than continuance in the city.

These remonstrances had some influence, and he at length consented to put his ability to the test. First, however, it was necessary to invigorate himself by a few hours' rest. To this, though with infinite reluctance, I consented.

This interval allowed him to reflect upon the past, and to inquire into the fate of Thetford and his family. The intelligence which Medlicote had enabled me to afford him was heard with more satisfaction than regret. The ingratitude and cruelty with which he had been treated seemed to have extinguished every sentiment but hatred and vengeance. I was willing to profit by this interval to know more of Thetford than I already possessed. I inquired why Wallace had so perversely neglected the advice of his uncle and cousin, and persisted to brave so many dangers when flight was so easy.

"I cannot justify my conduct," answered he. "It was in the highest degree thoughtless and perverse. I was confident and unconcerned as long as our neighbourhood was free from disease, and as long as I forbore any communication with the sick; yet I should have withdrawn to Malverton, merely to gratify my friends, if Thetford had not used the most powerful arguments to detain me. He laboured to extenuate the danger.

"'Why not stay,' said he, 'as long as I and my family stay? Do you think that we would linger here, if the danger were imminent? As soon as it becomes so, we will fly. You know that we have a country-house prepared for our reception. When we go, you shall accompany us. Your services at this time are indispensable to my affairs. If you will not desert me, your salary next year shall be double; and that will enable you to marry your cousin immediately. Nothing is more improbable than that any of us should be sick; but, if this should happen to you, I plight my honour that you shall be carefully and faithfully attended.'

"These assurances were solemn and generous. To make Susan Hadwin my wife was the scope of all my wishes and labours. By staying, I should hasten this desirable event, and incur little hazard. By going, I should alienate the affections of Thetford; by whom, it is but justice to acknowledge, that I had hitherto been treated with unexampled generosity and kindness; and blast all the schemes I had formed for rising into wealth.

"My resolution was by no means steadfast. As often as a letter from *Malverton* arrived, I felt myself disposed to hasten away; but this inclination was combated by new arguments and new entreaties of Thetford.

"In this state of suspense, the girl by whom Mrs. Thetford's infant was nursed fell sick. She was an excellent creature, and merited better treatment than she received. Like me, she resisted the persuasions of her friends, but her motives for remaining were disinterested and heroic.

"No sooner did her indisposition appear, than she was hurried to the hospital. I saw that no reliance could be placed upon the assurances of Thetford. Every consideration gave way to his fear of death. After the girl's departure, though he knew that she was led by his means to execution, yet he consoled himself by repeating and believing her assertions, that her disease was not *the fever*.

"I was now greatly alarmed for my own safety. I was determined to encounter his anger and repel his persuasions; and to depart with the market-man next morning. That night, however, I was seized with a violent fever. I knew in what manner patients were treated at the hospital, and removal thither was to the last degree abhorred.

"The morning arrived, and my situation was discovered. At the first intimation, Thetford rushed out of the house, and refused to re-enter it till I was removed. I knew not my fate, till three ruffians made their appearance at my bedside, and communicated their commission.

"I called on the name of Thetford and his wife. I entreated a moment's delay, till I had seen these persons, and endeavoured to procure a respite from my sentence. They were deaf to my entreaties, and prepared to execute their office by force. I was delirious with rage and terror. I heaped the bitterest execrations on my murderer; and by turns, invoked the compassion of, and poured a torrent of reproaches on, the wretches whom he had selected for his ministers. My struggles and outcries were vain.

"I have no perfect recollection of what passed till my arrival at the hospital. My passions combined with my disease to make me frantic and wild. In a state like mine, the slightest motion could not be endured without agony. What then must I have felt, scorched and dazzled by the sun, sustained by hard boards, and borne for miles over a rugged pavement?

"I cannot make you comprehend the anguish of my feelings. To be disjointed and torn piecemeal by the rack was a torment inexpressibly inferior to this. Nothing excites my wonder but that I did not expire before the cart had moved three paces.

"I knew not how, or by whom, I was moved from this vehicle. Insensibility came at length to my relief. After a time I opened my eyes, and slowly gained some knowledge of my situation. I lay upon a mattress, whose condition proved that a half-decayed corpse had recently been dragged from it. The room was large, but it was covered with beds like my own. Between each, there was scarcely the interval of three feet. Each sustained a wretch, whose groans and distortions bespoke the desperateness of his condition.

"The atmosphere was loaded by mortal stenches. A vapour, suffocating and malignant, scarcely allowed me to breathe. No suitable receptacle was provided for the evacuations produced by medicine or disease. My nearest neighbour was struggling with death, and my bed, casually extended, was moist with the detestable matter which had flowed from his stomach.

"You will scarcely believe that, in this scene of horrors, the sound of laughter should be overheard. While the upper rooms of this building are filled with the sick and the dying, the lower apartments are the scene of carousals and mirth. The wretches who are hired, at enormous wages, to tend the sick and convey away the dead, neglect their duty, and consume the cordials which are provided for the patients, in debauchery and riot.

"A female visage, bloated with malignity and drunkenness, occasionally looked in. Dying eyes were cast upon her, invoking the boon, perhaps, of a drop of cold water, or her assistance to change a posture which compelled him to behold the ghastly writhings or deathful *smile* of his neighbour.

"The visitant had left the banquet for a moment, only to see who was dead. If she entered the room, blinking eyes and reeling steps showed her to be totally unqualified for ministering the aid that was needed. Presently she disappeared, and others ascended the staircase, a coffin was deposited at the door, the wretch, whose heart still quivered, was seized by rude hands, and dragged along the floor into the passage.

"Oh! how poor are the conceptions which are formed, by the fortunate few, of the sufferings to which millions of their fellow-beings are condemned. This misery was more frightful, because it was seen to flow from the depravity of the attendants. My own eyes only would make me credit the existence of wickedness so enormous. No wonder that to die in garrets, and cellars, and stables, unvisited and unknown, had, by so many, been preferred to being brought hither.

"A physician cast an eye upon my state. He gave some directions to the person who attended him. I did not comprehend them, they were never executed by the nurses, and, if the attempt had been made, I should probably have refused to receive what was offered. Recovery was equally beyond my expectations and my wishes. The scene which was hourly displayed before me, the entrance of the sick, most of whom perished in a few hours, and their departure to the graves prepared for them, reminded me of the fate to which I, also, was reserved.

"Three days passed away, in which every hour was expected to be the last. That, amidst an atmosphere so contagious and deadly, amidst causes of destruction hourly accumulating, I should yet survive, appears to me nothing less than miraculous. That of so many conducted to this house the only one who passed out of it alive should be myself almost surpasses my belief.

"Some inexplicable principle rendered harmless those potent enemies of human life. My fever subsided and vanished. My strength was revived, and the first use that I made of my limbs was to bear me far from the contemplation and sufferance of those evils."

CHAPTER XIX.

HAVING gratified my curiosity in this respect, Wallace proceeded to remind me of the circumstances of our first interview. He had entertained doubts whether I was the person whom he had met at Lesher's. I acknowledged myself to be the same, and inquired, in my turn, into the motives of his conduct on that occasion.

"I confess," said he, with some hesitation, "I meant only to sport with your simplicity and ignorance. You must not imagine, however, that my stratagem was deep-laid and deliberately executed. My professions at the tavern were sincere. I meant not to injure but to serve you. It was not till I reached the head of the staircase that the mischievous contrivance occurred. I foresaw nothing, at the moment, but ludicrous mistakes and embarrassment. The scheme was executed almost at the very moment it occurred.

"After I had returned to the parlour, Thetford charged me with the delivery of a message in a distant quarter of the city. It was not till I had performed this commission, and had set out on my return, that I fully revolved the consequences likely to flow from my project.

"That Thetford and his wife would detect you in their bedchamber was unquestionable. Perhaps, weary of my long delay, you would have fairly undressed and gone to bed. The married couple would have made preparation to follow you, and, when the curtain was undrawn, would discover a robust youth, fast asleep, in their place. These images, which had just before excited my laughter, now produced a very different emotion. I dreaded some fatal catastrophe from the fiery passions of Thetford. In the first transports of his fury he might pistol you, or, at least, might command you to be dragged to prison.

"I now heartily repented of my jest, and hastened home, that I might prevent, as far as possible, the evil effects that might flow from it. The acknowledgment of my own agency in this affair would, at least, transfer Thetford's indignation to myself, to whom it was equitably due.

"The married couple had retired to their chamber, and no alarm or confusion had followed. This was an inexplicable circumstance. I waited with impatience till the morning should furnish a solution of the difficulty. The morning arrived. A strange event had, indeed, taken place in their bedchamber. They found an infant asleep in their bed. Thetford had been roused twice in the night, once by a noise in the closet, and afterwards by a noise at the door.

"Some connection between these sounds and the foundling was naturally suspected. In the morning the closet was examined, and a coarse pair of shoes was found on the floor. The chamber door, which Thetford had locked in the evening, was discovered to be open, as likewise a window in the kitchen.

"These appearances were a source of wonder and doubt to others, but were perfectly intelligible to me. I rejoiced that my stratagem had no more dangerous consequence, and admired the ingenuity and perseverance with which you had extricated yourself from so critical a state."

This narrative was only the verification of my own guesses. Its facts were quickly supplanted in my thoughts by the disastrous picture he had drawn of the state of the hospital. I was confounded and shocked by the magnitude of this evil. The cause of it was obvious. The wretches whom money could purchase were, of course, licentious and unprincipled. Superintended and controlled, they might be useful instruments; but that superintendence could not be bought.

What qualities were requisite in the governor of such an institution? He must have zeal, diligence, and perseverance. He must act from lofty and pure motives. He must be mild and firm, intrepid and compliant. One perfectly qualified for the office it is desirable, but not possible, to find. A dispassionate and honest zeal in the cause of duty and humanity may be of eminent utility. Am I not endowed with this zeal? Cannot my feeble efforts obviate some portion of this evil?

No one has hitherto claimed this disgustful and perilous situation. My powers and discernment are small, but if they be honestly exerted they cannot fail to be somewhat beneficial.

The impulse produced by these reflections was to hasten to the City Hall, and make known my wishes. This impulse was controlled by recollections of my own indisposition, and of the state of Wallace. To deliver this youth to his friends was the strongest obligation. When this was discharged, I might return to the city, and acquit myself of more comprehensive duties.

Wallace had now enjoyed a few hours' rest, and was persuaded to begin the journey. It was now noonday, and the sun darted insupportable rays. Wallace was more sensible than I of their unwholesome influence. We had not reached the suburbs, when his strength was wholly exhausted, and, had I not supported him, he would have sunk upon the pavement.

My limbs were scarcely less weak, but my resolutions were much more strenuous than his. I made light of his indisposition, and endeavoured to persuade him that his vigour would return in proportion to his distance from the city. The moment we should reach a shade, a short respite would restore us to health and cheerfulness.

Nothing could revive his courage or induce him to go on. To return or to proceed was equally impracticable.

But, should he be able to return, where should he find a retreat? The danger of relapse was imminent; his own chamber at Thetford's was unoccupied. If he could regain this house, might I not procure him a physician and perform for him the part of nurse?

His present situation was critical and mournful. To remain in the street, exposed to the malignant fervours of the sun, was not to be endured. To carry him in my arms exceeded my strength. Should I not claim the assistance of the first passenger that appeared?

At that moment a horse and chaise passed us. The vehicle proceeded at a quick pace. He that rode in it might afford us the succour that we needed. He might be persuaded to deviate from his course and convey the helpless Wallace to the house we had just left.

This thought instantly impelled me forward. Feeble as I was, I even ran with speed, in order to overtake the vehicle. My purpose was effected with the utmost difficulty. It fortunately happened that the carriage contained but one person, who stopped at my request. His countenance and guise was mild and encouraging.

"Good friend," I exclaimed, "here is a young man too indisposed to walk. I want him carried to his lodgings. Will you, for money or for charity, allow him a place in your chaise, and set him down where I shall direct?" Observing tokens of hesitation, I continued, "You need have no fears to perform this office. He is not sick, but merely feeble. I will not ask twenty minutes, and you may ask what reward you think proper."

Still he hesitated to comply. His business, he said, had not led him into the city. He merely passed along the skirts of it, whence he conceived that no danger would arise. He was desirous of helping the unfortunate; but he could not think of risking his own life in the cause of a stranger, when he had a wife and children depending on his existence and exertions for bread. It gave him pain to refuse, but he thought his duty to himself and to others required that he should not hazard his safety by compliance.

This plea was irresistible. The mildness of his manner showed that he might have been overpowered by persuasion or tempted by reward. I would not take advantage of his tractability; but should have declined his assistance, even if it had been spontaneously offered. I turned away from him in silence, and prepared to return to the spot where I had left my friend. The man prepared to resume his way.

In this perplexity, the thought occurred to me that, since this person was going into the country, he might, possibly, consent to carry Wallace along with him. I confided greatly in the salutary influence of rural airs. I believed that debility constituted the whole of his complaint; that continuance in the city might occasion his relapse, or, at least, procrastinate his restoration.

I once more addressed myself to the traveller, and inquired in what direction and how far he was going. To my unspeakable satisfaction, his answer informed me that his home lay beyond Mr. Hadwin's, and that this road carried him directly past that gentleman's door. He was willing to receive Wallace into his chaise, and to leave him at his uncle's.

This joyous and auspicious occurrence surpassed my fondest hopes. I hurried with the pleasing tidings to Wallace, who eagerly consented to enter the carriage. I thought not at the moment of myself, or how far the same means of escaping from my danger might be used. The stranger could not be anxious on my account; and Wallace's dejection and weakness may apologize for his not soliciting my company, or expressing his fears for my safety. He was no sooner seated, than the traveller hurried away. I gazed after them, motionless and mute, till the carriage, turning a corner, passed beyond my sight.

I had now leisure to revert to my own condition, and to ruminate on that series of abrupt and diversified events that had happened during the few hours which had been passed in the city: the end of my coming was thus speedily and satisfactorily accomplished. My hopes and fears had rapidly fluctuated; but, respecting this young man, had now subsided into calm and propitious certainty. Before the decline of the sun, he would enter his paternal roof, and diffuse ineffable joy throughout that peaceful and chaste asylum.

This contemplation, though rapturous and soothing, speedily gave way to reflections on the conduct which my duty required, and the safe departure of Wallace afforded me liberty, to pursue. To offer myself as a superintendent of the hospital was still my purpose. The languors of my frame might terminate in sickness, but this event it was useless to anticipate. The lofty site and pure airs of Bush Hill might tend to dissipate my languors and restore me to health. At least while I had power, I was bound to exert it to the wisest purposes. I resolved to seek the City Hall immediately, and, for that end, crossed the intermediate fields which separated Sassafras from Chestnut Street.

More urgent considerations had diverted my attention from the money which I bore about me, and from the image of the desolate lady to whom it belonged. My intentions, with regard to her, were the same as ever; but now it occurred to me, with new force, that my death might preclude an interview between us, and that it was prudent to dispose, in some useful way, of the money which would otherwise be left to the sport of chance.

The evils which had befallen this city were obvious and enormous. Hunger and negligence had exasperated the malignity and facilitated the progress of the pestilence. Could this money be more usefully employed than in alleviating these evils? During my life, I had no power over it, but my death would justify me in prescribing the course which it should take.

How was this course to be pointed out? How might I place it, so that I should effect my intentions without relinquishing the possession during my life?

These thoughts were superseded by a tide of new sensations. The weight that incommoded my brows and my stomach was suddenly increased. My brain was usurped by some benumbing power, and my limbs refused to support me. My pulsations were quickened, and the prevalence of fever could no longer be doubted.

Till now, I had entertained a faint hope that my indisposition would vanish of itself. This hope was at an end. The grave was before me, and my projects of curiosity or benevolence were to sink into oblivion. I was not bereaved of the powers of reflection. The consequences of lying in the road, friendless and unprotected, were sure. The first passenger would notice me, and hasten to summon one of those carriages which are busy night and day in transporting its victims to the hospital.

This fate was, beyond all others, abhorrent to my imagination. To hide me under some roof, where my existence would be unknown and unsuspected, and where I might perish unmolested and in quiet, was my present wish. Thetford's or Medlicote's might afford me such an asylum, if it were possible to reach it.

I made the most strenuous exertions; but they could not carry me forward more than a hundred paces. Here I rested on steps, which, on looking up, I perceived to belong to Welbeck's house.

This incident was unexpected. It led my reflections into a new train. To go farther, in the present condition of my frame, was impossible. I was well acquainted with this dwelling. All its avenues were closed. Whether it had remained unoccupied since my flight from it, I could not decide. It was evident that, at present, it was without inhabitants. Possibly it might have continued in the same condition in which Welbeck had left it. Beds or sofas might be found, on which a sick man might rest, and be fearless of intrusion.

This inference was quickly overturned by the obvious supposition that every avenue was bolted and locked. This, however, might not be the condition of the bath-house, in which there was nothing that required to be guarded with unusual precautions. I was suffocated by inward and scorched by external heat; and the relief of bathing and drinking appeared inestimable.

The value of this prize, in addition to my desire to avoid the observation of passengers, made me exert all my remnant of strength. Repeated efforts at length enabled me to mount the wall; and placed me, as I imagined, in security. I swallowed large draughts of water as soon as I could reach the well.

The effect was, for a time, salutary and delicious. My fervours were abated, and my faculties relieved from the weight which had lately oppressed them. My present condition was unspeakably more advantageous than the former. I did not believe that it could be improved, till, casting my eye vaguely over the building, I happened to observe the shutters of a lower window partly opened.

Whether this was occasioned by design or by accident there was no means of deciding. Perhaps, in the precipitation of the latest possessor, this window had been overlooked. Perhaps it had been unclosed by violence, and afforded entrance to a robber. By what means soever it had happened, it undoubtedly afforded ingress to me. I felt no scruple in profiting by this circumstance. My purposes were not dishonest. I should not injure or purloin any thing. It was laudable to seek a refuge from the well-meant persecutions of those who governed the city. All I sought was the privilege of dying alone.

Having gotten in at the window, I could not but remark that the furniture and its arrangements had undergone no alteration in my absence. I moved softly from one apartment to another, till at length I entered that which had formerly been Welbeck's bedchamber.

The bed was naked of covering. The cabinets and closets exhibited their fastenings broken. Their contents were gone. Whether these appearances had been produced by midnight robbers, or by the ministers of law and the rage of the creditors of Welbeck, was a topic of fruitless conjecture.

My design was now effected. This chamber should be the scene of my disease and my refuge from the charitable cruelty of my neighbours. My new sensations conjured up the hope that my indisposition might prove a temporary evil. Instead of pestilential or malignant fever, it might be a harmless intermittent. Time would ascertain its true nature; meanwhile, I would turn the carpet into a coverlet, supply my pitcher with water, and administer without sparing, and without fear, that remedy which was placed within my reach.

CHAPTER XX.

I LAID myself on the bed and wrapped my limbs in the folds of the carpet. My thoughts were restless and perturbed. I was once more busy in reflecting on the conduct which I ought to pursue with regard to the bank-bills. I weighed, with scrupulous attention, every circumstance that might influence my decision. I could not conceive any more beneficial application of this property than to the service of the indigent, at this season of multiplied distress; but I considered that, if my death were unknown, the house would not be opened or examined till the pestilence had ceased, and the benefits of this application would thus be partly or wholly precluded.

This season of disease, however, would give place to a season of scarcity. The number and wants of the poor, during the ensuing winter, would be deplorably aggravated. What multitudes might be rescued from famine and nakedness by the judicious application of this sum!

But how should I secure this application? To enclose the bills in a letter, directed to some eminent citizen or public officer, was the obvious proceeding. Both of these conditions were fulfilled in the person of the present chief-magistrate. To him, therefore, the packet was to be sent.

Paper and the implements of writing were necessary for this end. Would they be found, I asked, in the upper room? If that apartment, like the rest which I had seen, and its furniture, had remained untouched, my task would be practicable; but, if the means of writing were not to be immediately procured, my purpose, momentous and dear as it was, must be relinquished.

The truth, in this respect, was easily and ought immediately to be ascertained. I rose from the bed which I had lately taken, and proceeded to the *study*. The entries and staircases were illuminated by a pretty strong twilight. The rooms, in consequence of every ray being excluded by the closed shutters, were nearly as dark as if it had been midnight. The rooms into which I had already passed were locked, but its key was in each lock. I flattered myself that the entrance into the *study* would be found in the same condition. The door was shut, but no key was to be seen. My hopes were considerably damped by this appearance, but I conceived it to be still possible to enter, since, by chance or by design, the door might be unlocked.

My fingers touched the lock, when a sound was heard as if a bolt, appending to the door on the inside, had been drawn. I was startled by this incident. It betokened that the room was already occupied by some other, who desired to exclude a visitor. The unbarred shutter below was remembered, and associated itself with this circumstance. That this house should be entered by the same avenue, at the same time, and this room should be sought, by two persons, was a mysterious concurrence.

I began to question whether I had heard distinctly. Numberless inexplicable noises are apt to assail the ear in an empty dwelling. The very echoes of our steps are unwonted and new. This, perhaps, was some such sound. Resuming courage, I once more applied to the lock. The door, in spite of my repeated efforts, would not open.

My design was too momentous to be readily relinquished. My curiosity and my fears likewise were awakened. The marks of violence, which I had seen on the closets and cabinets below, seemed to indicate the presence of plunderers. Here was one who laboured for seclusion and concealment.

The pillage was not made upon my property. My weakness would disable me from encountering or mastering a man of violence. To solicit admission into this room would be useless. To attempt to force my way would be absurd. These reflections prompted me to withdraw from the door; but the uncertainty of the conclusions I had drawn, and the importance of gaining access to this apartment, combined to check my steps.

Perplexed as to the means I should employ, I once more tried the lock. This attempt was fruitless as the former. Though hopeless of any information to be gained by that means, I put my eye to the keyhole. I discovered a light different from what was usually met with at this hour. It was not the twilight which the sun, imperfectly excluded, produces, but gleams, as from a lamp; yet its gleams were fainter and obscurer than a lamp generally imparts.

Was this a confirmation of my first conjecture? Lamplight at noonday, in a mansion thus deserted, and in a room which had been the scene of memorable and disastrous events, was ominous. Hitherto no direct proof had been given of the presence of a human being. How to ascertain his presence, or whether it were eligible by any means to ascertain it, were points on which I had not deliberated.

I had no power to deliberate. My curiosity impelled me to call,—"Is there any one within? Speak."

These words were scarcely uttered, when some one exclaimed, in a voice vehement but half-smothered, "Good God!"—

A deep pause succeeded. I waited for an answer; for somewhat to which this emphatic invocation might be a prelude. Whether the tones were expressive of surprise, or pain, or grief, was, for a moment, dubious. Perhaps the motives which led me to this house suggested the suspicion which presently succeeded to my doubts,—that the person within was disabled by sickness. The circumstances of my own condition took away the improbability from this belief. Why might not another be induced like me to hide himself in this desolate retreat? Might not a servant, left to take care of the house, a measure usually adopted by the opulent at this time, be seized by the reigning malady? Incapacitated for exertion, or fearing to be dragged to the hospital, he has shut himself in this apartment. The robber, it may be, who came to pillage, was overtaken and detained by disease. In either case, detection or intrusion would be hateful, and would be assiduously eluded.

These thoughts had no tendency to weaken or divert my efforts to obtain access to this room. The person was a brother in calamity, whom it was my duty to succour and cherish to the utmost of my power. Once more I spoke:—

"Who is within? I beseech you answer me. Whatever you be, I desire to do you good and not injury. Open the door and let me know your condition. I will try to be of use to you."

I was answered by a deep groan, and by a sob counteracted and devoured as it were by a mighty effort. This token of distress thrilled to my heart. My terrors wholly disappeared, and gave place to unlimited compassion. I again entreated to be admitted, promising all the succour or consolation which my situation allowed me to afford.

Answers were made in tones of anger and impatience, blended with those of grief:—"I want no succour; vex me not with your entreaties and offers. Fly from this spot; linger not a moment, lest you participate my destiny and rush upon your death."

These I considered merely as the effusions of delirium, or the dictates of despair. The style and articulation denoted the speaker to be superior to the class of servants. Hence my anxiety to see and to aid him was increased. My remonstrances were sternly and pertinaciously repelled. For a time, incoherent and impassioned exclamations flowed from him. At length, I was only permitted to hear strong aspirations and sobs, more eloquent and more indicative of grief than any language.

This deportment filled me with no less wonder than commiseration. By what views this person was led hither, by what motives induced to deny himself to my entreaties, was wholly incomprehensible. Again, though hopeless of success, I repeated my request to be admitted.

My perseverance seemed now to have exhausted all his patience, and he exclaimed, in a voice of thunder, "Arthur Mervyn! Begone. Linger but a moment, and my rage, tiger-like, will rush upon you and rend you limb from limb."

This address petrified me. The voice that uttered this sanguinary menace was strange to my ears. It suggested no suspicion of ever having heard it before.

Yet my accents had betrayed me to him. He was familiar with my name. Notwithstanding the improbability of my entrance into this dwelling, I was clearly recognised and unhesitatingly named!

My curiosity and compassion were in no wise diminished, but I found myself compelled to give up my purpose. I withdrew reluctantly from the door, and once more threw myself upon my bed. Nothing was more necessary, in the present condition of my frame, than sleep; and sleep had, perhaps, been possible, if the scene around me had been less pregnant with causes of wonder and panic.

Once more I tasked memory in order to discover, in the persons with whom I had hitherto conversed, some resemblance, in voice or tones, to him whom I had just heard. This process was effectual. Gradually my imagination called up an image which, now that it was clearly seen, I was astonished had not instantly occurred. Three years ago, a man, by name Colvill, came on foot, and with a knapsack on his back, into the district where my father resided. He had learning and genius, and readily obtained the station for which only he deemed himself qualified; that of a schoolmaster.

His demeanour was gentle and modest; his habits, as to sleep, food, and exercise, abstemious and regular. Meditation in the forest, or reading in his closet, seemed to constitute, together with attention to his scholars, his sole amusement and employment. He estranged himself from company, not because society afforded no pleasure, but because studious seclusion afforded him chief satisfaction.

No one was more idolized by his unsuspecting neighbours. His scholars revered him as a father, and made under his tuition a remarkable proficiency. His character seemed open to boundless inspection, and his conduct was pronounced by all to be faultless.

At the end of a year the scene was changed. A daughter of one of his patrons, young, artless, and beautiful, appeared to have fallen a prey to the arts of some detestable seducer. The betrayer was gradually detected, and successive discoveries showed that the same artifices had been practised, with the same success, upon many others. Colvill was the arch-villain. He retired from the storm of vengeance that was gathering over him, and had not been heard of since that period.

I saw him rarely, and for a short time, and I was a mere boy. Hence the failure to recollect his voice, and to perceive that the voice of him immured in the room above was the same with that of Colvill. Though I had slight reasons for recognising his features or accents, I had abundant cause to think of him with detestation, and pursue him with implacable revenge, for the victim of his acts, she whose ruin was first detected, was—*my sister*.

This unhappy girl escaped from the upbraidings of her parents, from the contumelies of the world, from the goadings of remorse, and the anguish flowing from the perfidy and desertion of Colvill, in a voluntary death. She was innocent and lovely. Previous to this evil, my soul was linked with hers by a thousand resemblances and sympathies, as well as by perpetual intercourse from infancy, and by the fraternal relation. She was my sister, my preceptress and friend; but she died—her end was violent, untimely, and criminal! I cannot think of her without heart-bursting grief; of her destroyer, without a rancour which I know to be wrong, but which I cannot subdue.

When the image of Colvill rushed, upon this occasion, on my thought, I almost started on my feet. To meet him, after so long a separation, here, and in these circumstances, was so unlooked-for and abrupt an event, and revived a tribe of such hateful impulses and agonizing recollections, that a total revolution seemed to have been effected in my frame. His recognition of my person, his aversion to be seen, his ejaculation of terror and surprise on first hearing my voice, all contributed to strengthen my belief.

How was I to act? My feeble frame could but ill second my vengeful purposes; but vengeance, though it sometimes occupied my thoughts, was hindered by my reason from leading me, in any instance, to outrage or even to upbraiding.

All my wishes with regard to this man were limited to expelling his image from my memory, and to shunning a meeting with him. That he had not opened the door at my bidding was now a topic of joy. To look upon some bottomless pit, into which I was about to be cast headlong, and alive, was less to be abhorred than to look upon the face of Colvill. Had I known that he had taken refuge in this house, no power should have compelled me to enter it. To be immersed in the infection of the hospital, and to be hurried, yet breathing and observant, to my grave, was a more supportable fate.

I dwell, with self-condemnation and shame, upon this part of my story. To feel extraordinary indignation at vice, merely because we have partaken in an extraordinary degree of its mischiefs, is unjustifiable. To regard the wicked with no emotion but pity, to be active in reclaiming them, in controlling their malevolence, and preventing or repairing the ills which they produce, is the only province of duty. This lesson, as well as a thousand others, I have yet to learn; but I despair of living long enough for that or any beneficial purpose.

My emotions with regard to Colvill were erroneous, but omnipotent. I started from my bed, and prepared to rush into the street. I was careless of the lot that should befall me, since no fate could be worse than that of abiding under the same roof with a wretch spotted with so many crimes.

I had not set my feet upon the floor before my precipitation was checked by a sound from above. The door of the study was cautiously and slowly opened. This incident admitted only of one construction, supposing all obstructions removed. Colvill was creeping from his hiding-place, and would probably fly with speed from the house. My belief of his sickness was now confuted. An illicit design was congenial with his character and congruous with those appearances already observed.

I had no power or wish to obstruct his flight. I thought of it with transport, and once more threw myself upon the bed, and wrapped my averted face in the carpet. He would probably pass this door, unobservant of me, and my muffled face would save me from the agonies connected with the sight of him.

The footsteps above were distinguishable, though it was manifest that they moved with lightsomeness and circumspection. They reached the stair and descended. The room in which I lay was, like the rest, obscured by the closed shutters. This obscurity now gave way to a light, resembling that glimmering and pale reflection which I had noticed in the study. My eyes, though averted from the door, were disengaged from the folds which covered the rest of my head, and observed these tokens of Colvill's approach, flitting on the wall.

My feverish perturbations increased as he drew nearer. He reached the door, and stopped. The light rested for a moment. Presently he entered the apartment. My emotions suddenly rose to a height that would not be controlled. I imagined that he approached the bed, and was gazing upon me. At the same moment, by an involuntary impulse, I threw off my covering, and, turning my face, fixed my eyes upon my visitant.

It was as I suspected. The figure, lifting in his right hand a candle, and gazing at the bed, with lineaments and attitude bespeaking fearful expectation and tormenting doubts, was now beheld. One glance communicated to my senses all the parts of this terrific vision. A sinking at my heart, as if it had been penetrated by a dagger, seized me. This was not enough: I uttered a shriek, too rueful and loud not to have startled the attention of the passengers, if any had, at that moment, been passing the street.

Heaven seemed to have decreed that this period should be filled with trials of my equanimity and fortitude. The test of my courage was once more employed to cover me with humiliation and remorse. This second time, my fancy conjured up a spectre, and I shuddered as if the grave were forsaken and the unquiet dead haunted my pillow.

The visage and the shape had indeed preternatural attitudes, but they belonged, not to Colvill, but to—Welbeck.

CHAPTER XXI.

He whom I had accompanied to the midst of the river; whom I had imagined that I saw sink to rise no more, was now before me. Though incapable of precluding the groundless belief of preternatural visitations, I was able to banish the phantom almost at the same instant at which it appeared. Welbeck had escaped from the stream alive; or had, by some inconceivable means, been restored to life.

The first was the most plausible conclusion. It instantly engendered a suspicion, that his plunging into the water was an artifice, intended to establish a belief of his death. His own tale had shown him to be versed in frauds, and flexible to evil. But was he not associated with Colvill? and what, but a compact in iniquity, could bind together such men?

While thus musing, Welbeck's countenance and gesture displayed emotions too vehement for speech. The glances that he fixed upon me were unsteadfast and wild. He walked along the floor, stopping at each moment, and darting looks of eagerness upon me. A conflict of passions kept him mute. At length, advancing to the bed, on the side of which I was now sitting, he addressed me:—

"What is this? Are you here? In defiance of pestilence, are you actuated by some demon to haunt me, like the ghost of my offences, and cover me with shame? What have I to do with that dauntless yet guiltless front? With that foolishly-confiding and obsequious, yet erect and unconquerable, spirit? Is there no means of evading your pursuit? Must I dip my hands, a second time, in blood; and dig for you a grave by the side of Watson?"

These words were listened to with calmness. I suspected and pitied the man, but I did not fear him. His words and his looks were indicative less of cruelty than madness. I looked at him with an air compassionate and wistful. I spoke with mildness and composure:—

"Mr. Welbeck, you are unfortunate and criminal. Would to God I could restore you to happiness and virtue! but, though my desire be strong, I have no power to change your habits or rescue you from misery.

"I believed you to be dead. I rejoice to find myself mistaken. While you live, there is room to hope that your errors will be cured; and the turmoils and inquietudes that have hitherto beset your guilty progress will vanish by your reverting into better paths.

"From me you have nothing to fear. If your welfare will be promoted by my silence on the subject of your history, my silence shall be inviolate. I deem not lightly of my promises. They are given, and shall not be recalled.

"This meeting was casual. Since I believed you to be dead, it could not be otherwise. You err, if you suppose that any injury will accrue to you from my life; but you need not discard that error. Since my death is coming, I am not averse to your adopting the belief that the event is fortunate to you.

"Death is the inevitable and universal lot. When or how it comes, is of little moment. To stand, when so many thousands are falling around me, is not to be expected. I have acted an humble and obscure part in the world, and my career has been short; but I murmur not at the decree that makes it so.

"The pestilence is now upon me. The chances of recovery are too slender to deserve my confidence. I came hither to die unmolested, and at peace. All I ask of you is to consult your own safety by immediate flight; and not to disappoint my hopes of concealment, by disclosing my condition to the agents of the hospital."

Welbeck listened with the deepest attention. The wildness of his air disappeared, and gave place to perplexity and apprehension.

"You are sick," said he, in a tremulous tone, in which terror was mingled with affection. "You know this, and expect not to recover. No mother, nor sister, nor friend, will be near to administer food, or medicine, or comfort; yet you can talk calmly; can be thus considerate of others—of me; whose guilt has been so deep, and who has merited so little at your hands!

"Wretched coward! Thus miserable as I am and expect to be, I cling to life. To comply with your heroic counsel, and to fly; to leave you thus desolate and helpless, is the strongest impulse. Fain would I resist it, but cannot.

"To desert you would be flagitious and dastardly beyond all former acts; yet to stay with you is to contract the disease, and to perish after you.

"Life, burdened as it is with guilt and ignominy, is still dear—yet you exhort me to go; you dispense with my assistance. Indeed, I could be of no use; I should injure myself and profit you nothing. I cannot go into the city and procure a physician or attendant. I must never more appear in the streets of this city. I must leave you, then." He hurried to the door. Again, he hesitated. I renewed my entreaties that he would leave me; and encouraged his belief that his presence might endanger himself without conferring the slightest benefit upon me.

"Whither should I fly? The wide world contains no asylum for me. I lived but on one condition. I came hither to find what would save me from ruin,—from death. I find it not. It has vanished. Some audacious and fortunate hand has snatched it from its place, and now my ruin is complete. My last hope is extinct.

"Yes, Mervyn! I will stay with you. I will hold your head. I will put water to your lips. I will watch night and day by your side. When you die, I will carry you by night to the neighbouring field; will bury you, and water your grave with those tears that are due to your incomparable worth and untimely destiny. Then I will lay myself in your bed, and wait for the same oblivion."

Welbeck seemed now no longer to be fluctuating between opposite purposes. His tempestuous features subsided into calm. He put the candle, still lighted, on the table, and paced the floor with less disorder than at his first entrance.

His resolution was seen to be the dictate of despair.

I hoped that it would not prove invincible to my remonstrances. I was conscious that his attendance might preclude, in some degree, my own exertions, and alleviate the pangs of death; but these consolations might be purchased too dear. To receive them at the hazard of his life would be to make them odious.

But, if he should remain, what conduct would his companion pursue? Why did he continue in the study when Welbeck had departed? By what motives were those men led hither? I addressed myself to Welbeck:—

"Your resolution to remain is hasty and rash. By persisting in it, you will add to the miseries of my condition; you will take away the only hope that I cherished. But, however you may act, Colvill or I must be banished from this roof. What is the league between you? Break it, I conjure you, before his frauds have involved you in inextricable destruction."

Welbeck looked at me with some expression of doubt.

"I mean," continued I, "the man whose voice I heard above. He is a villain and betrayer. I have manifold proofs of his guilt. Why does he linger behind you? However you my decide, it is fitting that he should vanish."

"Alas!" said Welbeck, "I have no companion; none to partake with me in good or evil. I came hither alone."

"How?" exclaimed I. "Whom did I hear in the room above? Some one answered my interrogations and entreaties, whom I too certainly recognised. Why does he remain?"

"You heard no one but myself. The design that brought me hither was to be accomplished without a witness. I desired to escape detection, and repelled your solicitations for admission in a counterfeited voice.

"That voice belonged to one from whom I had lately parted. What his merits or demerits are, I know not. He found me wandering in the forests of New Jersey. He took me to his home. When seized by a lingering malady, he nursed me with fidelity and tenderness. When somewhat recovered, I speeded hither; but our ignorance of each other's character and views was mutual and profound.

"I deemed it useful to assume a voice different from my own. This was the last which I had heard, and this arbitrary and casual circumstance decided my choice."

This imitation was too perfect, and had influenced my fears too strongly, to be easily credited. I suspected Welbeck of some new artifice to baffle my conclusions and mislead my judgment. This suspicion, however, yielded to his earnest and repeated declarations. If Colvill were not here, where had he made his abode? How came friendship and intercourse between Welbeck and him? By what miracle escaped the former from the river, into which I had imagined him forever sunk?

"I will answer you," said he, with candour. "You know already too much for me to have any interest in concealing any part of my life. You have discovered my existence, and the causes that rescued me from destruction may be told without detriment to my person or fame.

"When I leaped into the river, I intended to perish. I harboured no previous doubts of my ability to execute my fatal purpose. In this respect I was deceived. Suffocation would not come at my bidding. My muscles and limbs rebelled against my will. There was a mechanical repugnance to the loss of life, which I could not vanquish. My struggles might thrust me below the surface, but my lips were spontaneously shut, and excluded the torrent from my lungs. When my breath was exhausted, the efforts that kept me at the bottom were involuntarily remitted, and I rose to the surface.

"I cursed my own pusillanimity. Thrice I plunged to the bottom, and as often rose again. My aversion to life swiftly diminished, and at length I consented to make use of my skill in swimming, which has seldom been exceeded, to prolong my existence. I landed in a few minutes on the Jersey shore.

"This scheme being frustrated, I sunk into dreariness and inactivity. I felt as if no dependence could be placed upon my courage, as if any effort I should make for self-destruction would be fruitless; yet existence was as void as ever of enjoyment and embellishment. My means of living were annihilated. I saw no path before me. To shun the presence of mankind was my sovereign wish. Since I could not die by my own hands, I must be content to crawl upon the surface, till a superior fate should permit me to perish.

"I wandered into the centre of the wood. I stretched myself on the mossy verge of a brook, and gazed at the stars till they disappeared. The next day was spent with little variation. The cravings of hunger were felt, and the sensation was a joyous one, since it afforded me the practicable means of death. To refrain from food was easy, since some efforts would be needful to procure it, and these efforts should not be made. Thus was the sweet oblivion for which I so earnestly panted placed within my reach.

"Three days of abstinence, and reverie, and solitude, succeeded. On the evening of the fourth, I was seated on a rock, with my face buried in my hands. Some one laid his hand upon my shoulder. I started and looked up. I beheld a face beaming with compassion and benignity. He endeavoured to extort from me the cause of my solitude and sorrow. I disregarded his entreaties, and was obstinately silent.

"Finding me invincible in this respect, he invited me to his college, which was hard by. I repelled him at first with impatience and anger, but he was not to be discouraged or intimidated. To elude his persuasions I was obliged to comply. My strength was gone, and the vital fabric was crumbling into pieces. A fever raged in my veins, and I was consoled by reflecting that my life was at once assailed by famine and disease.

"Meanwhile, my gloomy meditations experienced no respite. I incessantly ruminated on the events of my past life. The long series of my crimes arose daily and afresh to my imagination. The image of Lodi was recalled, his expiring looks and the directions which were mutually given respecting his sister's and his property.

"As I perpetually revolved these incidents, they assumed new forms, and were linked with new associations. The volume written by his father, and transferred to me by tokens which were now remembered to be more emphatic than the nature of the composition seemed to justify, was likewise remembered. It came attended by recollections respecting a volume which I filled, when a youth, with extracts from the Roman and Greek poets. Besides this literary purpose, I likewise used to preserve in it the bank-bills with the keeping or carriage of which I chanced to be intrusted. This image led me back to the leather case containing Lodi's property, which was put into my hands at the same time with the volume.

"These images now gave birth to a third conception, which darted on my benighted understanding like an electrical flash. Was it not possible that part of Lodi's property might be enclosed within the leaves of this volume? In hastily turning it over, I recollected to have noticed leaves whose edges by accident or design adhered to each other. Lodi, in speaking of the sale of his father's West-India property, mentioned that the sum obtained for it was forty thousand dollars. Half only of this sum had been discovered by me. How had the remainder been appropriated? Surely this volume contained it.

"The influence of this thought was like the infusion of a new soul into my frame. From torpid and desperate, from inflexible aversion to medicine and food, I was changed in a moment into vivacity and hope, into ravenous avidity for whatever could contribute to my restoration to health.

"I was not without pungent regrets and racking fears. That this volume would be ravished away by creditors or plunderers was possible. Every hour might be that which decided my fate. The first impulse was to seek my dwelling and search for this precious deposit.

"Meanwhile, my perturbations and impatience only exasperated my disease. While chained to my bed, the rumour of pestilence was spread abroad. This event, however, generally calamitous, was propitious to me, and was hailed with satisfaction. It multiplied the chances that my house and its furniture would be unmolested.

"My friend was assiduous and indefatigable in his kindness. My deportment, before and subsequent to the revival of my hopes, was incomprehensible, and argued nothing less than insanity. My thoughts were carefully concealed from him, and all that he witnessed was contradictory and unintelligible.

"At length, my strength was sufficiently restored. I resisted all my protector's importunities to postpone my departure till the perfect confirmation of my health. I designed to enter the city at midnight, that prying eyes might be eluded; to bear with me a candle and the means of lighting it, to explore my way to my ancient study, and to ascertain my future claim to existence and felicity.

"I crossed the river this morning. My impatience would not suffer me to wait till evening. Considering the desolation of the city, I thought I might venture to approach thus near, without hazard of detection. The house, at all its avenues, was closed. I stole into the back court. A window-shutter proved to be unfastened. I entered, and discovered closets and cabinets unfastened and emptied of all their contents. At this spectacle my heart sunk. My books, doubtless, had shared the common destiny. My blood throbbed with painful vehemence as I approached the study and opened the door.

"My hopes, that languished for a moment, were revived by the sight of my shelves, furnished as formerly. I had lighted my candle below, for I desired not to awaken observation and suspicion by unclosing the windows. My eye eagerly sought the spot where I remembered to have left the volume. Its place was empty. The object of all my hopes had eluded my grasp, and disappeared forever.

"To paint my confusion, to repeat my execrations on the infatuation which had rendered, during so long a time that it was in my possession, this treasure useless to me, and my curses of the fatal interference which had snatched away the prize, would be only aggravations of my disappointment and my sorrow. You found me in this state, and know what followed."

CHAPTER XXII.

THIS narrative threw new light on the character of Welbeck. If accident had given him possession of this treasure, it was easy to predict on what schemes of luxury and selfishness it would have been expended. The same dependence on the world's erroneous estimation, the same devotion to imposture, and thoughtlessness of futurity, would have constituted the picture of his future life, as had distinguished the past.

This money was another's. To retain it for his own use was criminal. Of this crime he appeared to be as insensible as ever. His own gratification was the supreme law of his actions. To be subjected to the necessity of honest labour was the heaviest of all evils, and one from which he was willing to escape by the commission of suicide.

The volume which he sought was mine. It was my duty to restore it to the rightful owner, or, if the legal claimant could not be found, to employ it in the promotion of virtue and happiness. To give it to Welbeck was to consecrate it to the purpose of selfishness and misery. My right, legally considered, was as valid as his.

But, if I intended not to resign it to him, was it proper to disclose the truth and explain by whom the volume was purloined from the shelf? The first impulse was to hide this truth; but my understanding had been taught, by recent occurrences, to question the justice and deny the usefulness of secrecy in any case. My principles were true; my motives were pure: why should I scruple to avow my principles and vindicate my actions?

Welbeck had ceased to be dreaded or revered. That awe which was once created by his superiority of age, refinement of manners, and dignity of garb, had vanished. I was a boy in years, an indigent and uneducated rustic; but I was able to discern the illusions of power and riches, and abjured every claim to esteem that was not founded on integrity. There was no tribunal before which I should falter in asserting the truth, and no species of martyrdom which I would not cheerfully embrace in its cause.

After some pause, I said, "Cannot you conjecture in what way this volume has disappeared?"

"No," he answered, with a sigh. "Why, of all his volumes, this only should have vanished, was an inexplicable enigma."

"Perhaps," said I, "it is less important to know how it was removed, than by whom it is now possessed."

"Unquestionably; and yet, unless that knowledge enables me to regain the possession, it will be useless."

"Useless then it will be, for the present possessor will never return it to you."

"Indeed," replied he, in a tone of dejection, "your conjecture is most probable. Such a prize is of too much value to be given up."

"What I have said flows not from conjecture, but from knowledge. I know that it will never be restored to you."

At these words, Welbeck looked at me with anxiety and doubt:—"You *know* that it will not! Have you any knowledge of the book? Can you tell me what has become of it?"

"Yes. After our separation on the river, I returned to this house. I found this volume and secured it. You rightly suspected its contents. The money was there."

Welbeck started as if he had trodden on a mine of gold. His first emotion was rapturous, but was immediately chastened by some degree of doubt:—"What has become of it? Have you got it? Is it entire? Have you it with you?"

"It is unimpaired. I have got it, and shall hold it as a sacred trust for the rightful proprietor."

The tone with which this declaration was accompanied shook the new-born confidence of Welbeck. "The rightful proprietor! true, but I am he. To me only it belongs, and to me you are, doubtless, willing to restore it."

"Mr. Welbeck! It is not my desire to give you perplexity or anguish; to sport with your passions. On the supposition of your death, I deemed it no infraction of justice to take this manuscript. Accident unfolded its contents. I could not hesitate to choose my path. The natural and legal successor of Vincentio Lodi is his sister. To her, therefore, this property belongs, and to her only will I give it."

"Presumptuous boy! And this is your sage decision. I tell you that I am the owner, and to me you shall render it. Who is this girl? Childish and ignorant! Unable to consult and to act for herself on the most trivial occasion. Am I not, by the appointment of her dying brother, her protector and guardian? Her age produces a legal incapacity of property. Do you imagine that so obvious an expedient as that of procuring my legal appointment as her guardian was overlooked by me? If it were neglected, still my title to provide her subsistence and enjoyment is unquestionable.

"Did I not rescue her from poverty, and prostitution, and infamy? Have I not supplied all her wants with incessant solicitude? Whatever her condition required has been plenteously supplied. This dwelling and its furniture was hers, as far as a rigid jurisprudence would permit. To prescribe her expenses and govern her family was the province of her guardian.

"You have heard the tale of my anguish and despair. Whence did they flow but from the frustration of schemes projected for her benefit, as they were executed with her money and by means which the authority of her guardian fully justified? Why have I encountered this contagious atmosphere, and explored my way, like a thief, to this recess, but with a view to rescue her from poverty and restore to her her own?

"Your scruples are ridiculous and criminal. I treat them with less severity, because your youth is raw and your conceptions crude. But if, after this proof of the justice of my claim, you hesitate to restore the money, I shall treat you as a robber, who has plundered my cabinet and refused to refund his spoil."

These reasonings were powerful and new. I was acquainted with the rights of guardianship. Welbeck had, in some respects, acted as the friend of this lady. To vest himself with this office was the conduct which her youth and helplessness prescribed to her friend. His title to this money, as her guardian, could not be denied.

But how was this statement compatible with former representations? No mention had then been made of guardianship. By thus acting, he would have thwarted all his schemes for winning the esteem of mankind and fostering the belief which the world entertained of his opulence and independence.

I was thrown, by these thoughts, into considerable perplexity. If his statement were true, his claim to this money was established; but I questioned its truth. To intimate my doubts of his veracity would be to provoke abhorrence and outrage.

His last insinuation was peculiarly momentous. Suppose him the fraudulent possessor of this money: shall I be justified in taking it away by violence under pretence of restoring it to the genuine proprietor, who, for aught I know, may be dead, or with whom, at least, I may never procure a meeting? But will not my behaviour on this occasion be deemed illicit? I entered Welbeck's habitation at midnight, proceeded to his closet, possessed myself of portable property, and retired unobserved. Is not guilt imputable to an action like this?

Welbeck waited with impatience for a conclusion to my pause. My perplexity and indecision did not abate, and my silence continued. At length, he repeated his demands, with new vehemence. I was compelled to answer. I told him, in few words, that his reasonings had not convinced me of the equity of his claim, and that my determination was unaltered.

He had not expected this inflexibility from one in my situation. The folly of opposition, when my feebleness and loneliness were contrasted with his activity and resources, appeared to him monstrous and glaring; but his contempt was converted into rage and fear when he reflected that this folly might finally defeat his hopes. He had probably determined to obtain the money, let the purchase cost what it would, but was willing to exhaust pacific expedients before he should resort to force. He might likewise question whether the money was within his reach. I had told him that I had it, but whether it was now about me was somewhat dubious; yet, though he used no direct inquiries, he chose to proceed on the supposition of its being at hand. His angry tones were now changed into those of remonstrance and persuasion:—

"Your present behaviour, Mervyn, does not justify the expectation I had formed of you. You have been guilty of a base theft. To this you have added the deeper crime of ingratitude, but your infatuation and folly are, at least, as glaring as your guilt. Do you think I can credit your assertions that you keep this money for another, when I recollect that six weeks have passed since you carried it off? Why have you not sought the owner and restored it to her? If your intentions had been honest, would you have suffered so long a time to elapse without doing this? It is plain that you designed to keep it for your own use.

"But, whether this were your purpose or not, you have no longer power to restore it or retain it. You say that you came hither to die. If so, what is to be the fate of the money? In your present situation you cannot gain access to the lady. Some other must inherit this wealth. Next to *Signora Lodi*, whose right can be put in competition with mine? But, if you will not give it to me on my own account, let it be given in trust for her. Let me be the bearer of it to her own hands. I have already shown you that my claim to it, as her guardian, is legal and incontrovertible, but this claim I waive. I will merely be the executor of your will. I will bind myself to comply with your directions by any oath, however solemn and tremendous, which you shall prescribe."

As long as my own heart acquitted me, these imputations of dishonesty affected me but little. They excited no anger, because they originated in ignorance, and were rendered plausible to Welbeck by such facts as were known to him. It was needless to confute the charge by elaborate and circumstantial details.

It was true that my recovery was, in the highest degree, improbable, and that my death would put an end to my power over this money; but had I not determined to secure its useful application in case of my death? This project was obstructed by the presence of Welbeck; but I hoped that his love of life would induce him to fly. He might wrest this volume from me by violence, or he might wait till my death should give him peaceable possession. But these, though probable events, were not certain, and would, by no means, justify the voluntary surrender. His strength, if employed for this end, could not be resisted; but then it would be a sacrifice, not a choice, but necessity.

Promises were easily given, but were surely not to be confided in. Welbeck's own tale, in which it could not be imagined that he had aggravated his defects, attested the frailty of his virtue. To put into his hands a sum like this, in expectation of his delivering it to another, when my death would cover the transaction with impenetrable secrecy, would be, indeed, a proof of that infatuation which he thought proper to impute to me.

These thoughts influenced my resolutions, but they were revolved in silence. To state them verbally was useless. They would not justify my conduct in his eyes. They would only exasperate dispute, and impel him to those acts of violence which I was desirous of preventing. The sooner this controversy should end, and I in any measure be freed from the obstruction of his company, the better.

"Mr. Welbeck," said I, "my regard to your safety compels me to wish that this interview should terminate. At a different time, I should not be unwilling to discuss this matter. Now it will be fruitless. My conscience points out to me too clearly the path I should pursue for me to mistake it. As long as I have power over this money, I shall keep it for the use of the unfortunate lady whom I have seen in this house. I shall exert myself to find her; but, if that be impossible, I shall appropriate it in a way in which you shall have no participation."

I will not repeat the contest that succeeded between my forbearance and his passions. I listened to the dictates of his rage and his avarice in silence. Astonishment at my inflexibility was blended with his anger. By turns he commented on the guilt and on the folly of my resolutions. Sometimes his emotions would mount into fury, and he would approach me in a menacing attitude, and lift his hand as if he would exterminate me at a blow. My languid eyes, my cheeks glowing and my temples throbbing with fever, and my total passiveness, attracted his attention and arrested his stroke. Compassion would take the place of rage, and the belief be revived that remonstrances and arguments would answer his purpose.

CHAPTER XXIII.

THIS scene lasted I know not how long. Insensibly the passions and reasonings of Welbeck assumed a new form. A grief, mingled with perplexity, overspread his countenance. He ceased to contend or to speak. His regards were withdrawn from me, on whom they had hitherto been fixed; and, wandering or vacant, testified a conflict of mind terrible beyond any that my young imagination had ever conceived.

For a time he appeared to be unconscious of my presence. He moved to and fro with unequal steps, and with gesticulations that possessed a horrible but indistinct significance. Occasionally he struggled for breath, and his efforts were directed to remove some choking impediment.

No test of my fortitude had hitherto occurred equal to that to which it was now subjected. The suspicion which this deportment suggested was vague and formless. The tempest which I witnessed was the prelude of horror. These were throes which would terminate in the birth of some gigantic and sanguinary purpose. Did he meditate to offer a bloody sacrifice? Was his own death or was mine to attest the magnitude of his despair or the impetuosity of his vengeance?

Suicide was familiar to his thoughts. He had consented to live but on one condition; that of regaining possession of this money. Should I be justified in driving him, by my obstinate refusal, to this fatal consummation of his crimes? Yet my fear of this catastrophe was groundless. Hitherto he had argued and persuaded; but this method was pursued because it was more eligible than the employment of force, or than procrastination.

No. These were tokens that pointed to me. Some unknown instigation was at work within him, to tear away his remnant of humanity and fit him for the office of my murderer. I knew not how the accumulation of guilt could contribute to his gratification or security. His actions had been partially exhibited and vaguely seen. What extenuations or omissions had vitiated his former or recent narrative; how far his actual performances were congenial with the deed which was now to be perpetrated, I knew not.

These thoughts lent new rapidity to my blood. I raised my head from the pillow, and watched the deportment of this man with deeper attention. The paroxysm which controlled him at length, in some degree, subsided. He muttered, "Yes. It must come. My last humiliation must cover me. My last confession must be made. To die, and leave behind me this train of enormous perils, must not be.

"O Clemenza! O Mervyn! Ye have not merited that I should leave you a legacy of persecution and death. Your safety must be purchased at what price my malignant destiny will set upon it. The cord of the executioner, the note of everlasting infamy, is better than to leave you beset by the consequences of my guilt. It must not be."

Saying this, Welbeck cast fearful glances at the windows and door. He examined every avenue and listened. Thrice he repeated this scrutiny. Having, as it seemed, ascertained that no one lurked within audience, he approached the bed. He put his mouth close to my face. He attempted to speak, but once more examined the apartment with suspicious glances.

He drew closer, and at length, in a tone scarcely articulate, and suffocated with emotion, he spoke:—"Excellent but fatally-obstinate youth! Know at least the cause of my importunity. Know at least the depth of my infatuation and the enormity of my guilt.

"The bills—surrender them to me, and save yourself from persecution and disgrace. Save the woman whom you wish to benefit, from the blackest imputations; from hazard to her life and her fame; from languishing in dungeons; from expiring on the gallows!

"The bills—oh, save me from the bitterness of death! Let the evils to which my miserable life has given birth terminate here and in myself. Surrender them to me, for——"

There he stopped. His utterence was choked by terror. Rapid glances were again darted at the windows and door. The silence was uninterrupted, except by far-off sounds, produced by some moving carriage. Once more he summoned resolution, and spoke:—

"Surrender them to me—for—*they are forged!*

"Formerly I told you, that a scheme of forgery had been conceived. Shame would not suffer me to add, that my scheme was carried into execution. The bills were fashioned, but my fears contended against my necessities, and forbade me to attempt to exchange them. The interview with Lodi saved me from the dangerous experiment. I enclosed them in that volume, as the means of future opulence, to be used when all other and less hazardous resources should fail.

"In the agonies of my remorse at the death of Watson, they were forgotten. They afterwards recurred to recollection. My wishes pointed to the grave; but the stroke that should deliver me from life was suspended only till I could hasten hither, get possession of these papers, and destroy them.

"When I thought upon the chances that should give them an owner; bring them into circulation; load the innocent with suspicion; and lead them to trial, and, perhaps, to death, my sensations were fraught with agony; earnestly as I panted for death, it was necessarily deferred till I had gained possession of and destroyed these papers.

"What now remains? You have found them. Happily they have not been used. Give them, therefore, to me, that I may crush at once the brood of mischiefs which they could not but generate."

This disclosure was strange. It was accompanied with every token of sincerity. How had I tottered on the brink of destruction! If I had made use of this money, in what a labyrinth of misery might I not have been involved! My innocence could never have been proved. An alliance with Welbeck could not have failed to be inferred. My career would have found an ignominious close; or, if my punishment had been transmuted into slavery and toil, would the testimony of my conscience have supported me?

I shuddered at the view of those disasters from which I was rescued by the miraculous chance which led me to this house. Welbeck's request was salutary to me and honourable to himself. I could not hesitate a moment in compliance. The notes were enclosed in paper, and deposited in a fold of my clothes. I put my hand upon them.

My motion and attention were arrested, at the instant, by a noise which arose in the street. Footsteps were heard upon the pavement before the door, and voices, as if busy in discourse. This incident was adapted to infuse the deepest alarm into myself and my companion. The motives of our trepidation were, indeed, different, and were infinitely more powerful in my case than in his. It portended to me nothing less than the loss of my asylum, and condemnation to an hospital.

Welbeck hurried to the door, to listen to the conversation below. This interval was pregnant with thought. That impulse which led my reflections from Welbeck to my own state passed away in a moment, and suffered me to meditate anew upon the terms of that confession which had just been made.

Horror at the fate which this interview had enabled me to shun was uppermost in my conceptions. I was eager to surrender these fatal bills. I held them for that purpose in my hand, and was impatient for Welbeck's return. He continued at the door; stooping, with his face averted, and eagerly attentive to the conversation in the street.

All the circumstances of my present situation tended to arrest the progress of thought and chain my contemplations to one image; but even now there was room for foresight and deliberation. Welbeck intended to destroy these bills. Perhaps he had not been sincere; or, if his purpose had been honestly disclosed, this purpose might change when the bills were in his possession. His poverty and sanguineness of temper might prompt him to use them.

That this conduct was evil, and would only multiply his miseries, could not be questioned. Why should I subject his frailty to this temptation? The destruction of these bills was the loudest injunction of my duty; was demanded by every sanction which bound me to promote the welfare of mankind.

The means of destruction was easy. A lighted candle stood on a table, at the distance of a few yards. Why should I hesitate a moment to annihilate so powerful a cause of error and guilt? A passing instant was sufficient. A momentary lingering might change the circumstances that surrounded me, and frustrate my project.

My languors were suspended by the urgencies of this occasion. I started from my bed and glided to the table. Seizing the notes with my right hand, I held them in the flame of the candle, and then threw them, blazing, on the floor.

The sudden illumination was perceived by Welbeck. The cause of it appeared to suggest itself as soon. He turned, and, marking the paper where it lay, leaped to the spot, and extinguished the fire with his foot. His interposition was too late. Only enough of them remained to inform him of the nature of the sacrifice.

Welbeck now stood, with limbs trembling, features aghast, and eyes glaring upon me. For a time he was without speech. The storm was gathering in silence, and at length burst upon me. In a tone menacing and loud, he exclaimed,—

"Wretch! what have you done?"

"I have done justly. These notes were false. You desired to destroy them, that they might not betray the innocent. I applauded your purpose, and have saved you from the danger of temptation by destroying them myself."

"Maniac! Miscreant! To be fooled by so gross an artifice! The notes were genuine. The tale of their forgery was false and meant only to wrest them from you. Execrable and perverse idiot! Your deed has sealed my perdition. It has sealed your own. You shall pay for it with your blood. I will slay you by inches. I will stretch you, as you have stretched me, on the rack."

During this speech, all was frenzy and storm in the countenance and features of Welbeck. Nothing less could be expected than that the scene would terminate in some bloody catastrophe. I bitterly regretted the facility with which I had been deceived, and the precipitation of my sacrifice. The act, however lamentable, could not be revoked. What remained but to encounter or endure its consequences with unshrinking firmness?

The contest was too unequal. It is possible that the frenzy which actuated Welbeck might have speedily subsided. It is more likely that his passions would have been satiated with nothing but my death. This event was precluded by loud knocks at the street door, and calls by some one on the pavement without, of—"Who is within? Is any one within?"

These noises gave a new direction to Welbeck's thoughts. "They are coming," said he. "They will treat you as a sick man and a thief. I cannot desire you to suffer a worse evil than they will inflict. I leave you to your fate." So saying, he rushed out of the room.

Though confounded and stunned by this rapid succession of events, I was yet able to pursue measures for eluding these detested visitants. I first extinguished the light, and then, observing that the parley in the street continued and grew louder, I sought an asylum in the remotest corner of the house. During my former abode here, I noticed that a trap-door opened in the ceiling of the third story, to which you were conducted by a movable stair or ladder. I considered that this, probably, was an opening into a narrow and darksome nook formed by the angle of the roof. By ascending, drawing after me the ladder, and closing the door, I should escape the most vigilant search.

Enfeebled as I was by my disease, my resolution rendered me strenuous. I gained the uppermost room, and, mounting the ladder, found myself at a sufficient distance from suspicion. The stair was hastily drawn up, and the door closed. In a few minutes, however, my new retreat proved to be worse than any for which it was possible to change it. The air was musty, stagnant, and scorchingly hot. My breathing became difficult, and I saw that to remain here ten minutes would unavoidably produce suffocation.

My terror of intruders had rendered me blind to the consequences of immuring myself in this cheerless recess. It was incumbent on me to extricate myself as speedily as possible. I attempted to lift the door. My first effort was successless. Every inspiration was quicker and more difficult than the former. As my terror, so my strength and my exertions increased. Finally my trembling hand lighted on a nail that was imperfectly driven into the wood, and which, by affording me a firmer hold, enabled me at length to raise it, and to inhale the air from beneath.

Relieved from my new peril by this situation, I bent an attentive ear through the opening, with a view to ascertain if the house had been entered or if the outer door was still beset, but could hear nothing. Hence I was authorized to conclude that the people had departed, and that I might resume my former station without hazard.

Before I descended, however, I cast a curious eye over this recess. It was large enough to accommodate a human being. The means by which it was entered were easily concealed. Though narrow and low, it was long, and, were it possible to contrive some inlet for the air, one studious of concealment might rely on its protection with unbounded confidence.

My scrutiny was imperfect by reason of the faint light which found its way through the opening; yet it was sufficient to set me afloat on a sea of new wonders and subject my fortitude to a new test.—

Here Mervyn paused in his narrative. A minute passed in silence and seeming indecision. His perplexities gradually disappeared, and he continued:—

I have promised to relate the momentous incidents of my life, and have hitherto been faithful in my enumeration. There is nothing which I more detest than equivocation and mystery. Perhaps, however, I shall now incur some imputation of that kind. I would willingly escape the accusation, but confess that I am hopeless of escaping it.

I might, indeed, have precluded your guesses and surmises by omitting to relate what befell me from the time of my leaving my chamber till I regained it. I might deceive you by asserting that nothing remarkable occurred; but this would be false, and every sacrifice is trivial which is made upon the altar of sincerity. Besides, the time may come when no inconvenience will arise from minute descriptions of the objects which I now saw, and of the reasonings and inferences which they suggested to my understanding. At present, it appears to be my duty to pass them over in silence; but it would be needless to conceal from you that the interval, though short, and the scrutiny, though hasty, furnished matter which my curiosity devoured with unspeakable eagerness, and from which consequences may hereafter flow, deciding on my peace and my life.

Nothing, however, occurred which could detain me long in this spot. I once more sought the lower story and threw myself on the bed which I had left. My mind was thronged with the images flowing from my late adventure. My fever had gradually increased, and my thoughts were deformed by inaccuracy and confusion.

My heart did not sink when I reverted to my own condition. That I should quickly be disabled from moving, was readily perceived. The foresight of my destiny was steadfast and clear. To linger for days in this comfortless solitude, to ask in vain, not for powerful restoratives or alleviating cordials, but for water to moisten my burning lips and abate the torments of thirst; ultimately to expire in torpor or frenzy, was the fate to which I looked forward; yet I was not terrified. I seemed to be sustained by a preternatural energy. I felt as if the opportunity of combating such evils was an enviable privilege, and, though none would witness my victorious magnanimity, yet to be conscious that praise was my due was all that my ambition required.

These sentiments were doubtless tokens of delirium. The excruciating agonies which now seized upon my head, and the cord which seemed to be drawn across my breast, and which, as my fancy imagined, was tightened by some forcible hand, with a view to strangle me, were incompatible with sober and coherent views.

Thirst was the evil which chiefly oppressed me. The means of relief was pointed out by nature and habit. I rose, and determined to replenish my pitcher at the well. It was easier, however, to descend than to return. My limbs refused to bear me, and I sat down upon the lower step of the staircase. Several hours had elapsed since my entrance into this dwelling, and it was now night.

My imagination now suggested a new expedient. Medlicote was a generous and fearless spirit. To put myself under his protection, if I could walk as far as his lodgings, was the wisest proceeding which I could adopt. From this design, my incapacity to walk thus far, and the consequences of being discovered in the street, had hitherto deterred me. These impediments were now, in the confusion of my understanding, overlooked or despised, and I forthwith set out upon this hopeless expedition.

The doors communicating with the court, and, through the court, with the street, were fastened by inside bolts. These were easily withdrawn, and I issued forth with alacrity and confidence. My perturbed senses and the darkness hindered me from discerning the right way. I was conscious of this difficulty, but was not disheartened. I proceeded, as I have since discovered, in a direction different from the true, but hesitated not till my powers were exhausted and I sunk upon the ground. I closed my eyes, and dismissed all fear, and all foresight of futurity. In this situation I remained some hours, and should probably have expired on this spot, had not I attracted your notice, and been provided, under this roof, with all that medical skill, that the tenderest humanity could suggest.

In consequence of your care, I have been restored to life and to health. Your conduct was not influenced by the prospect of pecuniary recompense, of service, or of gratitude. It is only in one way that I am able to heighten the gratification which must flow from reflection on your conduct:—by showing that the being whose life you have prolonged, though uneducated, ignorant, and poor, is not profligate and worthless, and will not dedicate that life which your bounty has given, to mischievous or contemptible purposes.

END OF VOL I.

STEREOTYPED BY L. JOHNSON & CO.
PHILADELPHIA.

www.ingramcontent.com/pod-product-compliance
Lightning Source LLC
LaVergne TN
LVHW011216110826
845150LV00006B/1440

* 9 7 8 1 4 2 5 5 1 7 3 0 4 *